HOME PORT

THE LONG ROAD HOME / LIGHTHOUSE SECURITY INVESTIGATIONS WEST COAST

MARYANN JORDAN

USA TODAY BESTSELLING AUTHOR

ISBN ebook: 978-1-947214-99-6

ISBN print: 978-1-956588-00-2

❀ Created with Vellum

Author's Note

Please remember that this is a work of fiction. I have lived in numerous states as well as overseas, but for the last thirty years have called Virginia my home. I often choose to use fictional city names with some geographical accuracies.

These fictionally named cities allow me to use my creativity and not feel constricted by attempting to accurately portray the areas.

It is my hope that my readers will allow me this creative license and understand my fictional world.

I also do quite a bit of research on my books and try to write on subjects with accuracy. There will always be points where creative license will be used in order to create scenes or plots.

Chris squatted at the edge of the mountain overlook, staring out into the dark. A dark so black it was hard to see his hand in front of his face. But when he lifted his chin, the stars above glistened with a brilliance that made him wonder if he'd ever noticed them before. *What the hell? Christ, I'm thinking about stars?* He figured if his former SEAL brothers could hear his thoughts now, they'd laugh their asses off.

He wasn't supposed to be there. *I should have been in California by now.* The road to get to this place had not been in his plans, and he always stuck to his plans. But ever since he'd left Virginia Beach several days ago, nothing had gone according to schedule. *What was it the strange lady in the Atlanta airport USO said?*

"The destination isn't as important as the road you take to get there. Learn to enjoy the journey." Blessing... that was her name.

Scrubbing his hand over his face, he squeezed his eyes shut, forcing those thoughts to the side. Taking another careful look around, he listened for any sound of danger. The night was quiet, and that should have eased the caution holding a grip on him. Instead, it just made him more aware of possible dangers. Someone was out there... someone who wanted them dead.

A movement and the sound of a soft snore drew his attention to the rock slab next to him. His gaze drifted down to the woman curled up on her side, her head resting on her hands as her palms clasped together. She was sleeping soundly on the hard rock. A small smile curved his lips at the sight of her yellow-blonde curls escaping from her lopsided braid, her wildly printed shirt, and purple sneakers. And if her eyes were open, he knew he'd be staring at a blue so pure it was like looking at the ocean off the coast of Greece on a sunlit day. *Christ, I'm losing it.*

If he believed in voodoo shit, he'd wonder if Blessing had cast an incantation over him. Sighing, he shifted his ass to the ground next to her. He hoped the only danger that might get to them tonight was his own imagination.

TWO DAYS EARLIER

Chris Andrews had booked first-class airline tickets so that he could board early, get off the plane first, and have room for his carry-on. Not an extravagant person, it was a rare indulgence for someone used to military transport but worth every penny. Except now, sitting on the plane, waiting for it to pull up to the gate at the Atlanta airport, he clenched his teeth because even the extra money spent wouldn't help him.

When he'd sat in the plane for an hour and a half on the tarmac of the Norfolk Airport while the maintenance crew worked on what the pilot assured them was a minor mechanical issue, he'd watched each minute pass, knowing the odds of making his connecting flight in Atlanta were decreasing.

As they rolled to the gate and came to a stop, the passengers further back in the plane began filling the aisle, and grumblings over the delay reverberated inside the cabin. As soon as they were allowed, he stood quickly and reached up for his bag, aware that his large size could naturally move people out of the way, and yet he didn't want to accidentally elbow someone in the head. Dipping his chin in acknowledgment and thanks to the crew, he walked swiftly to the gate, hustling with the hope that if his next flight was also delayed, he just might make it on board.

It took several minutes, but he refused to run through the airport like so many others were doing. Approaching the gate, he spied the closed door, and peering through the wall of windows, it was evident the plane had already pulled away from the terminal. Sighing heavily, he wondered if his trip was cursed.

Walking to the ticket counter, he stood in line as several pissed-off passengers in front of him berated the young woman as she tapped away on her computer, her fingernails clicking at a furious rate, attempting to placate the others who'd missed the flight as well. The words, "Everything today is full, I can get you on a flight first thing in the morning," and, "I'm sorry, there is nothing I can do," were heard numerous times.

By the time he made it to her, he'd already made up his mind to find the USO, get some food, and chill out.

"Yes, sir, may I help you?" Her head had been lowered as she stared at her computer screen, but when her gaze lifted, her eyes widened as though expecting a man his size to unleash a fury on the hapless situation.

"Andrews. Chris Andrews." He handed her his boarding pass. "I was flying to San Francisco. Non-stop flight from here. First class."

"I'm sorry, sir, but there's only one other flight to San Francisco today, and it's booked full. I can place you

4

on a standby list. I will be able to get you on a flight first class tomorrow morning, or I can make connecting flights for you that leave later today."

He hesitated for a moment. He much preferred a straight flight but also hated the idea of finding a hotel near the airport. "Connecting flight today, please."

She blinked, her fingers halting over the keyboard. "You're fine with that?"

"I don't see that I have any choice. You can't create a straight flight at the snap of your fingers, and neither can I. So, yes, ma'am, that's fine."

"Thank you!" The words rushed from her, and she began tapping furiously on her keyboard again, almost as though she was afraid that he would change his mind and decide to berate her as well.

"Can you direct me to the USO?"

"Yes, sir. Follow signs that take you outside of security, and the USO is located on level three. You will need to claim your bags and then recheck them before you can fly out again. If you give me just a moment, I'll have your new boarding passes ready for you."

In another minute, her printer began to chug, the piece of machinery protesting with each line of print. With a huge smile on her face, she ripped off the paper and handed it to him. "Your flight leaves in four hours. I hope you have a lovely day, Mr. Andrews."

Chris dipped his chin in acknowledgment and stepped to the side, rolling his eyes as the person behind him immediately began berating the young woman. *Jesus, when did people get wrapped so fuckin' tight?*

No longer in a hurry, he still felt like a salmon swimming upstream as he made his way to the baggage claim. By now, the signs had already flashed for his flight's luggage arrival, and he headed directly to the carousel. He spied his bags but refused to push others out of the way to get to them. On its second go-around, most of the travelers had already claimed their suitcases, giving him room to snag his bags off the conveyor.

It seemed most of the travelers in baggage claim had left through the sliding doors leading to the outside, making it easier for him to maneuver his bag to the escalator. Arriving at the third level, he glanced up at the signs above, following the arrows pointing toward the USO. Finding it easily, he stepped through the glass doors, leaving behind the hustle and bustle of the major US airport, immediately appreciating the conversational tones inside.

As he stepped to the desk to sign in, a woman approached wearing a bright red apron with the letters 'USO' embroidered across the front and a wide smile on her face. Her dark brown hair swung just above her shoulders, and her assessing gaze moved over him.

"Hello! Welcome to the Atlanta Airport USO!"

"Thank you, ma'am. I'm Chris Andrews, U.S. Navy. Or rather, recently retired U.S. Navy and flying home."

"How nice to meet you, Chris. I'm Blessing." She laughed, her eyes twinkling. "I know that's a strange name, but it's the one my parents gave me. At least I'm not easily forgotten."

His lips curved, and he nodded. "I'm sure, ma'am." He glanced down at the desk. "Is this where I sign in?"

"Absolutely. Once you've done that, I'll show you around. We usually close at nine. Will you need accommodations outside the airport for tonight?"

He signed his name, then turned to her and shook his head. "No, ma'am, I'll have a connecting flight that leaves in about four hours. I missed my earlier flight, and that was the best they could do."

"Please, call me Blessing," she said, and with a swoop of her arm indicated that he should walk with her down a hall painted red, white, and blue. On one side was a large shelving unit with a few bags, duffels, suitcases, and even a stroller parked next to it. "You may leave your bags here. I assure you that they'll be completely safe."

He hefted his luggage and carry-on bags onto one of the higher shelves, leaving the lower ones for those with children so they wouldn't have to reach so far. As they continued down the hall, he glanced into a room with several children playing or napping and harried-looking parents. Another room's chairs and sofas had uniformed men and women reading, sleeping, or chatting.

Blessing had stopped, her gaze on him once again assessing. "Recently retired and just going home to California. Such a time of change and new adventures for you."

It was an odd thing for her to say considering most people immediately asked if he was injured. Then, when finding out that he wasn't, they wanted to know what he would be doing or if he had any plans. *As though I'd give up my paying job without having something else lined up.*

He'd always hated assumptions. Or rather, he hated those who voiced their assumptions about him or what he should be doing. *Like my father.* He sighed. *Nope... not going there.*

Blessing patted him on the arm and turned to continue down the hall before he realized she'd mentioned California. Glancing down at the boarding passes in his hand, he couldn't believe how good her eyesight must be in order to have seen the destination in the small print.

"Coming, Chris?" she called out, smiling over her shoulder.

Jolting slightly, he easily caught up with his long stride. "Yes, ma'am... Blessing."

She waved her hand toward the left. "Showers and toilets are there, and there is food in the room we just passed. We keep snacks and drinks out all the time, and we'll have food for meals in just a bit." Stopping just outside another doorway, she smiled up at him. "I'm taking you somewhere special. We call it the library. There, you will find a few others, and I think you'll enjoy their company. All are travelers, heading home or somewhere, but all are looking to see where the journey will take them. I think you'll find your journey to be as important as the destination although most people are more focused on where they're going. Ursula Le Guin said, 'It is good to have an end to journey toward, but it is the journey that matters, in the end.' Don't you agree?"

He stared, uncertain what to say, but it seemed Blessing didn't have that problem.

She laughed and patted his arm once again. "Of course, William Shakespeare said, 'Journeys end in lovers meeting.'"

Now completely lost in what she was talking about, he merely nodded and mumbled, "Yes, ma'am."

Her faraway expression settled into one of contentment. "Come, this way."

He was grateful to follow her into the room and glanced around at the smaller lounge. Plush leather sofas sat facing each other with a recliner against the wall. Three other men were already comfortably ensconced in the seats and looked up as Blessing and he entered.

"Gentlemen," she greeted warmly. "This is Chris Andrews, U.S. Navy. And this is Calvin Swenson, but he prefers to go by Cal. He's also in the Navy. I think perhaps your paths are similar."

Cal stood and reached his hand out. Chris was tall, but Cal was taller with his Nordic DNA clearly written in his size, blond hair, and sharp blue eyes that held Chris' in greeting before narrowing as he glanced toward Blessing.

She continued with the other two men who'd stood, as well. "This is Dylan Grant, U.S. Army. He's transitioning also, and what an end he'll find on his journey. And here we have Nolan O'Rourke. Former SEAL, like yourself, but he already knows the strange paths life can take us on."

The four men hesitated after greeting each other,

their glances toward Blessing seemingly going unnoticed by her. "Well, gentlemen, I'll leave you to get acquainted." With that, she turned and walked out of the room.

He sat on one side of the sofa, the soft leather cushion more comfortable than he'd imagined it would be. Sinking back, a long sigh slipped out as his back cracked. Casting a look at the doorway where Blessing disappeared, his brow furrowed. "She was... interesting."

Dylan said, "I have no idea what she means by me finding something at the end of my journey."

"Probably nothing." Chris rubbed his chin and shook his head.

"Where are you heading?" Cal asked. "I thought it might be the same place as me since she mentioned that our paths were similar."

"California." Even though these men were strangers, it didn't seem right to just leave his answer at one word with these men. "Home to California. I'm getting out. Retiring."

Cal's brow furrowed. "I'm leaving California, so I don't know what she meant. Heading home to New York. Want to see my grandmother before she passes."

"I'm sorry to hear that," Chris replied.

"Yeah, well, the trip sucks even more from just having to spend time with my old man."

Chris offered a rueful nod but remained quiet. Blessing had mentioned that he and Cal had similar paths but there was no way she could know about the contentious relationship he'd had with his father.

"Medical?" Dylan asked, snapping Chris' attention back to the men in the room.

Shaking his head, he snorted. "No. Although if you ask my back and knees, they'd give you a different answer."

The others chuckled, nodding in understanding.

Still feeling the strange desire to explain his reasons, he continued, "The truth is I was on the best team with the best camaraderie for me. I got to do a job that I loved. I know a lot of people go all the way, twenty-plus years before they get out. But for me, it was time. Time for something new. Time to let some fresh blood take my place." What he didn't say was how the last mission had stolen pieces of him that he wasn't sure he'd get back. The death of a team member. The serious injury of two others. And a mission that may have been counted as successful in the end but sure as fuck wasn't successful to those in the middle of the shitstorm. Looking at the faces of the other men, he had the feeling that he didn't need to explain. They'd been there. Done that. Bought the fuckin' T-shirt and burned it.

"Got plans or just winging it for now?" Nolan asked.

"I've got a job lined up. Security. With a company run by a man I'd heard of from a buddy."

Nolan lifted a brow. "So, different and yet the same?"

Chuckling, he nodded. "Yeah. Guess some things don't change, and considering I'm a medic, I figured my skills still had use."

"Were you ever stationed in California?" Cal asked, shifting in his seat.

"No. Virginia Beach. But I was raised in California.

My mom is still there." That was another thing he kept abbreviated. The last time he was in California two years ago, he'd been there to bury his father. The time before that had been when he turned eighteen and his dad had ranted when Chris joined the Navy instead of planning on medical school.

"What about you?" He threw out the general question to them all, figuring anyone who wanted to keep their own secrets could.

"Heading back to Jasper, Tennessee," Nolan said. "I've got... well, I've got some family business there to take care of."

"Birch Falls for me," Dylan said. "Time to settle back home."

Blessing walked back into the room with another man in tow. "Dylan, Nolan, Cal, and Chris, this is Scott Evers. He's a SEAL transitioning out of the Navy. I'm needed up front, but I'll come to check on you later."

After Blessing bestowed a smile on each of them, she turned and left the room as Scott settled into one of the deep-cushioned chairs, his gaze staying on her retreating back. The look on Scott's face reminded Chris of her comment to him. Turning to the others, he inclined his head toward the door. "Blessing? Did she seem a bit..."

"Odd?" Dylan said as Nolan added, "Nice but kinda weird."

"Yeah. Told me something about my journey and then quoted Shakespeare."

The others laughed as Scott snorted. "The woman knew I was leaving the military."

"By choice?" Cal asked.

"Yeah. Not medical. It was time."

Chris silently agreed. After a few minutes, Cal, Dylan, and Nolan tossed a deck of cards onto the footstool between them. He and Scott declined, settling back in their seats as the other three began a friendly game.

Looking toward Scott, he asked, "So, you're transitioning? SEAL?"

"Made the decision a couple of weeks ago."

"Any idea what you're going to do?"

Scott nodded. "I know some people who work with Guardian. Recently, I've thought I might look in that direction."

He'd heard of Guardian and knew things had been devastating for them. "They got slammed a couple of months ago."

"They did." Sighing, Scott asked, "What about you? Traveling to a new base or on leave?"

"I'm getting out and heading to California. Met someone who has a security company opening there."

"No kidding?" Scott angled in his seat, facing him more fully. "I'm heading to Coronado to out-process on terminal leave."

"I made it to Coronado a couple of times. I was stationed in Virginia Beach."

"Which team?"

Chris grinned. He knew Scott would have no problem discerning he was a former SEAL. "Four. You?"

"I did six years enlisted, diving specialty. On Team Six, also out of Virginia Beach. I got my commission and took over as platoon commander on Team One in Coronado."

"Medic, enlisted. Good to meet you, sir."

"Cut the shit. I'm Vader."

"Doc, but I don't go by that." He winced, hating that he'd added that last comment.

"Can I ask why?"

Chuckling, he admitted, "Nothing dramatic. My old man was a cardiothoracic surgeon. He was the only doc in the family. What I did wasn't medicine according to him."

A scowl crossed Scott's face. "Then he's never seen a medic in the field. I've watched you guys work. You're fucking magicians. So much so we called our medic Merlin."

Chris shrugged. "Thanks, but it is what it is. He's gone now. Still..."

Cal looked over from the game. "Same with my old man. I never could get his respect when I joined. But, in my case, he's still around."

Chris shot him a sympathetic gaze, not knowing which was the better situation. Maybe if he thought his father would have ever come around... *Nah, that was never going to happen.*

Scott nodded. "I get it. So, just time to get out?"

"Yes and no. It was for me. The last mission we went on was FUBAR, you know?" He sighed, the pain still evident even talking to another SEAL who would understand.

"Been there, done that. Sort of the reason I'm heading out, too."

"I just… it was time."

Scott sighed along with him. "That tug in your gut that wakes you up in the middle of the night telling you to move on."

They were silent for a moment before Scott asked, "Tell me about the company you're going to work with."

"Lighthouse Security Investigations. They originated in Maine and were started by a former Special Forces officer who also ran CIA operations. He got out and replicated what was successful about his team for his business. He's opening another division on the west coast, as well. It's my understanding that they'll have more soon. I was lucky to know one of the guys working there and got in for an interview. I'll start as soon as I get to California."

"Sounds solid. Are they still taking on people?"

"I'm not sure. Give me your number, and I'll shoot you a text with the point of contact. His name is Carson Dyer. That's the guy in California. The one in Maine is Mace Hanover. I can shoot you both."

Scott leaned forward. "I appreciate that. I can send you a POC for Guardian."

Chris appreciated the gesture but shook his head. "Not unless they have something full-time in California. I need to be there for my mom. She hasn't had anyone for the last two years. I need to step up." In truth, he really wanted to be there for her. She'd been the sunshine in the family to counter his father's cloudy moods.

Holding his gaze, Scott nodded. "Sounds like you already have."

They traded phone numbers, joined by Dylan, Nolan, and Cal.

Blessing appeared at the door again, this time her gaze seeking him out. "Chris? I checked with the ticket agent for your airline, and they've been able to accommodate you on their next flight. I took the liberty to tell them that you'd take it." His chin jerked back slightly, and before he had a chance to speak, she lifted her hands and quickly said, "I know it was high-handed of me, but I truly feel that this is the journey you should take."

Pressing his lips tightly together, he could hardly deny that he'd like to get to California as soon as possible. He dismissed the idea of the journey. For him, it was all about the destination. California. New job. New opportunities. And a chance to forge a new relationship with his mom. The journey? Not important. He pushed himself to a stand and nodded. "Okay, I'll take it. Dylan, you'll have to let me know what you find when you get home." He grinned, shaking the man's hand. Turning to Cal, he added, "Good luck with your old man. Hope the family situation turns out all right, Nolan." Shaking his hand as well, he then turned and said his goodbyes to Scott.

As he walked back down the hall, he grabbed his bags from the high shelf and moved toward the desk where Blessing was waiting for him. He stopped and looked down as she beamed her smile up toward him and reached out to clutch his forearms.

"Oh, Chris, I'm so excited about your trip."

"Thank you, Blessing, but I'm just heading home."

She patted his arm, a benevolent smile curving her face. "Yes, but remember that home is the destination. You have such a journey in front of you. Take advantage of it. Learn from it. And most of all, enjoy it! Izaak Walton said, 'Good company on a journey makes the way seem shorter.'"

He was about to tell her that he was traveling by himself but simply nodded and mumbled his goodbye. He turned to walk through the sliding doors back into the main airport when he suddenly stopped and turned back toward Blessing. For a man used to controlling his actions, he dropped his bags onto the floor and lifted his hand toward her.

She glanced down and laughed. "I'm a hugger, Chris," she said, throwing her arms out wide.

He accepted her hug, surprising himself once again. She patted his back, then loosened her arms and winked. Before he had a chance to ponder his actions, she turned to greet the next serviceman who'd just entered the USO.

Feeling strangely lighthearted, he hefted his bags from the floor and headed out into the hustle and bustle. First destination on his journey: finding his flight's gate. *Who knows? Maybe Blessing is right and this will be a real journey.* He snorted. *Yeah, right. Hell, it's just to get me to my final home port. Nothing special about that.*

3

An hour later, Chris was prepared to wait until the end to board since he had a first-class seat and knew his carry-on would fit underneath the seat, but a chance call to the check-in counter where he showed his boarding pass coincided with the announcement for first-class boarding.

"Here's your new pass, and you can go right on," the cheerful ticket agent said.

She must be new. No way someone can work this job and stay cheerful. Taking advantage of the timing, he walked down the ramp and straight onto the plane. He had an aisle seat and quickly sat to accommodate the others lining up behind him. The attendant immediately offered him a beverage, and soon he had juice placed in his hand. The seat next to him remained empty, and as the plane continued to fill, he wondered if his seatmate was coming. *If not, they'll fill it with someone on the waiting list. No way I could be lucky enough to have the privacy of no seatmate.*

The long line of people boarding had finally slowed, and still, no one had taken the seat. He sipped his juice, wishing it was stronger, but refused to drink alcohol on a flight... at least not a commercial flight. A beer with his teammates after a mission when they were flying home? *Hell yeah*. But he trusted them.

Just when he thought the doors were about to close, the sound of running feet could be heard, and a woman popped through the door, her chest heaving as she showed her boarding pass to the attendant. "Oh, God, I made it. I'm just over there... in seat 3B... in first class."

He couldn't see her face yet but everything else about her screamed for attention. Thick, wavy, yellow-blonde hair that was partially in a long braid hanging over her shoulder with lots of loose curls flying about her face creating a wild halo. Her shirt was tie-dyed in colors of pink, purple, and teal, and her stretchy black pants cupped her curves. And with her feet encased in bright purple sneakers, he sucked in a quick breath. *A teenager? Christ, was I ogling a teenager?* A grimace settled on his face, and now the idea of sitting next to an adolescent for the whole trip to California suddenly seemed daunting. *Please, if there's a god of airline travel, let her listen to music and not talk.*

The attendant looked at the papers in the girl's hands and then inclined her head toward the side. As the girl turned, his eyes widened. She was no teenager.

She quickly made it to his side, and a wide smile split her face. "Hi! So sorry to make you move. I was trying to make this connection and almost didn't! I had to run all the way through the airport only to discover they'd changed the gate. But thank God, it was in the same terminal. I should have stopped to check my phone because I have that app that tells you all the up-to-date stuff about your flight, but I was more focused on running than looking. But then, I made it, and here I am!"

As she babbled, she stopped next to him and lifted her bag to the overhead compartment. The movement raised her shirt slightly, just enough to expose a sliver of tanned skin between the wild colors of her shirt and her pants. Why the fuck he was staring, he had no idea, but the torture continued as she struggled to get the bag into the bin.

"Here, let me." He stood, and she scrambled to move backward. Taking the bag from her hands, he easily lifted it and then closed the door to the bin.

"Wow, thank you." Her smile was still wide as she shoved a lock of hair behind her ear. She lifted on her toes as she peered up at him, leaning in to whisper, "It's sometimes a pain in the ass to be short."

He wasn't sure why she whispered considering her lack of height was evident to all. He opened his mouth to respond but snapped it closed, having nothing to add to her declaration.

She hurried around him, and another bag haphazardly slung over her shoulder slapped against his ribs as she settled into her window seat. Sighing, he followed and took his seat again, now able to stretch his legs out in front of him after stowing his under-the-seat bag.

She buckled her seat belt and then turned toward him. "I'm Stella. Stella Parker, by the way."

Feeling forced to comply with the overt introduction, he dipped his chin. "Christopher Andrews."

Turning his attention to the attendant giving the safety instructions as though they were state secrets imparted just for him, he effectively shut down any further interaction with his seatmate. Soon they were in the air, and he closed his eyes, ready to sleep for the rest of the trip. After several minutes, he relaxed. The ding of the seatbelt sign went off, and he felt a nudge from the side.

"I'm so sorry, Christopher, but I need to get out."

Plastering a blank expression onto his face to make sure his features didn't form a scowl, he shifted upward and pulled his legs in.

With her back to him, she stepped over his legs, placing her ass directly in his line of sight. Thank goodness, she was quick-footed, and she soon disappeared to the front lavatory. She wasn't gone for a moment when she reappeared, and they did the same dance again as she slid into her seat.

"Thank you," Stella said, puffing a strand of hair that had fallen over her eyes. "But I should warn you that I'll probably have to disturb you several times." She crinkled her nose as she hefted her shoulders. "My dad always said I had a peanut bladder. I guess he wasn't wrong."

Once again struck dumb and not having a clue what to say, the attendant saved him as she came around for drink orders.

"Another cranberry juice, please," he replied.

"Oh, I'll take diet soda and another bottled water,

please," Stella said. As the attendant left, she leaned closer to Chris. "I know I should slow down on the liquid, but it's important to stay hydrated."

Soon the drinks were served as well as a tray with fruit, cheese, meats, and crackers. The crunching immediately started next to him as Stella dove into the food.

"Sorry," she mumbled. "I look like a little piggy, but I missed breakfast when I left early this morning and then didn't have a chance to stop in the airport considering I was hoofing it through."

He offered a slight nod that he hoped was simultaneously polite and conversation-ending. No luck.

"And isn't it funny that even when food isn't all that good, somehow someone else fixing it and handing it to you makes you ravenous! Of course, I live by myself, so cooking for one isn't all that much fun. But when others come over, it's a real treat."

The attendant made the rounds in first class to take their dinner order and whisk away their snack trays.

"I don't usually fly first class... but then, I don't usually fly. I prefer to drive so that I can see things more clearly, but," she shrugged again, "on this trip, I was stuck without my car, so my parents encouraged me to splurge, which in my line of work was an extravagance."

By now, he'd lost count how many polite nods he'd offered and breathed a sigh of relief when she turned toward the window. She appeared to be peering down toward the ground, so he took the opportunity to slip on his headphones, pull up the soft music, and close his eyes. *Ah, yes... the universal sign to someone on a plane that you don't want to talk.* The motion of the plane was smooth, and he felt his body relax.

A gentle nudge jolted his body awake. Years of having to be combat-ready at an instant, his eyes jerked open as he swung his gaze to the side, seeing Stella's nose scrunching.

"Sorry, Christopher. I need to slip out again."

Trying and failing to hide his sigh, he pulled his legs up and closed his eyes so that the delicious torture of her ass in front of his face wouldn't be such a temptation to stare at. A slight movement to the side grabbed his attention. The man directly across the aisle had leaned to the side, his leering gaze pinned on the back of Stella as she disappeared into the lavatory.

The man looked toward Chris and grinned. "Wouldn't mind joining that little piece in close quarters."

Dropping his gaze to the man's beer gut, it was on the tip of Chris' tongue to tell the man to dream on at the chance of *joining* with anyone in the lavatory, but then the fire of anger that simmered flamed higher as the man unbuckled his seatbelt.

Without giving him the opportunity, Chris stood quickly and blocked the aisle, pretending to get something from the overhead bin. Just as quickly as the first time, Stella hurried back and slid into her seat. As Chris joined her, she smiled.

"I'm so sorry to be a bother."

Shaking his head, he replied, "No worries." He almost suggested she take the aisle seat, but the idea of her being closer to the still-leering man across the aisle had him keep his mouth shut.

She reached inside her purse and pulled out her phone. Holding it to the window and aiming down, she began to snap pictures. He couldn't imagine there was much to see, knowing at this height, clouds were often below them. But she seemed excited, snapping away and then peering some more, her smile widening.

"It's amazing to see the shapes and patterns from up here. The colors are so different from when you're on the ground. Quite inspirational!"

Her comments once again took him by surprise, and he wondered if she wasn't a distant relative to Blessing. Both seemed to have the gift of seeing things unusually, leaving him to feel both surprised and somewhat idiotic. But Stella didn't seem to expect a response. Instead, she pulled out her laptop and began tapping away.

Curious, he tried to close his eyes again but found his gaze drifting to her screen. Photographs and images were moved and manipulated. She appeared to be cropping, copying and pasting, changing lighting, and even altering colors. Having no clue what she could possibly be working on—and not about to ask—he forced his eyes shut and fell into a peaceful rest again.

Another nudge had him shift his legs, but a slight laugh from Stella, who was still in her seat, had him open his eyes to see the attendant with his dinner tray. She handed one to Stella, who had put away her laptop, and then offered the next tray to him.

"I hope you don't mind me waking you," Stella said,

unwrapping her silverware and immediately spreading butter over her hot roll. "But if you didn't wake, they would just pass you by. I figure if you're paying for first class, you need to take advantage of all the perks!"

She bit into the roll and her eyes closed as she moaned. He forced his attention to his meal and off the sounds she made while her tongue slipped over her lips.

She glanced at his plate, and her eyes got bigger. "Oh, that chicken looks good. I was afraid it might be dry. I got the beef stroganoff. And while I know it's just airplane food, it's not bad."

She laughed, and it struck him that her laugh was nice. It sounded *real*. He'd spent enough time in bars near military bases listening to women as they sharpened their flirting skills with fake laughs that somehow managed to make their boobs shake in hopes of catching the eye of a SEAL. If they only knew that the ones they got were only in it for a good time. And if they had higher aspirations, such as becoming a girlfriend, the fake laugh was never going to get them what they hoped it would.

She continued to chatter during dinner, and he nodded at appropriate times. It wasn't that he was trying to be rude, but small talk had never been his strong suit.

Finishing his meal, he caught the attention of the attendant and handed his tray to her. Stella handed hers as well, but she snagged the rest of her roll and dessert off her plate and placed them on a napkin. She caught him looking and shrugged. "Can't see letting it go to waste. I'll snack on it later."

Leaning back, he started to stretch his legs out again, then realized that Stella would probably need to take another trip to the lavatory. Hoping it would be sooner rather than later, she must have read his mind—or he was reading hers because she slipped out again.

"Lucky man."

He turned to see the man across the aisle leering again.

"I get stuck with someone snoring, and you get to sit next to that—"

"Don't say it," he growled, leaning forward, not minding using his size to intimidate when needed.

The man's eyes widened. "Hell, I was just kidding around." The man slumped back in his seat.

Stella returned, her smile bright. Slipping back into her seat, she thanked him. Still pissed at the other passenger, he tightened his jaw and nodded.

She wiped her mouth and peered at him. He could feel her stare boring into the side of his head and gave in and turned toward her, finally allowing his gaze to fully take in her face. Heart-shaped. Lightly tanned. A smattering of pale freckles across her nose and cheeks. Full, pink lips curved into a smile. Up close, he could see her face had a maturity that he'd first missed. Smile lines that emanated from her eyes. Which were the clearest blue eyes he'd ever seen.

As he stared, her smile slipped. "I'm sorry, Christopher. I tend to talk a lot. Um… I'll try to be quiet so you can… um… do whatever."

She leaned back in her seat and turned her face toward the window.

The urge not to be an asshole filled him. "No, really, Stella, it's okay."

She looked over her shoulder, and her lips curved gently, but it didn't reach her eyes before she turned back to peer down out of the window.

And the strangest emotion passed through him as he stared at the back of her messy-ponytailed head.

I'd like to see her really smile again.

4

Chris sat with his headphones on, but his gaze continued to stray to the side to see Stella still looking out the window. Wondering if she was going to ignore him for the rest of the flight, he tried to tell himself that it didn't matter.

Suddenly, she whirled around, her smile back in place, lighting her eyes. "Don't you ever wonder who's down there?"

He blinked, uncertain who the *who* was that she was referring to. "I'm sorry?"

"Down below. You know, the streets and the roads. The houses and the schools. Sometimes, when you look down and you see a car on a road, you wonder who they are and where they're going. Whenever I fly, I wonder if the person down there is looking up at the plane and wondering who *we* are and where *we're* going."

He opened his mouth, then snapped it shut as his brow lowered. Her gaze was still on him, and he felt sure that a response was necessary. "Well, I have to admit that I've never thought about it."

She sighed and nodded. "I'm not surprised. It seems like I often wonder about things that no one else seems to care about." Her nose scrunched. "Weird, I know."

His gaze seemed stuck on her cute expression, once again finding her so different from most women he'd spent time with. Unlike some men, he didn't have a *type*, and yet he had to admit that she didn't fall into any category he'd ever met before. Still uncertain what to say, he nodded, then realized that made it appear as though he were agreeing with her being weird. "I'd say more unique would be a better description."

Her eyes widened, and her smile grew. "Unique. That does sound better." Jerking her head toward the window, she said, "Lean over and look down. You'll see what I mean."

From another woman's lips, that invitation might seem like a contrived method to have him get close, but it was apparent Stella simply wanted him to look out the window. It wasn't an easy maneuver with the armrest between them, but he shifted so that he could lean closer to the window and look down. While he didn't have the best vantage point, he could see what she had been referring to: farmland with roads criss-crossing between small towns.

Shifting back into his seat, he nodded. "Looking out an airplane window isn't what I typically do when I fly, but I can see for someone with an imagination how it would appeal."

She threw her head back and laughed. "That's a very

politically correct response instead of making fun of my uniqueness!"

His lips curved at her unabashed delight. She reached down and pulled up her laptop again, and his attention was drawn to her screen as she brought up images of large pottery vases, then superimposed some of the graphics she'd worked on earlier. He tried to read but found his gaze shifting to her screen, wondering what she was working on.

Before he had a chance to ask, the captain announced over the intercom that due to a non-emergency mechanical issue, the flight was being diverted to Kansas City. A collective groan emerged from the passengers, and Chris closed his eyes for a few seconds, wondering how many more delays he would have to face before getting to California.

The attendant moved through the cabin, assuring everyone that they were safe but letting them know that the passengers would need to disembark once they landed at the airport and that the ticket agents would be available to assist with new arrangements.

Stella's hand landed on his arm, and he looked over to see her wide eyes peering at him. "Do you think they're telling us everything? Are we really safe?"

"I don't think there's anything we can do unless they suddenly go into emergency procedures," he said, keeping his voice calm as he held her gaze.

She stared intently, then must have found the answer she needed to hear as she sucked in a breath before letting it out slowly and nodded. "You're right."

The plane began descending, and after he put away

his headphones and she stowed her laptop, he noticed her looking out the window again. Hoping to take her mind off her fears, he asked, "What do you see out there?"

She looked over her shoulder, but her easy smile was gone. "It's easier to see the cars on the road now. I know sometimes parts of a plane fall off, and I just keep hoping that doesn't happen to us and something lands on someone."

Her answers always surprised him, giving him pause as he pondered her reasoning. Instead of panicking about falling from the sky, she was worried about someone on the ground being in danger.

A few minutes later, the sound of the wheels lowering met their ears, and her hand reached out to clutch his wrist. Normally hating unbidden physical contact, he turned his hand up, extending the silent offer. She accepted, sliding her palm into his, holding tightly until the wheels touched down and the plane slowed to a roll, safely on the ground.

Her grip eased as her shoulders slumped, and she released his hand. Looking at her, he expected embarrassment or a flirty grin, but she simply blew out a long breath, puffing her hair out of her face.

"Wow, thank you. I always hate landings, but I have to confess, that one worried me. I wondered if the pilot was just bullshitting about being safe when he knew we were really going to plummet to the ground!" Without giving him a chance to respond, she bent and picked up her carry-on bag, setting it in her lap, now with an easier smile on her face. "And thanks for being such a nice seatmate."

His fingers twitched as he realized his hand was still on the armrest, his palm still facing upright. And strangely, he missed the warmth from her touch. *Jesus, I must be tired... or hallucinating.* The desire to regain control slid easily onto his shoulders once again, and as soon the plane began disembarking, he moved forward whereas normally he would have stepped into the aisle and backward, allowing his seatmate to go first. Swallowing down his chagrin over his brusque dismissal, he used his long stride to maneuver past people to get to the ticket counter.

Listening to their apologies for not having another flight leaving that evening plus the difficulties of getting one out first thing in the morning, he nodded and turned away. The idea of getting a hotel near the airport was no more appealing in Kansas City than it had been in Atlanta, but with no choice, he headed to the baggage claim.

Being taller than many, it wasn't hard to locate Stella's bright blonde hair, and he moved to the other side of the carousel, hoping to avoid her. He winced at that thought, knowing she'd done nothing to warrant his avoidance. But there was something about her, something so natural and unaffected that had captured his attention. That made her different... and complicated. And starting a new life, including a new career, he didn't want a complication.

She looked up as he was staring in her direction, and her face lit as she tossed a little wave his way. Offering a chin lift in response, he fought the urge to wince again. *Christ, I just met her... I don't have to act like we're friends.*

Seeing his bag, he grabbed it and, unable to stop himself, looked to see if she'd had any difficulty with her luggage. He spied the leering passenger standing next to her, pressing close, offering to help with her bags. So used to Stella's smile, it hit Chris right in the chest to see her blink up at the man, no smile on her face, leaning away from him. That reaction only made the man lean closer.

Stalking around the end of the carousel, he approached to hear the man say, "Come on, dollface. We can share a taxi over to a hotel."

"Not interested," Stella said, standing to her full height, which was inconsequential. "Anyway, I'm heading to the rental car facility."

"Then we can share a taxi that far—"

Grabbing the handle of her luggage, she shook her head as she turned to walk away. "Still not interested."

Chris hesitated as it seemed that she had made her point clear. Stella walked through the doors that led to the airport buses. A quick glance at the jerk showed that his red-faced expression was more anger than leering, and Chris watched as the man followed Stella out the door.

"Fuck," he grumbled under his breath. No way in hell was he going to leave her unprotected with that asshole following. Moving through the door, he watched as the man bypassed the taxis and continued following Stella as she waited for the next bus to take her to the rental car facility. She glanced over her shoulder, seeing the man nearby, her brow lowering.

Elbowing past the man, Chris walked up to her and smiled. "Hey, I got my bag early so we can go get a car together."

She blinked, then smiled widely, her eyes twinkling with mirth. "That'd be great! I was hoping you'd get here in time."

The sound of mumbled cursing behind them met their ears, and she leaned to the side to peer around Chris' much larger body. A little gasp of laughter slipped out as she looked back up at him. "That did the trick. Thank you! I'm pretty sure I could've handled him, but you never know. Some men just don't like being told 'no.'"

"I thought maybe he was just an asshole, but I sure as hell didn't like the look on his face when he started walking after you," Chris admitted.

Her head swung around to look up at him, eyes wide. "Really? Damn. I just thought he was going to be a nuisance."

As the airport bus rolled to a stop in front of them, she reached out and patted his arm. "Thanks again, Christopher. For being a great seatmate, not getting too pissed about me running to the lavatory or talking too much, and for making sure that guy stayed away."

He hesitated once again. She was getting on the bus, and all he had to do was turn and head to the taxi queue to get a ride to the hotel. And yet, his feet moved forward, and he climbed up into the bus, claiming the seat next to her.

Once again, her eyes jerked open wide as she looked up at him. "You're going to get a rental car, too?"

Shrugging, he said, "I just figured I could make sure you get off safely. Then I'll head over to a hotel to fly out tomorrow morning." Her nose scrunched again, and he battled the description *adorable* that settled in his brain.

"You don't have to do that. I promise I've traveled by myself lots of times."

He glanced down at her petite stature and lifted his brows. "I'm sure you have, and I'm not trying to be insulting. But I'd feel better if I knew that guy was gone for good."

She shrugged and nodded. "I was looking on my phone to see how long it would take to drive to California—"

"You're going to drive to California? I thought maybe you'd changed your plans and were going to stay local."

"I feel like I've been in airplanes and airports all day, and after we landed safely, I decided that perhaps I should keep my feet on the ground for a little while."

Not following her train of thought, he shook his head. "Stella, it's a long way to drive to California!"

"Yep, twenty-eight hours, and that's driving straight."

"You can't drive that long straight through!"

"I know! I'll take breaks along the way. But just think of all the amazing sights I'll see."

He opened his mouth to refute her reasoning, then pinched his lips together as he had done several times since meeting her. It shouldn't matter what she wanted to do. They weren't even friends, just two people who passed some time while sitting next to each other on a plane ride.

She gently placed her hand on his arm, giving a little squeeze as the bus came to a stop. "Hey, Christopher, I'll be fine. I love to travel, and driving is a great way to experience things. Slower than flying, but at least I can go at my own pace." Laughing, she added, "I read somewhere that 'It's the journey that matters, in the end.'"

She stood, grabbed her bags, and made her way to the exit, tossing a smile over her shoulder. Mouthing, 'Goodbye,' she walked toward the building.

The air left his lungs, and he stared at the back of her as she disappeared into the rental car facility. Where she would rent a car and drive off. By herself. God knew what trouble she might land in. He was aware his thoughts sounded condescending, but while she seemed to glide along in her own little happy place, he knew the shadows that could come out at night and what dangers could hide in the dark. Years as a SEAL taught him that.

Jumping to his feet, he grabbed his bags and followed her inside.

I must be fuckin' losing my mind.

5

Stella managed to balance her bag with her laptop on top of her rolling suitcase, slinging her purse across her body as she got off the bus. Used to making impulsive decisions based on a whim, she'd decided she'd like to see the Midwest from the ground. But, instead of her typical excitement, her mind was in disarray. Not because of the obvious reasons like interrupted travel, running through airports, emergency landings, and dealing with a creepy man who she'd caught leering at her every time she headed to the airplane lavatory. No, her whirling emotions had everything to do with the gorgeous man she'd sat next to on the plane. Tall. Built. Dark-haired. Blue eyes that captivated her artist's inter-est... as well as made her try to decide if it was his mouth or his eyes that made her want to jump him.

While she didn't often fly, whenever she did, her luck would usually have her next to someone who either rolled their eyes when she spoke, grumbled every time she needed to pee, glared when she took extra time to choose a snack, or leaned so close they were in her personal space. But Christopher wasn't like that at all. Not only was he a beautiful specimen of a man, but he'd also quietly shifted whenever she needed to exit into the aisle, didn't roll his eyes or huff when she chattered, and didn't leer one single time.

Add in the fact that he'd moved protectively toward her and then accompanied her on the airport bus to ensure her safety and it was no wonder her mind was racing with thoughts of gratitude mixed with surprise and covered in a healthy dose of lust.

Pushing through the doors, she glanced around to see the variety of car rental businesses stationed around the counters. Much to her dismay, most of them had signs that displayed the words 'No Vehicles Available.'

Hurrying to the closest one that indicated an availability, she walked straight up to the counter. Offering what she hoped was a 'please help me' smile toward the young man, she opened her mouth to speak, but he jumped in first.

"Before you ask, yes, I do have a vehicle. Last one on my lot. Probably the most expensive, and that's why it's still there."

Blinking at his rather brusque sales pitch, she cocked her head to the side. "What's going on?"

"NASCAR race this weekend. Two sporting events and three big-name concerts. We've been booked up and sold out, and that includes getting all the rental cars we could from the city."

"Oh. I never thought about a run on rental cars.

Well," she shrugged, "at least you've got something. I hope it's small. An economy size would be great."

He barked out a laugh. "Nope. It's the biggest SUV we've got. Looks like a tank." He glanced down at her petite stature and shook his head. "You'd probably need a ladder just to get up into it."

Irritated that he'd made assumptions based on her size, she started to let him know she could handle any vehicle when suddenly, another thought hit her. Scrunching her nose in distaste, she sighed. "It probably guzzles gasoline, doesn't it?"

"Yep. It's got a full tank and would need to be returned with a full tank. Where are you going?"

"California."

He barked out another laugh and shook his head. "That'll cost you a fortune!"

Plopping her hands onto her hips, she looked up at him. "You're not doing a very good sales job!"

"Lady, I get paid whether or not that last vehicle gets rented—" He stopped in mid-sentence as his eyes lifted to a point above her head and then widened.

"Is there a problem here?"

Recognizing the low, smooth voice even though she'd only heard it a few times, she turned around and looked up, smiling at the sight of Christopher standing behind her. "Hi! Long time no see."

His lips twitched as his gaze moved down to her. "Hello again." He inclined his head toward the counter. "Problem?"

"As you can see, the rental lot is almost decimated," she said, swiping a lock of hair back from her face.

"Something about NASCAR, sports, and concerts. I take it everyone has decided that Kansas City is the place to be, and they've wiped out most of the vehicles. He's got one but says it's a huge SUV, expensive, and the gas will kill me going to California." Chris kept his gaze fixed on her face, giving her his full attention, a trait she appreciated. Suddenly curious as to why he was in the car rental building, she raised her eyebrows. "What are you doing here?"

He hesitated for a few seconds, then replied, "Checking to make sure you're being taken care of."

Uncertain of his meaning, she nodded, nonetheless. The man behind the counter appeared cowed now that Christopher was around. Pressing her lips together, she knew she could handle herself, but it was nice to have Christopher around to make sure she wasn't being taken advantage of. She wasn't so independent that she didn't appreciate having someone in her corner.

"As I told the little lady—" His voice cut off suddenly when she speared him with a glare. He cleared his throat and began again. "As I told... her... this was the only vehicle I had and probably the only one she'll find here this evening."

"Excuse me!" came a voice from a counter to the left. "I can help you. I just had a cancellation of my last vehicle. It's still an SUV, but smaller and much more economical!"

Stella turned and grinned widely at the older man waving her over. Looking back at the first man, she wiggled her fingers, and still smiling, glanced over her shoulder toward Christopher. "I swear, you must be my good luck charm!" She'd only known him for a short time but knew he'd have no reply. *Man of few words but big with action.* Rolling her luggage down the counter, she dug for her wallet and struggled to pull out her driver's license. "Got it!" she exclaimed.

She didn't have to turn around to know that Christopher had moved down the counter with her and was now standing at her back again. Hating for him to miss getting to a hotel, she said, "It's okay, Christopher. I can take care of everything from here."

"May I have your credit card, please?" the nice man asked.

She reached into her wallet, but before she was able to pull it out, she heard the slap of a card on the countertop. Jumping slightly, she spied Christopher's hand in front of her, pushing his credit card and driver's license toward the man. She jerked her head around so fast her braid swung over her shoulder, hitting his arm before landing on her chest. "You don't need to pay! I've got this!"

His gaze dropped to her, his blue eyes full of thoughts she couldn't discern but kept her mesmerized.

"I'll pay for the car. And the gas."

His words slowly penetrated the mental fog, and she blinked. "You're… what?"

"You're going to California. I'm going to California. You're tired of flying, and I really don't care how I get there. But I wouldn't mind making sure you get there in one piece."

She sucked in her lips and pinched them tightly, her

brow lowering. "Are you inviting yourself on my impromptu road trip?"

His lips quirked upward on one side. "I guess I am."

"And did it occur to you to ask if I wanted any company on this road trip?" He continued to hold her gaze, and she struggled to find any serial killer vibes. *Presumptuous but not killer.* Scrunching her nose, she said, "You already know I'm not the easiest passenger to travel with."

"And you already know I'm not a big conversationalist."

She glanced toward the man behind the counter, finding his attention riveted on the two of them. Turning back to Christopher, she asked, "So, why exactly are you making this journey proposition?"

Instead of answering, he reached inside his wallet and pulled out his military ID and special investigator's license and snagged his driver's license off the counter. Handing them all to her, he waited.

She looked down, seeing that they all matched his photograph. *Well, he's who he says he is.*

"I recently retired from the U.S. Navy. Former SEAL. Heading to California to start my new job with Lighthouse Security Investigations." His words were clipped, given in an official manner.

She swallowed, her mind sifting through the information. *I don't mind traveling alone. I also like to have company. Is it smart to share a ride with somebody I don't know?* She snorted slightly. *No. But then, I once traveled across Europe with people I didn't know either.* She chewed on her bottom lip for a moment. *He's gorgeous but a lot more stoic than I'm used to being around.*

He leaned forward, his face now close and his voice soft. "I don't blame you for being cautious, Stella. In fact, I'd be pissed if you weren't. I just hate the idea of you traveling alone."

Her tongue darted out to moisten her suddenly dry lips. "If the only reason you're coming is because you hate for me to travel alone, then that makes me feel indebted."

He shook his head slowly from side to side. "I have no problem following plans, but as a former SEAL, I'm used to reevaluating situations and making changes instantly. For me, making sure you get to California safely just feels like the right thing to do. And I assure you, you would not be indebted to me in any way."

A tiny seed of a possible new friendship was planted deep inside her chest. Her smile widened. "You know, I read a meme the other day that went something like 'good company on a journey makes the way seem better...' or maybe it was shorter."

"'Good company on a journey makes the way seem shorter.' Izaak Walton."

Her chin jerked back. "How the hell did you know that?"

She could have sworn a blush hit his face when he mumbled, "I heard it somewhere recently."

Throwing her head back, she laughed. "Wow... what a coincidence. So, it looks like I've got a travel companion!"

Turning back to her, he inclined his head toward his

IDs still in her hand. "Take a picture. Send it to someone you trust."

She did as he instructed and then handed her driver's license to him. "You should do the same."

He looked at her license and then nodded.

Glancing toward the man behind the counter, she said, "We'll split the cost right down the middle."

The man was smiling but shook his head. "I'm sorry, but my system can only take one credit card, and I've already run Mr. Andrews' card through."

"Oh. Well, okay."

She looked up at Christopher. "When we get to California, I'll pay you back for half."

She placed her wallet back into her purse, then grabbed the handle to her rolling luggage. Walking next to each other as they moved through the side doors to the mostly empty parking lot toward the small SUV sitting alone, she looked up, seeing his intense gaze on her.

"If we're traveling together, you might as well call me Chris. All my friends do."

Grinning, she tried to shoulder bump him, but considering how tall he was, it was more like her shoulder bumped into his ribcage. Sucking in a deep breath of air, glad to be out of the stuffy airplane and airport, she felt light. "You know, Chris, this is going to be fun."

6

―――――――

"This is going to be fun." As Chris started the vehicle after he and Stella stored their belongings in the back, her words resounded in his head. It was all he could do to keep from rolling his eyes. *Fun?* A long-ass road trip with a woman who had a penchant for saying what she thought, changed her mind quickly, didn't appear to pay attention to dangers in her surroundings... *and is beautiful.*

He shoved that thought down. *I'm not a fuckin' teenager thinking with his dick. Nope, I just want to make sure she gets where she's going safely, and since she's determined to travel by car, then so be it.* He'd been surprised when she showed him her driver's license. Stella Parker. Twenty-eight years old. She was so youthful in appearance, she could have easily passed for much younger.

"Okay, my phone GPS says we should turn right at the next light—"

"I've got it," he said.

"Huh?"

Tapping the computer screen on the dashboard, he repeated, "I've got it."

"Oh… well. My car is so old, I have to use my phone's GPS." She leaned over and looked at the map. "So, we turn right—"

"I've got it," he reiterated for the third time.

She quieted for a moment, then went back to tapping on her phone. "We didn't really talk about which direction we were going to take."

"I assumed we'd go west."

He felt her eyes staring at the side of his head before she laughed. "Oh, my God, Chris, I think you just made a joke!"

His lips quirked. "Not really a joke, Stella."

"You know what I mean." She play-slapped his arm. "Although, we've got a long way to go to get you really loosened up!"

"I figure we can take Highway 70 west through Kansas and stop for the night somewhere."

"Um… speaking of stopping…"

He swung his head around in surprise. "Seriously?"

"I didn't go after we landed because I was trying to get my luggage. And then I wanted to get away from Mr. Creep. I thought about going at the rental facility, but then you showed up, and all my thoughts went out of my head. So, yeah, I need a pit stop."

Glad they hadn't gotten so far down the road that it would be hard to find a place to stop, he pulled off at the next exit, easily finding a gas station and market. Stella hopped out of the car and hustled through the front door. He'd parked where he could keep an eye on her and through the glass window saw her head to the back hallway. A moment later, she reemerged, then disappeared behind an aisle. Just when he was ready to get out of the car and look for her, she popped over to the checkout counter, and his eyes bugged at the arm full of junk she was buying. The young man behind the counter was laughing, and he watched as she waved her hands around, talking nonstop. He wondered if she'd ever met a stranger. *At least her antenna was up with the letch in the airport.*

Tossing the young man a wave while shaking her head, giving Chris the feeling that she'd just been asked out, she pushed her way through the door and beamed her smile toward him as she carried her bags to their vehicle. Climbing in, she set the bags at her feet and turned toward him. "Score!"

Lifting a brow, he repeated, "Score?"

"They had chili corn chips as well as ranch sour cream nachos. Best taste in the world is to chomp on those two kinds of chips at the same time."

He kept his gaze on her, wondering if she was joking, but as she opened both bags, he realized she was serious. "You do know that sounds disgusting, right?"

She crunched, then swallowed, shaking her head. "No! It's like a party in your mouth!"

While Chris didn't ascribe to the idea that his body was a temple, he took his physical training seriously and couldn't imagine what would happen if he shoved in as much processed junk as Stella was doing right now.

"I also have soda, diet and regular, but both with caffeine 'cause I figure we'll be up late driving. But if drinking soda will be a shock to your system, then I have water and juice, also."

His lips twitched. "We can go for a couple of hours before finding a hotel, then be ready to start tomorrow morning."

Her hand reached out to land on his arm. "Thank you! I'd so much rather travel during the day so that I can find places to take pictures."

His arm tingled even after she removed her hand. Shaking his head, he dismissed the ridiculous notion that one had anything to do with the other. He focused on the drive, fighting the urge to speed along the sparsely traveled highway leading west as it cut through the middle of Kansas. Settling into the feel of the vehicle, he tried to ignore the crunching coming from the passenger seat.

Suddenly, chips were placed at his mouth, and he startled.

"Come on. Open up. These are great."

He opened his mouth to deny that he wanted a snack when two chips were pushed past his lips. Unless he wanted to spit them out, he had no choice but to chew and swallow. An explosion of flavor hit his taste-buds. *Damn... that's good.*

"See, I told you," she said, holding more out for him to take from her fingers.

Not used to eating food that someone else placed into his mouth—in fact, he couldn't ever remember eating food from someone else's fingers—he none-theless opened at her command and accepted several more chips. He'd barely chewed and swallowed again when an opened bottle was held up next.

"It's water," she said. "I was going to offer soda, but I have a feeling the chips might be enough of a junk-shock to your system."

Another smile played about his lips. Taking the bottle, he drank deeply before handing it back. "Thanks."

She laughed as she screwed the cap back on, then took a large sip from her soda. "After I saw the look on your face when I handed you the chips, it dawned on me that my idea of travel food and yours are probably very different. But this was the best I could do under the circumstances."

"Don't worry about it, Stella. But I'm good."

"How far are we going to get tonight?"

"We'll get past Topeka. Honestly, I could drive for hours, but Salina isn't a bad place to stop. We should be able to get a hotel for tonight and start fresh in the morning."

"I'm an early riser, so that won't be a problem. And if we get a hotel that has a breakfast buffet, we can eat before we get on the road."

Lifting a brow, he glanced over at her. "Are you sure your body can handle anything healthy?"

An exaggerated huff met his ears. "I'll have you know I can eat healthily! It's just that when it comes to snacks, I'm very serious about those."

A smile crossed her lips, and he realized it was matched by one of his own. Shaking his head, he turned his attention back to the road. She began fiddling with the radio, and he hoped she wouldn't land on a station where he'd feel like his ears were being assaulted, surprised when she settled on 1970s music.

"Is this okay?" she asked. "I know you probably hate this, don't you?"

As her hand reached for the console again, he quickly said, "No, it's fine."

"Really? I like all kinds of music but thought this would be fun."

"My mom loved music and often played the songs she remembered as a teenager."

"Oh, my God! My parents are the same! Growing up, I was always hearing Doobie Brothers, Chicago, Boston, Aerosmith, and all the other groups they remembered. They'd start dancing around the living room and pull me into their crazy dance party."

The smile on her face was nostalgic, and he felt glad that she had those memories, mixed with a small pang of envy. God knows he didn't have any memories of his parents dancing together in their home.

The next hour passed easily as Stella continued to snack, occasionally offering a few more chips and water to him. The sun had set by the time they arrived in Salina, Kansas, and he easily found a hotel. They walked into the lobby together, and he made arrangements for two rooms next to each other. She whipped out her credit card, paying for hers, then moved to the side and stretched her arms over her head, bending and twisting. His gaze snagged on her, ensnared by her invisible web, and he stared as the movement pushed her breasts forward and lifted her shirt just enough to show off the strip of skin. Irritated at his lack of control, he turned back to the receptionist, glaring as the young man behind the desk stared wide-eyed and slack-jawed toward Stella. Growling, he recaptured the man's attention. The young man blushed bright red, ran their credit cards, and shoved the key cards back toward Chris.

The growl that had erupted surprised even Chris, but as he and Stella walked to the elevator, he convinced himself that he was simply making sure she was safe in all ways. *God knows she had no idea she was being stared at, once again proving she has no idea of her own beauty. And all the more reason for me to make sure I'm here to... to... to what?* Stella wasn't a mission. She hadn't even asked for his help. And yet, something about her called to him. *This is not the time to get attached... not with a new job and a new life!*

"Hey, we're here!"

His feet stumbled to a halt at her words, realizing he hadn't paid attention to his surroundings and had passed her door. Irritation flooded him. *How the hell can I keep her at a distance if thinking about her makes me lose attention?* Grumbling, "I know where we are!" He opened her door and then scanned the inside, avoiding her gaze. His words had erupted, sounding clipped even to his own ears. Turning, he handed the key card to her, then chanced a glance to see her furrowed brow as she appeared to hide the effect of his sharp words.

"Thank you, Chris. For everything. I'll see you in the morning," she said softly, closing the door on him.

He stood in the hallway for a minute, his fists planted on his hips and his chin down as he stared at his boots. He'd only known Stella for about twelve hours, and in that time, she'd managed to twist him inside out and upside down. He'd entered a conversation with an airplane seatmate, something he'd never done. He'd reacted protectively when he felt she might be in need. He'd altered his plans in an impromptu desire to help. He'd listened as she sang along to old songs, loving the sound of her voice while laughing at a few of her mis-sung phrases. And he'd actually let her feed him a crazy-ass chip combination from her fingers.

She hadn't asked for any of that but had managed to draw him in, nonetheless. And he'd repaid her by snapping. He lifted his hand to knock on the door, then hesitated. The desire to apologize was strong, and yet... *Maybe it's better this way. We're travel companions heading in the same direction, that's all.*

With another sigh, he grabbed his bag from the floor and moved to the next door. Unlocking his room, he stepped into a mirror image of her room. Suddenly tired, he dropped his bag and sat on the edge of the bed.

Needing a distraction, he pulled out his phone and called a good friend, soon to be a coworker. "Hey, Rick. Thought I'd call and give you an update." Richard Rankin had also been a SEAL, but they'd served on different teams. Their paths had crossed numerous times over the years, and a friendship had developed. Rick's brother left the military and now worked for the original Lighthouse Security Investigation firm in Maine. Rick followed in his brother's footsteps but recently relocated to California to the new LSI-West Coast office, where Chris was heading.

"I thought your flight would have been in by now," Rick said.

"Change of plans, man. Delays, mechanical problems, you name it, the day was one dumbass thing after another. Finally made it to Kansas City and decided to take a couple of days to drive the rest of the way."

"Driving? Damn, you did get sick of airports, didn't you?"

Chuckling, he agreed. "Since I had a few extra days, I figured I'd take a chance to enjoy the sights and not have to be packed into another plane. I should be in California in two days and will head straight to the apartment. Once I get close, I'll give you a call."

"A nice long drive by yourself on the open road sounds good. Carson is excited to have you on board, and you'll have plenty of time to get acclimated before you're sent out on a mission."

It was on the tip of his tongue to mention Stella, but he remained quiet about having a traveling companion. He knew the assumption would be he was hooking up on the road with some random woman or he'd lost his mind by agreeing to travel for a couple of days with a perfect stranger. He definitely wasn't hooking up, but neither did he think he'd lost his mind. Stella was just… well, Stella. Hard to define, and right now, talking to his friend, he didn't want to. "Can't wait to get started with LSI-WC. Thanks again for the recommendation, both to me and for me."

"Not a problem. Carson only wants to hire the best, and as far as I'm concerned, that includes you."

With promises to share a beer as soon as he got to

California and with goodbyes said, Chris disconnected the call. He remained quiet for a moment but heard no sounds coming from Stella's room. There might just be a wall between where they'd be sleeping, but his words had created a much larger breach. Wincing, he headed into the bathroom, ready to wash off the day's travel from his body. And hopefully, the regret would go down the drain, as well.

Later, as he lay in bed, he finally fell asleep with his regret still just as large.

7

Stella walked out of the bathroom having showered, her naturally bouncing walk a little more subdued than normal. She jerked down the covers on the bed, piled the pillows up against the headboard, and climbed in. Leaning back, she stared at the empty room, aware that the wall behind her was all that separated her from Chris.

She winced, scrunching her nose at the memory of his growling words in the hall. She sighed, her shoulders slumping as she thought back on the entire day.

Rising early, she'd made it to the airport in time only to be held up by an extra-long line at security. Having rushed through the terminal, she'd made it onto her first flight only to have it be delayed for takeoff. Reaching Atlanta, she'd had to race through that airport, barely making it onto the plane before the doors closed.

When she'd seen her seat companion, her feet had nearly stumbled, and she was stunned that she hadn't landed in his lap in her attempt to sit quickly. Long legs.

Long, thick-thighed legs. *Is thick-thighed a word? Doesn't matter, it's the appropriate word.* Broad shoulders. Biceps that stretched the material of his shirt. Dark-brown hair, neatly trimmed. Blue, piercing eyes. Lips that looked firm although they didn't turn up into a smile nearly as often as she would have liked to have seen. And yet, when they did, it was mesmerizing.

Her art anatomy professor would have loved having Chris as a model. And even though she'd never planned on using the human form for her art, she could easily make an exception in his case.

Sighing again, she thought of how she'd blabbed while he'd tried to put on his headphones. She wasn't flirting, not ever really knowing how to flirt, but just being around him made her nervous.

The idea of driving had been an inspiration that came over her as she'd stared out the airplane window, wishing she could have been on the ground to take photographs of the scenes after having collected a group of pictures showing scenic shapes and patterns from above.

Once at the baggage claim, she'd been aware of the creep once he'd leaned into her space. She'd handled creeps before but didn't mind admitting it was nice when Chris stepped in. *And then escorted me to the rental facility. And then said he'd come along, too.* She knew that to some people, that could seem just as creepy, but she didn't get that feel from him at all. She knew enough about SEALs to know that he could be trusted. Even insisting she take his ID and send the information to someone.

Of course, she got the feeling that he'd rather be anywhere other than with her. *Although, we did bond a little over music.*

Chewing on her bottom lip, she startled when her phone rang. Grinning, she connected. "Mom!"

"I see you weren't attacked by a serial killer pretending to be a good guy!"

Scrunching her nose, she picked at the edge of the comforter. "God, I know, Mom. I guess my decisions today make me sound like I'm one of those stupid girls in a horror movie. But seriously, he really is a great guy."

"Well, just so you know, your father had Joe check out his credentials."

"Oh, God," she groaned. Joe was her uncle who'd worked for the FBI until his recent retirement. The two brothers couldn't be more different in personalities, but they'd remained close throughout their adult lives.

"He was pleased to report that this Chris Andrews is who he says he is although he wasn't happy that you drove off with him before checking him out."

"I've got good instincts about people. Mom, you know that. You're the same way." She thought back to the stories of her mom and dad meeting at a concert where they'd bonded over music, art, and a lot of pot. Her mom and dad had traveled the country shortly after in search of more music, art, and probably a lot more pot. The occasional craft beer had now become their vice of choice, but their love of music and art had remained.

"Yeah, baby, I know," her mom chuckled.

"Anyway, it's not like you and Dad. He's just a really nice if somewhat uptight man who's heading to California also and was willing to share the costs and driving."

"So, no butterflies?"

Her mother was a big believer in butterflies and always said that was how she'd known Stella's father was the one for her. That was why Stella had once dated one of her art professors, a four-month relationship that didn't end well when he became possessively jealous of any of her friends. Those butterflies were also the reason why she'd dated the lead musician of a band that was only marginally successful. He'd continued to live off her earnings while promising that one day he'd pay her back. After a year and then finding out she was not the only woman he'd made those promises to, she'd kicked him out. She'd finally decided that perhaps butterflies in the stomach were not always a good indicator of deep feelings—or at least not the only reason to start a relationship.

Pressing her lips together, she wasn't in the habit of lying to her mom. Finally, she forced out a laugh which she hoped was convincing and said, "Nah. He's too stuck in his ways for me, and I'm certainly not his cup of tea. But he's a perfect gentleman and a really cool guy who wants to make sure I'm okay."

As she said the words, she realized she wasn't just feeding her mom a line, but the sentiment was true. Chris had been nothing but a gentleman, and it was really cool that he was helping to share the costs and the driving on the trip. And right then, she decided that for the rest of the trip, she would be polite, friendly, and try to be the perfect traveling companion.

"I'll talk to you tomorrow, Mom, and let you know where we are. I love you."

"Love you too, Stella sweetheart."

Disconnecting the call, she placed her phone onto the nightstand after setting her alarm. When she'd told Chris she was an early riser, it was the truth, but she wanted to make sure she didn't oversleep and make them late. *After all, the perfect traveling companion would never be late.*

Turning out the light, she slid down under the covers and closed her eyes. Lifting her hand, she placed her palm against the headboard, knowing he was just on the other side of the wall. *Sleep tight, Chris.* Rolling to her side, she fell asleep feeling strangely safe in the middle of Kansas, knowing she wasn't completely alone.

"Hi!" Stella greeted as Chris walked into the hotel's breakfast buffet. "I went ahead and got some juice and coffee for you." She inclined her head to his side of the table before smiling up at him again.

"Uh... thanks. You didn't have to do that, but it's appreciated."

"Caffeine, the nectar of the gods. Actually, I always wondered where that phrase came from. Who knows if the gods had nectar, but..." *Oh, shit, I'm rambling.* Her smile wobbled, but instead of seeming irritated, Chris' lips curved slightly.

"Well, I don't know if the gods have nectar, but this'll do it for me," he replied.

The air whooshed from her lungs, her smile wide once again.

He looked down at her plate and his brows lifted. She followed his gaze, spying her piled-high plate. Scrunching her nose, she leaned forward and whispered, "It's all you can eat. So, if we have to pay the exorbitant fee they charge for this buffet, I'm going to eat *all* I can eat!"

"Then I guess I'd better get up there before you make a second round."

Laughter burst forth. "You must have slept well to be ready to make jokes first thing in the morning."

His smile slipped ever so slightly before he offered a nod and then headed over to the buffet. A moment later, he returned, his plate full although not quite as full as hers. Settling into his seat, they ate in companionable silence for a few minutes. When she was well-stuffed and had pushed her plate back, she grabbed her coffee cup and sipped the creamed and sweetened brew, sighing in contentment.

"I… well, I want to apologize for snapping at you last evening—"

Her gaze jumped to his, but she waved her hand dismissively. "There's no need, really."

"But there is to me, Stella."

She sucked in her lips and nodded.

Now that she'd given her full attention to him, the unflappable Chris appeared uncertain. Finally, he cleared his voice and lifted his gaze to her. "I'm not a very spontaneous man, which might seem odd considering that, as a former Seal, we had to make spontaneous and often life-and-death decisions instantaneously. Perhaps that's why in my personal life I prefer to make a plan and stick with it. I suppose it gives me a sense of control which I find comfortable. Yesterday, there were a lot of things that were out of my control, making the trip less than optimum."

Stella listened carefully, not only wanting Chris to get off his chest everything he was feeling but really wanting to gain more understanding of this fascinating man in front of her. Even now, as he spoke, he seemed to be in complete control. She offered a slight nod, encouraging him to continue.

"In truth, I wasn't looking forward to having to go through the irritation of commercial flying again today but had not considered any other option. You'd been so friendly on the flight and so unaware of the attention of the man who I didn't trust. At first, I just wanted to make sure you were safe. I found that I was uncomfortable with the idea of you driving halfway across the country by yourself, which is not indicative of an assumption that you weren't able." He lifted his shoulders and shook his head. "Honestly, I have no idea why I suggested that I come with you. It was a spur-of-the-moment decision that shocked me. And I suppose that by last night when we arrived, I was wondering why I acted in a way that was not my normal self. I snapped at you, and I apologize for that. It wasn't you... that was all on me."

A warm sense of comfort moved through her at his

confession and explanation. In front of her was a man who exuded power and strength, intelligence and control. And stepping out of his comfort zone with her yesterday, he'd had to question his motives. She leaned forward, her elbows on the table, then reached out one hand and placed it on his arm. "Are you sorry you made the choice? Because I would never want you to feel obligated. We can drive to the next airport and—"

"No, absolutely not. I want to take this trip with you." He shook his head with vehemence, his intense gaze never leaving her face. He winced, then added, "I can't promise to be great company, but we'll get to California in one piece. I can drive, and you can just enjoy the journey." Before she had a chance to respond, he softened his voice. "Really, Stella. I'd like to do this."

Squeezing his arm, she smiled. "Then I'd love to have you continue this journey with me. And for the record, you really weren't all that snappish last night. I think we can chalk it all up to just a crappy air travel day." Shrugging, her smile widened. "And today is the start of a brand-new day filled with the glories of sights to see, great companionship, and road snacks!"

8

Road snacks. Chris grinned.

Walking into the buffet, it had been easy to spot Stella. While other hotel guests were wandering sleepily around the small restaurant, her blond braid hung over her shoulder, and it was the wavy tendrils that created a golden halo that caught his attention. Then his eyes traveled to the bright purple shirt paired with jeans that cupped her hips and led down to the same purple sneakers she'd worn yesterday.

He'd shown up at breakfast to apologize for being so brusque the night before, not having a clue how she was going to react. He half-expected her to greet him with a cold shoulder or extract whatever she could out of his apology, but in what appeared to be true Stella fashion, she'd accepted him graciously, had already gotten him coffee, and had generously planned for their day of driving.

Now, he lifted a brow hearing Stella mention snacks and glanced down at her previously-filled-and-now-empty breakfast plate. He wondered where all the food went because she was tiny. But with the way she flitted around like a hummingbird, he figured she burned off the calories.

Her gaze followed his, and she laughed. "I know. Breakfast is barely over, and I'm talking about snacks. But we won't have to stop right away because I went to the snack bar next to the registration desk and loaded up. More chips. More cookies. And I filled the water bottles from yesterday with ice water, so we're good to go!"

Smiling, he nodded. "Then it sounds like we're ready. We can head back to our rooms and get our things." Standing, he hesitated as he glanced at the to-go coffee cups in her hand and added, "Uh… you might want to make sure to… um…"

"Yep… bathroom break before we leave. Check!"

With her laughter ringing in his ears, he noticed the envious gazes of other men in the restaurant. Placing his hand on her lower back as they walked out, he refused to analyze why he felt the need to claim her, but there was no denying his fingers tingled as she twisted around and speared him with a beaming smile.

"Oh, here! Here!" Stella cried out.

"Again?" Chris glanced to the side, her excitement palpable, and yet at this rate, they'd get to California sometime next year instead of a couple of days. They had only been on the road for four hours and had just crossed over the state line into Colorado, but they'd already stopped three times, once for a bathroom break and twice so that she could hop out of the car and take pictures of the vista. As far as Chris could see, the vista was the same—flat, dry grassy land that extended forever. Watching her turn slowly as she snapped pictures with her phone, it dawned on him that he'd never asked her *why*. Why did she take pictures out the window of the plane? Why did she take pictures of the sunsets over the rolling hills of eastern Kansas? Why was she taking pictures of the same flat, unremarkable scenes now? His mother used to say that he was inquisitive as a child, but then he'd learned that if something didn't fit his father's idea of worth knowing, there was no reason to ask. And in the SEALs, it wasn't his job to ask why but to just follow the commands.

The SUV door opened, and the Stella-whirlwind hopped inside, her smile wide. "I promise that is the last picture I'll take for a little while," she gushed, twisting to buckle her seatbelt. The ever-present Midwest wind had whipped her hair into a larger halo. The heavier tendrils fell back onto her shoulders, but the shorter hair around her face stood straight up.

He waited to pull back onto the highway until she was ready, which he had learned meant buckling, getting her snack back out of the bag that was at her feet, sipping her drink, shifting in her seat until she was comfortable, and then flipping through the photographs on her camera. Granted, none of these things took much time, but he once again wondered if he was going to have to call LSI and get an extension on his starting date based on Stella's travel idiosyncrasies.

"So," he began, glancing to the side, seeing her bent over her phone, her fingers gliding over the screen. "Can I ask about the pictures you're taking?"

A snort erupted from the passenger seat. "Can you ask? It's not like I'm taking secret spy pictures and would have to kill you if you knew what they were!" She grinned and held up her phone.

At a glance, he spied the very same vista that they'd stared at for almost four hours. "Okay… um, I guess a better question would be what do you do with those pictures? I saw you download some to your computer on the airplane but wasn't sure what you were doing."

"You could have asked," she said softly, her head cocked to the side.

"I guess I figured that I'd never see you after the plane trip and that it wouldn't matter to me what you were doing." As soon as the words left his mouth, he realized they made him sound harsh and uncaring. "Not that I wasn't curious…"

She laughed. "It's okay, Chris. I'm just messing with you. Anyway, I use the photographs for inspiration. Kind of my muse."

"Muse? For what?"

"My art. I'm a potter."

"A potter?"

Laughter rang out again. "Are you going to parrot everything I say?"

The heat of blush raced up his neck. "Sorry. I guess I am. But potter? As in you make pottery?" Just then, he remembered seeing her computer screen on the airplane, and it appeared as though she were superimposing some of the pictures that she'd taken out her window onto a large clay vase.

"Yes," she nodded with enthusiasm. "I'm an artist. I have a small studio in California but love to travel when possible to obtain inspiration from the scenes around me."

"Wow… I'm impressed. Artistic is probably the last word anyone would use to describe me, so this is all new. How does that work?"

She twisted in her seat, facing him more fully. "I get inspiration from the colors I see around me, but also the lines and shapes. It might be from clouds, or trees, or just the way the sky meets the horizon."

Her eyes were bright, and as she talked, her hands waved in front of her, excitement filling each word in motion. His lips curved upward, enjoying her explanation even if it didn't mean a lot to his non-artistic mind. As a medic, he'd put his training to use, saving the lives of several team members more than once and certainly patching up many others who had less serious injuries. His medical skills had also been used for civilians they'd encountered on missions. But he'd learned to keep his emotions under wraps. After all, his team needed his concentration as much as his care.

He tried to remember the last time he was that excited about something. He loved his job, enjoyed the people he worked with, and strove to do the best he could with every mission, but Stella seemed to approach everything with an excitement that he found strangely refreshing. "I can tell your creative mind is in overdrive, but it's still hard to imagine. Maybe you can show me what was on your computer sometime."

"I'd love that!" Turning back toward the front, she was quiet for a moment, then pointed out the windshield. "Look at the view out the window and note the variety of colors. Right now, there are no clouds in the sky, but earlier, there were. We first stopped this morning, and I wanted to get the colors of the sky as the sun was rising behind us. Then there were clouds when we stopped the second time, and I wanted to capture their shapes. The past hour, there haven't been any clouds, but look at the blues." She leaned forward and pointed upward. "Higher in the sky is more of a cerulean blue. Then, as you come closer to the ground, it becomes lighter and lighter until it's very pale right before it meets the line of green."

He followed along with what she was saying, nodding. "I have to admit, I never thought much about the sky other than its indication of the weather."

"That would be important as a SEAL, wouldn't it?"

"Absolutely. So, it's not that I don't pay attention to detail, I suppose it's all in the context."

"Now that we're into Colorado, we'll start seeing hints of the mountains along the horizon."

He glanced over and grinned. "Is that your way of letting me know that we're going to need to make some more stops?"

She play-slapped his arm and nodded. "That, plus I'm getting hungry. Will it be time to stop for lunch soon?"

Because of the snacks she'd generously shared, they'd driven into the early afternoon. "Yeah, we can stop anytime." He glanced at the GPS. "Were almost to Flagler. Take a look and see if there's a good place to eat."

She bent over her phone, tapping away. "Oh! There's a diner right at the exit. They have a drive-through, but if it's okay, I'd rather get out of the car."

"No, that's fine. I could use a pitstop, too."

"The menu looks great. They make breakfast all day, which I normally go for, but since we ate such a huge breakfast this morning, I think I'd rather get one of their famous burgers. Oh, and fries. Or onion rings. Or one of us can get fries and the other one gets onion rings, and then we can eat both!"

"Sounds good to me," he said, surprised by the sliver of excitement that moved through him just listening to her talk about lunch.

It didn't take long to arrive, and just as she said, the diner was located right after they'd exited the highway. Parking, he climbed out and stretched, looking over the top of the SUV to where she was doing the same. A glance toward the diner showed several people in booths next to the window, and every male there was staring out at her.

She closed her door and walked around to him, her beaming smile and eyes never leaving his face. *She's the center of attention wherever she goes and has no clue.* He found it incredibly refreshing, definitely sexy, and also disquieting that she saw beautiful colors and shapes in the world around her—but not the dangers. *And I'd like to be the one to keep the danger away.* That notion flashed through his mind, causing his chin to jerk back slightly in surprise.

"Come on! I'm starving!" she exclaimed, grabbing his hand and tugging slightly. Allowing her to lead him to the door while keeping their fingers linked, he tried to push down the thought of them being more than just traveling companions.

"My parents are artists," Stella said, her mouth closing around a big bite of burger.

Chris had asked how she got into art, but as she chewed, he was continually distracted by the way her mouth moved, wondering how eating a hamburger could appear so sensual. Dragging his gaze from her mouth, he tried to remember what she'd just told him. "So, your parents? Artists?"

She swallowed as she nodded. "My dad is a painter, and my mom is a sculptor. They'd gone to different art schools but met when they were both at a concert. My mom's art is more abstract, and she sells pieces all over the world. My dad is inspired by nature, and his art is a type of hyperrealism."

Brows lifted, his fries halted on their way to his mouth. "Hyperrealism? Remember, you're talking to an art neophyte. You're going to have to give me more explanation."

Stella's blue eyes sparkled. "That's so cool that you're asking!" Wiping her mouth, she took a sip of soda, then leaned forward, elbow on the table and her chin resting on her hand. "His painting resembles a high-resolution photograph. He's painted people but prefers nature scenes. His art is so precise that many people assume he's a photographer when he's actually painted the entire picture, capturing the realism perfectly. When I talked to them last night, I promised him that I would take some pictures for him." She scrunched her nose and shrugged. "Of course, I really should have my best camera with me, but I didn't know I was going to be taking a road trip!"

"That's interesting that your whole family is involved in art. Obviously, there are family businesses where everyone's involved, but art has to be a profession that requires not only interest but incredible talent. Sounds like that kind of creative talent runs in your family."

Her face softened, and she reached out her hand to place it on his arm. He tried to ignore the warmth that her touch exuded, but all his attention was captured by the feeling in their connection.

"That's true. What runs in your family?"

He blinked, realizing he'd walked into that line of questioning by asking about her family. Shaking his head, he shrugged. "Can't say anything runs in my family. Not anything like that."

"So, I take it your dad wasn't also in the military."

It was all he could do to keep from snorting at the image of his father *lowering* himself to wear the uniform. "No. Furthest thing from his mind." Not ready to continue a discussion of his parents' merits or lack thereof, he glanced down at their now-empty plates. "I'll go pay, then hit the men's room." She held his gaze for a few seconds, and he found it hard to breathe under her assessing stare.

Her lips curved, and she patted his arm, then turned to grab her purse. Pulling out some bills, she laid them on the table. "I'll go to the restroom, also, and meet you back at the car."

She slid from the booth, and his chest eased. Stella was different from anyone he'd been around in a long time. Teammates didn't give a shit about who his parents were or what they did. For SEALS, it was all about what you brought to the team. The women that hung out at the bars hoping to bang a SEAL also weren't interested in family dynamics. But he had a feeling that Stella was the type of woman who could worm her way under a man's skin and into his heart. *But not mine. There's no room for her in mine.* For the first time since he'd met her the previous day, the idea that he'd never see her again after the trip was over didn't make him happy.

Grabbing her bills, he shoved them into his pocket to sneakily return them to her later. Using his card to pay at the counter, he then detoured to the men's room. Heading out to the SUV, he hoped they could make it several hours down the road before she had to stop again. When he stepped out into the sunshine, he saw her leaning against the side of the SUV, her head tilted back facing the sun with her eyes closed and her face settled into a peaceful expression as though soaking up the sunshine was her favorite pastime. His gaze landed on her arms that now held a new assortment of soda bottles and a bag of doughnuts, and he chuckled.

Opening the door, he assisted her in with her bounty of snacks and realized he didn't care how often she wanted to stop. This journey was turning out to be a lot more enjoyable than he'd ever thought it could be.

9

Stella had excitedly pointed out the change in the horizon as the flat land gave way to gently rolling hills, and in the distance, what started out appearing as low, gray clouds eventually rose into the Rocky Mountains. Soon, the highway cut through hills on either side as they steadily rose in altitude. By now, the brilliant blue sky was dotted with white fluffy clouds. Trees replaced the scrub brush and fields, and soon, forests were surrounding the road.

She'd offered to drive when they'd left the diner, but Chris insisted on staying behind the wheel, saying he'd prefer her to be free to view their surroundings. She wasn't sure if he was telling the truth, just preferred to drive, or perhaps didn't trust her driving, but it didn't matter. She'd loved their journey so far. He'd suggested pulling off so that she could take pictures without waiting for her to ask.

Glancing surreptitiously to the side as often as possible while hoping he didn't catch on to her perusal, she could not help but be fascinated by him. Easy on the eyes, he was the most handsome man she'd spent any length of time with. And now that the stoic layers were slowly being pulled back so that the true man was more accessible, she found that she wanted to know every-thing about him. And if his family and his career as a SEAL were off-limits, she wondered how to discover more.

Deciding to go for the mundane, she asked, "I know you're heading to California, but where were you born?"

He glanced to the side, his lips curving slightly, and she breathed easier at the sight.

"I was born in California. Outside of Los Angeles, actually."

"I was, too. Well," she shook her head, "not in Los Angeles. Further north in the Santa Cruz and San Jose area. My parents live near there, and both teach and exhibit at several of the art centers. I have a small apart-ment and studio just south of town and teach pottery design at several art centers, also."

His head swung around, his eyes wide. Blinking, she tilted her head to the side, waiting to see what prompted his surprised expression.

"Then we're heading almost in the same direction. My new employment is less than two hours south of there."

"That's crazy! To think we're practically neighbors," she laughed. "Well, neighbors in a big-ass state."

Chuckling, he nodded. "Yeah, I hardly think we'll be bumping into each other in the grocery store at that distance, but still, it'll make our journey's end easier."

The idea of their journey coming to an end sent an ache into the left side of her chest. Forcing her smile to remain, she was determined to make the most of their short time together. "Did you always want to go into the military?"

The long moment of silence that followed had her wondering if she'd squelched their conversation. Just as she was about to tell him he didn't need to reveal anything, he glanced over again. This time, his expression was so mixed that she had no idea how to interpret it.

"Not really. I sort of stumbled into it. If I'm honest, I probably joined initially to piss off my father. But I scored well in the math and science portion of the entrance test and was offered medic school after basic training, so I jumped at the opportunity."

Realizing Chris was on the verge of pulling back more layers, she barely breathed, hoping he'd continue.

"After serving a couple of years as a medic, I was accepted into BUD/S. That's the training for becoming a SEAL. Once I completed all training and schools, then I was assigned to a team."

"And you were the medic for your team?"

His lips curved as though fond memories were passing through his mind. "Yes and no. I was the medic, but all the team members have some training in all areas so that we are able to complete missions seamlessly."

"You loved it." Her statement was simple, but she knew it was true without him having to confirm. *And yet, something drove him away.* She wanted more layers pulled back but knew to pry them off might possibly leave him raw underneath. "So, are you ready for another snack?"

He laughed, shaking his head. "I think I'm good for now."

It didn't take long for them to continue climbing as the highway wound around the mountains to the west of Denver. The traffic wasn't heavy, and Stella loved seeing the ever-changing view out the windows. She leaned forward, her hands on the dashboard, and exclaimed, "Oh, look! Snow!!"

They continued climbing and winding over the mountain passes, snow covering the trees and ground everywhere they looked. Chris turned the heat on in the SUV, the colder air now seeping in.

"I don't have a good place to stop for pictures," he said, and she could have sworn she heard regret in his voice.

"That's fine, honestly! I can snap a few shots out the window just for memory's sake." She lifted her phone and tapped on the camera app, taking pictures all around. She turned toward her left, and Chris filled the screen. He was facing forward, concentration etched into his expression, and glad that the sound was off so that her camera app could take a picture undetected, she snapped several of him. *Our travels will be over in a couple of days, and I want to steal a memory.* Before she had a chance to lower her phone, he glanced to the side and grinned. Her finger pressed the button once again.

"Did you get what you wanted?" he asked.

"Yeah—" She cleared her throat and nodded. "Yes, thank you. I was able to grab some shots that will make it easy to remember this part of our trip." She slid her phone back down into her bag and faced forward again, her mind swirling, no longer on the view. The butterflies she'd tried to deny when talking to her mom had returned, and she placed her hand against her stomach.

"Are you okay? You got kinda quiet over there."

Her lips curved. "I'm fine. Probably just snacked too much."

"You?" he asked with mock surprise.

She continued smiling, and they drove in silence for a while as they reached the peak and continued on, leaving the thick clouds and snow-covered vista behind. She continued to steal glances toward Chris, wondering what kind of women he usually went for. *Certainly not me.*

Self-esteem was not a problem for Stella but neither was self-honesty. She knew she was decent looking but could never seem to tame her hair or take the time to worry about playing up her features with a lot of makeup. Her clothes were chosen for comfort rather than style. And she knew she rambled, often talking too much and about things that she found fascinating but sometimes forgot that others didn't. And most of the time, that was fine. But high in the Rocky Mountains on a beautiful day with a gorgeous man at the wheel of their vehicle, she suddenly wished she had something that would make a man like Chris look at her the way she was looking at him.

"I thought we'd stop at Glenwood Springs," he said.

"We could easily make it to Grand Junction, but we need to get gas and eat dinner."

She grabbed her phone and started tapping again, her eyes landing on a website that caught her attention. "Let's stay at a campground tonight!"

"A campground?"

"Here's one where we can stay in a little log cabin. It's off-season, so they have vacancies. They come with two bedrooms, a bathroom, a little kitchenette, and there's a restaurant right there on the campground. It's no more expensive than two hotel rooms, and they have a campfire each night! Won't that be fun?" She looked over when he didn't reply and realized her idea of fun and his were probably very different. "But... um... a hotel would be fine..."

"No. A campground is fine."

"Really?"

"Sure." He glanced over at her. "Just give me the directions."

Excitement speared through her at the idea of sitting around a campfire. "Oh, maybe they'll have s'mores."

Laughter rang out from Chris, and Stella grinned at the sound, then looked over at him, and her breath caught in her throat. His face relaxed in mirth was gorgeous. Blowing out a long breath, she turned her attention back to her phone, calling out the directions.

The campground was close to the highway, and they were soon pulling up to the log cabin reception building. Moving inside, they walked to the counter where Chris registered them, but she managed to sneak in her credit card before him. His gaze landed on the card, then swung down to her, a scowl on his face.

She elbowed him in the ribs, eliciting a grunt. "You always pay. This one's on me," she whispered.

Soon armed with their cabin key, a map of the small resort, and a list of activities, they drove a short distance and parked outside a small log cabin with a breathtaking view of the west side of the Rocky Mountains and the sunset sky brilliant with colors.

"Oh, my," she breathed as she stood on the front porch, staring out over the vista. She grabbed her phone and turned slowly, snapping pictures. "I can't believe I don't have my good camera with me. Dad would so love this view."

"Maybe you can come back with your parents sometime," he suggested.

Lowering her phone, her eyes widened. "What a fabulous idea!"

He turned to unlock the door, and with the gold and orange sky behind him, she couldn't help but snap another picture. Guilt immediately hit her. "Um... I should tell you that I've taken a couple of pictures with you in them. Not in a stalkerish way. Just in an I-want-to-remember-this-trip sort of way. I can delete them if you want—"

He turned, his intense gaze pinning her to the wooden floor of the porch, but his face was impassive, and she had no idea what he was thinking. Swallowing deeply, she lifted her phone to delete the picture she'd just taken and the ones from the SUV.

His arm reached out, and he slipped the phone from

her hand. A gasp fell from her lips, and her eyes bugged at the idea he was taking her phone. "I—"

He stepped next to her and held the phone out with his long arm, the camera facing toward them. She looked toward the screen, seeing the two of them standing close to each other, his tall frame towering over her but bent slightly so his head was close to hers, and the glorious colors of the sky behind them.

"Smile," the order rumbled from his chest as his lips curved.

"Huh?" She blinked, then managed to smile at the last second before he pressed the camera button several times.

Before she could blink again, he stood straight and handed the phone back to her before throwing open the cabin door. Her mind whirled with the realization that he'd taken a selfie of them with the glorious sunset in the background. She knew enough about Chris by now to know he wasn't a selfie person. Nor someone who reveled in a sunset. But for her, he'd done both. Her gaze dropped to the screen of her phone, the image of the two of them filling her phone and her heart. For an instant, it was easy to pretend they were so much more than just traveling companions.

He stepped inside first, his head turning quickly from side to side, and it dawned on her what he was doing. Just like the previous night at her hotel room, he was scanning the interior for whatever threat he might deem was there. Her teeth landed on her bottom lip as she followed him into the cabin, realizing she'd never had someone so attentive before. Not in an overt, grandiose gesture of attentiveness but more of a quiet protectiveness. One that she noticed and made her insides feel warm.

Following him inside, she gasped again. The warm wood of the log cabin glowed with polish and smelled of lemon oil with a touch of smokiness from the fireplace. "Wow," she breathed. The small room held a kitchenette in one corner with a four-seater table. A sofa and two comfortable chairs were near the fireplace. A door toward the back opened to the bathroom, flanked by two side doors which she assumed led to the bedrooms. She was entranced but had no idea what Chris thought. "Is it okay for tonight?" Turning toward him, steeling herself in case his face held derision, the sight of his curved lips captured her.

"It's great, Stella," he said, his gaze landing on her. "Not a place I would have thought of staying, but I'm glad you did."

For a few seconds, she thought she spied not only appreciation for the accommodations but also for her, as well. Then he turned quickly and stalked to the bedroom, opening the doors and checking them out. The air rushed from her lungs, and she was forced to suck in a deep breath to keep from passing out.

Following, she spied two identical bedrooms on either side of the hall, both with a queen-size bed made of logs and covered with a spread designed to look like an heirloom quilt. She walked in, her hands trailing over the wood, her gaze taking in the mountain prints framed on the walls.

"I figure you're hungry," Chris said from her doorway.

She looked over her shoulder and smiled.

"Whenever you're ready," he continued, "we can head over to their restaurant. It looks like they've got barbecue."

She turned to face him, taking in this unique man whose path had crossed with hers and could have been no more than a seatmate on a flight and now was sharing a journey with her. A mixture of emotions rushed through her. Surprised that they'd trusted each other so quickly. Awe that a man like Chris would willingly spend so much time with her considering how opposite they seemed. Impressed with his integrity. Wanting to know more and yet willing to let him offer up bits of himself as he felt comfortable. Enjoying the way he teased her. Overwhelmed with his physical prowess and his need to protect and humbled by how she fell under that protection. And deep inside, she felt an attraction that she knew needed to stay buried, never wanting him to regret seeing her safely to California.

"Thank you," she said softly, the words barely above a whisper. Pulling herself out of her thoughts, she recognized his lowered brow as his silent way of questioning her. Feeling her cheeks heat, she offered a little smile. "Just... um... thank you for everything. You are really going out of your way on this trip for me, and I just wanted you to know that I appreciate it."

His brow relaxed, but his gaze on her remained intense. He pushed away from the doorframe, and for a second, she thought he was going to come closer.

Instead, he stepped back and said, "I'll wait out here until you're ready for dinner." With that, he turned and headed into the small living area.

Sucking in a deep breath, she let it out slowly. Hurrying into the bathroom, she took care of business, then washed her face and hands before running her brush through her hair and re-braiding the long waves. Stepping out, she moved into the room to find him with the front door open, standing on the front porch, his hands on his hips and his gaze pinned on the magnificent mountain vista in front of them. Almost hating to interrupt whatever thoughts he was having, she stepped closer and gently placed her hand on his arm. "Are you ready for barbecue?" she asked.

He twisted his neck and looked down, a smile on his face. With a nod, he pulled the door behind her closed and placed his hand on her lower back, guiding her down the short path to the restaurant.

10

Chris sat on one of the logs that circled the massive fire pit, his stomach full of large homemade rolls, baked potatoes, slaw, and some of the best barbeque he'd ever had. The fire was roaring, the flames were rising, and the smoke was curling into the air.

"Here you go! Best things ever!"

He smiled as Stella placed the toasted marshmallow on top of the graham cracker and layered it with a chocolate bar, then pressed it all together with another graham cracker before handing it to a little boy sitting nearby with his parents. So far, she'd made at least ten s'mores for the kids while charming them with tales of elves that lived in the mountain forests.

The campground director hadn't had to do anything for entertainment other than starting the fire and bringing out the ingredients for the gooey desserts. Stella had commanded the attention of the children, giving the tired-looking parents a little reprieve.

Blonde tendrils had escaped her braid again, their

waves flying about her head, creating the halo he'd come to expect. The firelight played up her bright eyes and rosy cheeks as she smiled. It was obvious she had no idea that every eye was on her, whether from an enchanted child, a grateful parent, a benevolent elder, or the few single men around who stared at her with unadulterated lust. The latter made him want to put his fist in their faces, but he settled for hard stares until they left the fire activities to the others and made their way back to their cabin, grumbling about not being able to drink in public.

As several families finally pulled their children off to their cabins, she returned to his side, a freshly made s'more in her hands. "Here, Chris. You haven't had one yet."

He lifted a brow, staring at the gooey-chewy confection. "You expect me to get that all over my mouth trying to eat that mess?"

Laughing, she took a huge bite out of one and nodded as she chewed. Bits of melted marshmallow clung to the sides of her mouth and her chin as she swallowed.

"Yes, I do. I don't mind eating one," she argued.

"Yeah, but on you, the mess looks cute." He lifted his finger and wiped her lip, suddenly wishing he could kiss off the sweet taste. Unsure where that thought came from, he reached for the proffered treat and, sighing, took a large bite. Sure enough, he felt the string of marshmallow land on his chin.

She burst out laughing and leaned closer, now wiping his chin with her fingers. He grabbed her finger and licked the confection off, causing her to squeal as she threw her head back and laughed harder.

"It's so nice to see a young couple having such fun."

Chris and Stella turned at the same time to the older couple sitting across from them. The man was mostly bald, and the woman had hair that was more white than silver. They sat next to each other, hands held with fingers linked.

"We're Claire and Henry," the woman said. "We've enjoyed watching you delight the children with your stories and s'more-making skills."

Stella laughed, tucking a wayward strand behind her ear. "I'm Stella, and this is Chris. I always liked sitting around the campfire with my parents when I was younger. My dad used to tell the most fantastical stories of woodland elves, goblins, daring princes, and ingenious princesses. And I'm not sure I've ever enjoyed a campfire that didn't include s'mores!"

"Well, when you have children of your own, I can imagine that they'll be just as enthralled."

Chris watched as Stella blinked, her mouth opening slightly before she said, "Oh, we're—"

"Thank you," Chris interrupted, ignoring Stella's wide-eyed expression turned toward him.

"I always said that couples should be able to have fun together," Claire said. "I wasn't sure about Henry at first. He was what we used to call a stick in the mud. That meant he didn't know how to have a lot of fun."

Henry chuckled and shook his head. "I'd like to deny it, but Claire is right. I was a planner. Thought everything had to be planned out just so. But Claire was like a breath of fresh air and taught me how to just go with the flow." He leaned forward, his smile still wide as he focused his attention on Chris. "Best thing I ever did was hang on to her and enjoy the ride. Looks like you're doing the same, young man." He turned to his wife and said, "Claire, darlin', you ready to head to the cabin?"

"Absolutely, sweetie," she said. Looking over her shoulder, she called out her goodnight, and he watched as they disappeared up the main path to one of the cabins.

By now, the campground activities director was putting out the fire, and Chris stood, reaching his hand toward Stella to pull her upward. She placed her hand in his, the warmth created from their simple touch moving up his arm. He'd meant to let go of her hand as soon as she was standing, but it felt right to follow Henry and Claire's example and walk hand-in-hand to their cabin. If Stella had pulled back, he would've let go immediately, but she didn't. And he didn't want to analyze why that made him feel so good.

Once inside, he had no choice but to let her go and immediately felt the loss. The soft light from the table lamps created a warm glow inside the log cabin. His chest squeezed at her beauty, and he couldn't pull his gaze away.

She fiddled with the bottom of her shirt, seeming unsure of what to do with her hands. Tilting her head to the side, she chewed on her lip and then asked, "Why didn't you let me correct their assumption that we were a couple?"

The real answer was that at that moment he wanted

to be with her, wanted to be the man who'd claimed her and was claimed by her. Tamping down the desire to blurt out that thought, he shrugged. "They appeared to like the notion that we were together, so it seemed harmless to let them think that."

He had no idea what her reaction would be, but in typical Stella style, she smiled. "That's sweet, Chris. You're right. I think they did like that." She sucked in a deep breath, then reached out to squeeze his hand. "Thank you for tonight. I had a great time."

"I did, too."

Her brow furrowed as though uncertain of the veracity of his admission. Scrunching her nose, she asked, "Really?"

He chuckled and nodded. "Granted, it's not how I usually spend an evening, but the food was delicious, the company was wonderful, and watching you made everything better. So, I really should thank you for letting me tag along on this journey of yours."

He didn't think it was possible for her face to become more beautiful, but as her smile widened and her eyes brightened, his world tilted. He wasn't sure when this trip was over if it would ever right itself again, and that thought scared the shit out of him.

Knowing he needed separation before he grabbed her, pulled her close, and kissed her, he took a step back, trying to ignore the slash of surprise that crossed her face. "Well, I'll see you in the morning. If we get a decent start after breakfast, we can be in Salt Lake City by early afternoon. We can grab lunch and then make it over halfway through Nevada before we stop tomorrow night. One more easy day after that, and we'll be in San Jose."

She jerked her head up and down, her smile faltering slightly. "Good, yeah, that'll be good. Two more days, and I'll be out of your hair." She also took a step back, her gaze darting toward the hall before coming back to him. "I'll be quick in the bathroom and then head to bed. I'll see you in the morning."

She turned and hustled away, and his gut clenched. Unused to the feelings that were churning through him, he called out, "Stella."

She stopped and looked over her shoulder at him. "Yes?"

"I... I hope you sleep well."

Her smile, while not nearly as bright as earlier, still made her appear angelic. "You, too." She turned and disappeared into the bathroom, the door closing with a final click.

He heard the water in the shower turn on, and he sighed heavily. With his hands planted on his hips, he dropped his chin to his chest and stared at his boots. *It's better this way. Stick to the plan. Accompany her to California. Then drive to Lighthouse Security Investigations and start my new job. There's no time for distractions.* No matter what his head told him, he knew it was a lie. "I'm a fuckin' moron."

Chris slept fitfully but rose early, as was his habit. He dressed quickly, made sure he gathered the few belongings he had with him, and stepped out into the main living area. The scent of coffee met him, and he was shocked to find Stella already dressed and her overnight bag sitting by the front door.

"I started to fix a cup for you, but it's not the greatest coffee. I was just sipping on this until you got up and we could go grab breakfast next door."

"I didn't expect to find you up so early."

She turned and dumped the rest of her coffee into the sink, rinsing out her cup. "I didn't want to delay our start today."

The Stella he was getting to know didn't seem like she'd hold a grudge, but it was obvious his brusque plans for finishing the trip had affected her. He hated that he'd doused her enthusiasm but had no idea how to backtrack. "Yeah, sure."

It didn't take long for them to get served, and the food and good coffee seemed to revive her mood. Her shoulders were less stiff, her smile more bright. Thirty minutes later, they were back on the road with a full tank of gas to go along with their full bellies... and the snacks she'd bought in the reception area of the campground.

After a while, they left the mountains behind them as they continued on their westward journey. The land flattened, and by the time they crossed into Utah, the blue sky met the brown earth with only bits of green scrub brush. Used to noting the topography of an area in relation to his previous missions as a SEAL, he now noticed the world a bit differently, mainly through Stella's eyes.

Her earlier reticence around him seemed to have relaxed, and they once again enjoyed the drive as she chatted about the area they were traveling through. She hadn't asked to stop at all for pictures, but the smile she bestowed on him when he made the suggestion loosened the tightness he'd felt in his chest since the previous evening.

He'd planned on staying on major highways but decided to take a less-traveled road off Hwy 70 heading north toward Provo. Just as he'd hoped, Stella was thrilled with the sights. By now, they were fully into cliffs and buttes, mountains in the background, and dry earth.

Leaning his back against the side of the SUV, he watched as she walked closer to the edge of a cliff. She appeared more interested in flipping through settings on her phone than where her feet were taking her. Launching forward, he called out, "Stella! Stop!" He hustled closer as she turned to look over her shoulder, her brow knitted.

"What's wrong?"

"You need to watch where you're going," he said. "You're close to the edge."

"Oh, sorry. I was trying to figure out how to erase part of the image, but I can do that once I get home."

"What are you trying to erase?" As he reached her, he glanced down at what she was pointing toward.

"It must be some Boy Scouts. I just wanted some pictures that showed the water at the bottom and where it had cut through thousands of years of rock."

Below them, he could see the strip of the river at the

bottom with the multicolored layers of rock lining each side of the cliffs that rose from the water. And at the bottom was a pickup truck parked near a larger panel van with Scouts moving back and forth carrying large duffels. The scene reminded him of many drills he'd been on while in the military. "If they weren't Scouts, I'd think they might be on a survivalist trip." Glancing down, he smiled as she turned her face up to him, her eyes wide.

"What's a survivalist trip?"

"Extreme roughing it," he laughed. "People who get taken to the middle of nowhere for a few days and hunt their own food and live off the land as they hike along."

Her nose scrunched as she shook her head. "Yuck. I'm all for seeing beautiful sights but sleeping outdoors with bugs and snakes is not my idea of a good time."

"Even if they have a campfire and make s'mores?"

She play-slapped his arm. "Chris Andrews, are you teasing me?"

"Maybe just a little," he said, enjoying her light-hearted smile. Inclining his head toward her phone, he asked, "Did you get enough pictures? We should be in Salt Lake City soon. We'll try to get to the other side before we stop for lunch."

She slapped her hand over her heart dramatically. "I don't know if I'll make it that long before we eat! I might keel over from hunger!"

Barking out a laugh, he slung his arm over her shoulder, turning them both back toward their SUV. "Then we better get you back to your snacks."

He didn't miss the confusion that passed through

her eyes. *Hell, I'm confused myself.* He liked spending time with her but knew there was no future beyond this trip. He was determined to enjoy his time left with her, hoping she did, as well, before they ended the journey and said goodbye. *Have good times, and we leave with hearts intact.* As they climbed into the SUV and he started the engine, he hoped his ideas would work.

11

Few cars had been on the road until they got closer to Salt Lake City and then the traffic picked up. Once they passed the main city, Stella looked out the window with interest as they drove near the southern tip of the huge lake. Stopping at one of the many exits, they topped off the gas in the SUV and had lunch at a local steakhouse.

Sitting at the table, finishing her iced tea as Chris hit the men's room before they got back on the road, she sighed. The truth was the many confusing thoughts about the trip were all bouncing around in her head at the same time.

While it was evident their personalities were very different, Chris had relaxed more and seemed to enjoy her company as the trip progressed. He'd even teased her about the multitude of bathroom and snack breaks along the way and pointed out places they could pull off so that she could capture the scenery. And the night before, around the campfire, it had almost felt as though they were a couple even though she'd known that was a dangerous idea to entertain.

It wasn't hard to start falling for a man like Chris. Strong, handsome, protective. She snorted, shaking her head. *Not like the typical guy I've gone out with.* She didn't have a type, but with her career, she tended to be around mostly men she'd met through work or school. Artists or art students. Musicians. Photographers. Videographers. And while she'd dated and had a few short-term relationships, she'd always felt as though the men were trying to compete with her. It was refreshing to spend time with a man who could appreciate her art without angling to see what she could do for their career or if their success could top hers.

The previous night, with the sparks from the campfire lifting into the night sky along with the curling smoke, she'd glanced over to see him as she entertained some of the children. And each time, his penetrating gaze was always on her. She'd grown warm deep inside and knew it wasn't from the campfire. Sitting close to him, she'd allowed her thoughts to drift into the dangerous territories of 'what if' and 'maybe.' What if they decided to have a vacation fling? Maybe even see each other after the trip? And the most dangerous of all... *What if we really were a couple?*

When he'd intimated that they were a couple even just to feed the imaginings of Claire and Henry, her heart had begun to pound in a staccato rhythm. Suddenly, the idea that they'd spend the night in a cabin, in the same room, sharing the same bed, sent nerves first to her stomach, and then tingles moved to the rest of her in hopeful anticipation. They were standing so close when she'd reached out to touch his hand, and she was sure that if he bent slightly toward her, she'd have to fight the urge to jump into his arms, knowing that kissing Chris would be every bit as amazing as she imagined.

Instead, as though a shutter slid down over his face, he'd stepped back and rattled off the rest of the trip's itinerary as though he couldn't wait for it to be over. She'd never been good at hiding her emotions but fought to keep the disappointment from her face. Disappointment—and embarrassment.

Then, standing under the hot shower, she'd washed away the smoky scent of the campfire that she loved, needing to rid her body and hair of the lingering memory of sitting next to him, feeling as though the start of something special was about to happen. *Something special*. She snorted, shaking her head. Chris was a gorgeous, smart former SEAL. She'd gone through a phase of reading military romances the previous year and had no doubt that just like the men in those books, he'd had his share of beautiful women. *And me? An artist who spends more time designing the perfect pottery than caring about hair, makeup, and clothes?* Stella knew she was special in her own way, not normally having a problem with self-confidence, but there was no doubt that Chris was not interested in anything more than travel buddies.

He reappeared at the end of the counter, and she watched as he stalked with panther-like grace toward the table. His gaze hit hers, and her heartbeat sped up again. *It's fine. I can do this. Enjoy the trip. Enjoy his company. Occasionally allow myself to wander down the what-if path. But ultimately say goodbye when we reach our destination.*

Jumping up from the booth, she grinned. "I'll hit the ladies' room and meet you at the car. By the way, I paid for our lunch." Scooting around him as a scowl crossed his face, she laughed.

A few minutes later, she stepped outside into the bright Utah sunlight and spied him leaning against the SUV. Willing her heart to stop its erratic flip-flops as he opened her door, she climbed into the vehicle. This trip wasn't a romance novel, but for her, it was a journey she'd remember fondly. *And that has to be enough.*

They'd driven for several more hours and were now nearing the middle of Nevada. The sun was lowering in the sky, and considering they were driving west, it made visibility difficult, at least for her. Chris was tall enough that with his sun visor down, his eyes were shaded. Even with her sunglasses on, her sun visor was still too high to provide any relief from the relentless sunlight. To keep from looking straight ahead, she'd spent the past hour watching the little-changing horizon.

It wasn't that she was no longer interested, but having slept little the night before, she was tired. Rolling her head to the side, she looked at Chris and asked, "Where are we stopping tonight?"

"We're just passing Elko right now. There are a couple of motels just beyond in Battle Mountain." He glanced toward her. "Is that okay?"

"Absolutely. I feel bad because you've done all the driving on this trip, Chris. When I started out renting a vehicle, I thought I'd be doing all the driving. When you said you wanted to come along, I thought I would be splitting the chore."

"Nah. I like driving."

"Are you sure you just don't want a woman behind the wheel?" she teased.

"I promise it's not a sexist opinion on women drivers. Or, for that matter, your driving ability. I enjoy driving, and you enjoy looking at the sights. I figure that makes it a good trade-off."

She nodded, smiling, glad that they were back to easy conversation. Looking out her window again, she said, "There's a sign for the Nevada Army National Guard. I confess that I know very little about the military other than what I've read in books, and I don't suppose fiction stories are always correct."

"The National Guard is a state-based military force that can become reserve components of the Army and Air Force when activated federally. Most people in the National Guard hold full-time civilian jobs while serving part-time in the Guard. What we just passed would be the base for Nevada." He glanced to the side and grinned. "I probably gave you more information than you wanted, didn't I?"

She shook her head, smiling in return. "No, I always like learning new things."

"The Navy is, of course, the federal maritime branch of the Armed Forces. And, I might add, the largest navy in the world."

"I can hear the pride in your voice," she said, turning to give her full attention to him.

"The Navy was good to me."

"And being a SEAL?"

"They were good to me, too. Being part of an elite special operations force not only gave me a career and great friends, but it opened the door to even more opportunities."

She wondered about her next question, then decided to go for it. "When you showed me your identification, you said you were getting ready to start working for a private security company. Why did you want to leave the SEALs?"

He was quiet for a moment, then replied, "The time just felt right. My team was... changing, and I decided that I was ready to try something new. I had a friend who was working for an elite security company and decided that was going to be the right next step for me."

"And that's why you're heading to California. To start your new job."

He nodded, then sighed. "My mother is still in California, and I plan on seeing her before I start work. It's been a while."

"Just your mother?"

"Yes, just my mother."

His voice was heavy, and she could tell there was more to the story but didn't want to push. The fact that he'd shared as much as he had thrilled her because she'd learned that Chris would talk when he was ready.

There was little traffic on the road by the time they pulled into the parking lot for a small hotel. The sun had lowered more in the sky, but there was still some daylight.

"I could have kept driving, and I'm sure we would have found another hotel, but there's no reason to push it," he said, turning to hold her gaze.

Glad that he no longer seemed anxious to end their time together, she nodded. "This is great, Chris. I'd rather not be traveling at night anyway. This gives us a chance to check in, find a place to eat, and maybe watch the sunset."

He grinned, and the breath caught in her throat as it always did when he smiled at her. *It should be illegal for someone to be that gorgeous!*

Once inside the small hotel's reception area, they checked in, getting rooms next to each other, and while Chris made the arrangements, she glanced at a poster on the wall proclaiming that Battle Mountain was the home of the most beautiful sunsets in the world. Their claim made her smile considering she'd often seen brilliant sunsets everywhere.

"You looking to see a pretty sunset, missy?"

She looked over her shoulder to see the elderly man behind the counter. His tanned skin and deep wrinkles indicated he'd spent a lot of time in the sun. "I never turn down a view of the sunset," she laughed.

"There's a little back road you can take. Go about five miles. You'll come to a spot where you can view the sunset, and you'll swear it's the prettiest thing you've ever seen."

She glanced up toward Chris, catching his smile. He turned to the man and got directions. Her heart did a little pitter-patter at the idea of a beautiful sunset with him. She hated to put more emphasis than she should on a simple side trip but couldn't deny that he must want to spend more time with her to consider this a special sunset view after having spent the past couple of days in their vehicle.

They checked into their rooms, and she noted that not only were they next to each other, but they had a connecting door. After quickly using the bathroom, she grabbed her purse and met him outside.

He cocked his elbow as he looked down. "Are you ready to go see the most beautiful sunset in the world?"

"Absolutely!" she laughed, looping her arm through his.

It didn't take long to get to the location. Parking on the side of the dirt road, they alighted and walked to the edge of the overlook. The sky had already turned brilliant shades of gold, orange, and red, interspersed with varying colors of blue. She stared for a moment, filled with awe. "Oh, my God. Isn't it beautiful?"

"Yes. It is."

Chris' voice was rough, and she looked over her shoulder to see his eyes pinned on her, not the sunset.

12

Chris had spent the day fighting his feelings. Fighting the pull he felt toward Stella. Fighting to keep his eyes on the road when all he wanted to do was glance to the side and drink her in. Fighting to keep his hands curved around the steering wheel when he longed to reach over and run his fingers through her hair and over her soft skin. Fighting to keep his mind just on the trip and not the woman that invaded every thought. Fighting the idea that it was the right time to see if there was anything between them. Fighting the realization that the carefree happiness she exuded would intrude into his well-ordered life.

He stared at her profile, his heart pounding in his chest, taking in the brilliant sunset in the background but focused on the beautiful woman in front of him. Her colorful shirt rivaled the sky and did nothing to hide her curves. Her hair waved in the breeze. Her eyes sparkled in the light of the setting sun. Her skin glowed.

And her lips curved as she stared over the buttes in the background.

He had no clue what to do, but he was tired of fighting.

When she turned around and looked at him, his gaze was filled with her and nothing else. Her mouth opened slightly, and her tongue darted out to moisten her bottom lip.

Stalking the few feet between them, her head tilted back to keep her gaze on him as he approached. Her top teeth worried her bottom lip, and he wanted to soothe the flesh with his mouth. Stopping when his body was almost to hers, he waited. The air around them vibrated with a distant thunderstorm. Or maybe it was the pounding of his heart. Bolts of need coursed through his body, and his fingers twitched at his sides. Yearning and fear warred within.

As much as he wanted to give, he needed her to show him what she was willing to take. Her lips curved upward even more, and she nodded.

Moving faster than he thought possible, his arms banded around her, and he bent just as she lifted on her toes, their mouths meeting. He angled his head, sealing his mouth over hers, then tightened his grip and lifted her easily. She wrapped her legs around his waist and her arms around his neck.

Her lips were soft, and as he swept his tongue over them, she groaned. He swallowed the sound and thrust his tongue inside, the velvet warmth sending shock-waves straight to his groin. Her taste was sweet, and he wanted more. More of her kiss and more of her body pressed against his.

And with the heat of her core nestled against his crotch and her breasts crushed against his chest, he wanted less. Less clothes between them.

Her arms tightened around his neck, and his scalp tingled as she dragged her short fingernails through his hair. Her tongue tangled with his, starting as a slow exploration, then quickly battling for dominance.

He gave as much as he took, memorizing her taste, the little sounds she made, and the feel of her in his arms. He couldn't remember the last time he'd kissed a woman this way but knew it had been years... if ever. He'd never been as much of a player as some of his teammates, and his occasional hookups had been for a good time and a physical release. The few women he'd seen more than once had been about convenience rather than romance. But holding Stella in his arms made him want more of everything she had to offer.

The kiss slowed to nibbles before they separated, both chests heaving as though they'd run up the mountain. "I've been wanting to do that all day," he confessed.

Her eyes sparkled, and she threw her arms into the air, leaning back slightly, shouting, "Me, too!"

He reared back to keep her from tipping them over, laughing at her exuberant reaction. The reds and oranges behind her had deepened in color as the sun continued to set. "Absolutely the best sunset in the world."

Still in his arms, she laughed and reached down to slip her phone from her pocket. Holding it out, she snapped several pictures of them with the brilliant sky in the background. He stared at the screen, amazed at the beautiful woman in his arms. A slight flash caught his eye in the camera, and he turned, glancing down toward the ravine below.

"What is it?" she asked, peering down. "Oh, it must be more Boy Scouts or maybe those survivalists you were talking about."

Two pickup trucks and a panel van were below, several people moving between them. Two men stopped and looked upward toward him and Stella. In her typical friendliness, she waved, and one of the men threw his hand up and waved in return.

"You're a goof," Chris said, letting her legs slide down but keeping his hands around her waist until she was steady on the rough ground.

"I just think it's important to be friendly, that's all," she laughed.

With his knuckle under her chin, he lifted her head and bent toward her, stopping when their lips were a whisper apart. "I like you being friendly to me."

Her eyes darkened. "Yeah," she breathed. "I like being friendly with you, too."

He grinned just before he kissed her again. "Are you ready to go back to the hotel?"

She nodded. "Yeah."

"We'll stop and grab something to eat before we get there."

Her face fell, and he laughed. "I think that's the first time the idea of food didn't make you happy."

She narrowed her eyes, tossing a pretend glower his

way. "I just thought maybe we could head straight back to the room."

"When we get to the room, I won't want to leave. Plus, we'll need our strength for all I've got planned."

Her eyes widened as she grabbed his hand and started to tug him toward the SUV. "Then what are we waiting for? Let's eat!"

They drove back to the small town and found a bar across the street from the hotel that served burgers and fries. Sitting at a small high-top table, they sipped their beer while waiting for the food. Music played in the background mixed with the sound of balls clanging together from the pool tables near the back and conversations all around, but Chris' singular focus was on Stella, and the way her gaze never left his, she was just as focused.

"If you don't stop staring at me like that, I'm tempted to drag you over the table and onto my lap," he said, his voice rumbling.

"If you don't stop staring at me like you are, you won't have to do that. I'll swipe this table clean of beer glasses, hop over, and land on your lap. After that, all bets are off," she quipped in return.

They were both startled as two plastic baskets were set in front of them filled with juicy hamburgers and crispy fries. "Here you go, folks. Enjoy!" The friendly server turned and headed to serve a new group of men who'd just come in.

Forcing his gaze to leave Stella, Chris cast a glance around the interior of the bar once again, the habit of checking his surroundings ingrained. The bar was tame, everyone eating or drinking, no tension evident, and yet his Spidey senses were alert. But from all he could discern, no one was paying him or Stella any attention.

Turning back, he found her mouth wrapped around her burger, taking a huge bite. Thinking of what he'd like her lips to be wrapped around, he sucked in a deep breath and counted to ten, willing his dick to calm down long enough for them to eat.

Stella chewed and swallowed, taking a healthy gulp of beer. "Are you okay?"

He grinned and nodded. "Just enjoying the view."

"What? Me shoving down a burger?"

"I don't think there's anything you could do I wouldn't enjoy watching."

She'd reached for another french fry, but her hand halted, suspended in the air as she slowly licked her lips. Finally, she inclined her head toward his meal. "You better eat up. Because if we're going to do what I hope we do, you're going to need your energy."

"Damn, woman," he groaned as the blood rushed south. He was tempted to grab her hand and say to hell with the food and drag her out of there, but she'd taken another bite of hamburger, rolled her eyes, and moaned in enjoyment. One thing he learned about Stella on this trip: he wasn't about to mess with her and her food.

As soon as they finished, he threw bills onto the table that more than paid for their dinner, drinks, and a hefty tip, grabbed her hand, and linked fingers as they made their way out of the bar. One more look around and he still saw nothing untoward. Shifting his gaze down to her, seeing a smile light her face, he grinned as they headed back to their rooms.

They stopped at the SUV parked outside and grabbed their bags before walking to his door. She glanced at the door right next to his, then looked up at him, a sliver of uncertainty moving through her eyes. "I guess I'll take these into my room?"

Her words came out more as a question than a statement, and he held her gaze. "Stella, we can do whatever you'd like to do. Keep separate rooms. Open the connecting door between them. Stay in one room. It's your call."

Her tongue darted out to moisten her bottom lip. "I know I liked kissing you earlier more than anything I've done in a really long time. And I know I'd like to do a whole lot more of that plus anything else we get into the mood for. As far as which room? It doesn't matter to me as long as we're together."

Stella's honesty pierced straight through him, and he lifted his hand to cup her face. Bending, he placed a gentle kiss on the very corner of her mouth, knowing if he kissed her fully, he wouldn't be able to take her as slowly as he wanted to go. "Then how about we go into my room? We can open the connecting door so you never feel trapped."

She leaned her cheek into his palm and grinned. "I don't need the connecting door open because being trapped with you just makes this journey all the better."

"Damn," he groaned, turning to the door, his fingers almost fumbling with the old-fashioned key. Finally getting the door open, he stepped in first, his gaze sweeping the dated but clean room, and then ushered her inside.

They dropped their bags onto the floor at the same time, then stood unmoving. He lost sense of time as they stared at each other. It could have been a few seconds or a few minutes. His gaze roved from the top of her head to her toes and back again, drinking in the view, anticipating when clothes would no longer stand in their way. He lifted his hand slowly just to touch her cheek, the barest hint of soft skin underneath his rough fingertip.

Then, caught in the magnetic force that pulled them together, they moved in unison, barely stopping as their bodies slammed into each other. His arms encircled her, lifting as his mouth sealed over hers. Just like before, she wrapped her legs around his waist, pressing her body tightly against his.

He turned, backing her up against the wall, nearly knocking off one of the cheap pictures hanging from an old nail. Her hands clutched his jaws, her fingertips digging into the back of his head, and their noses bumped as they twisted and turned through their kiss, tongues tangling, breathing each other in. With her body sandwiched between his and the wall, she used her leverage to shift her hips over his groin, his cock swelling to eagerly answer her demand.

Maneuvering one hand between them, he managed to unzip her shorts and shift them down just far enough that his hand could cover her mound, sliding her satin panties to the side. "Christ, you're wet for me," he mumbled through their kiss.

"Uh…" was all she got out before he glided his finger through her folds and slipped it deep inside. Her mouth left his as her head jerked back, hitting the wall and rattling the picture once again.

He wanted to get her to the bed. He wanted to get her out of all her clothes. But at the look on her face as she gasped for air and wiggled her hips against his finger, he lost all rational thought other than giving her pleasure.

"More… yeah…" she panted.

Her eyes were squeezed shut, but he didn't want anything hidden from him. "Look at me." His rumbled words came out as an order. She gasped again but dropped her chin and held his gaze. "Just like that, Stella. I want you. I want all of you, and that includes you watching me make you come."

He didn't know if it was his words or his finger hitting the special place deep inside, but her legs squeezed his waist as her entire body stiffened for a few seconds. A beautiful blush rose from the top of her shirt to her cheeks, making him wonder if her breasts held the same rosy glow. She shook in his arms, and he felt her release as her core gripped his finger, and her hands gripped his shoulders.

She rode out her orgasm, then, as he slid his finger from her body, she slumped forward, her cheek now resting on his shoulder and her legs limp as they relaxed. Her lips moved over his neck, little kisses that sent shivers down his spine. Lifting her head, she stared at him. Her hair was mostly out of its braid, wavy flyaway tendrils sticking out in every direction. Her lips were reddened and kiss swollen. Her eyes were bright, and her smile was wide albeit a little wonky.

He was certain he'd never seen anything so beautiful in his life. Reality crept in, and he grimaced. "Damn, babe, our first time shouldn't have been against the wall—"

"Shut up. It was fuckin' fabulous, and I don't want you messing it up by apologizing." She clutched his jaws and kissed him, her eyes dancing.

Laughter erupted from deep inside, and keeping her in his arms, he turned and stalked to his bed. Giving her a little bounce to show his intentions, she unhooked her ankles from around his lower back, and he tossed her gently onto the mattress. Her hands moved to her shorts which were halfway down her hips, and after toeing off her sneakers and a little wiggling, she shed her shorts and panties onto the floor. Her hands moved to the bottom of her T-shirt, and he reached out, wrapping his fingers around her wrist.

"Uh-uh. You unwrapped part of the gift, now I want to unwrap the rest."

An impish grin slid across her face, taking his breath away almost as much as her half-naked body. Bending forward, he slipped his hands underneath the bottom of her shirt, his fingertips meeting her warm, soft skin. Gliding upward, he chuckled as her stomach jerked. "Ticklish?"

Her brows lifted. "I'll never tell."

He danced his fingers over her stomach again, and the little shriek that flew from her lips answered his question.

His hands continued on their upward path, his thumbs sweeping over her breasts. She sucked in a quick breath, her eyelids lowered halfway, and her teeth landed on her bottom lip. Determined to give her breasts his full attention once they were free, he slowly pulled her T-shirt over her head and arms, dropping it somewhere behind him.

Her curves had been evident even with her modest clothing, but seeing her breasts spilling from her bra, he gave in to the urge and pressed his lips against one plump mound before nibbling his way to the other. Unhooking the back, the material gave way, and with her head thrown back, offering herself up to him, she gave him unfettered access to her rosy nipples. He latched onto one, sucking deeply, barely aware her hands landed on the mattress behind her. He drank her in as a man lost in the desert, then kissed his way to her neck, sucking lightly where her pulse fluttered underneath his lips. Finally making his way to her mouth, he dove in.

"Now," she moaned in the middle of the kiss.

He'd thought that he had more control. More finesse. But hearing her beg for what he wanted to give, he jerked upward and grabbed the back of his shirt, pulling it over his head. His hands went to his belt buckle, the sound of the leather sliding and the clink of the metal clasp mixing with their labored breaths. He bent and jerked off his boots, shucking his pants and boxers, a movement that might not have been smooth but got the job done. Sending up a grateful thanks that he always kept a condom in his wallet, he snagged it then rolled it on before crawling back over her naked, gorgeous body.

His hands skimmed over her breasts, but she reached up and grabbed his arms, her fingers digging into the muscles.

"Now," she repeated.

"I want to make sure you're ready—"

"I'm ready." Her fingers clutched even tighter.

He grinned slowly as her legs fell apart and he settled between her thighs. Unbidden thoughts moved through him, and he hesitated. *What is this? What does she expect? More importantly, can I give her what she deserves?*

Her fingers caressed his brow, and his attention moved back to her face. "Hey, Chris, where did you go?"

"I don't know what this is," he confessed. "I don't know what I can promise or what I can give."

Her warm touch continued to dance over his face as her expression softened. "We don't have to label it as anything. We can just be us for now. No expectations. No promises. No vows or declarations."

She was handing him what many men would love to hear—sex for the pleasure and nothing else. His chest felt tight because he wanted so much more. Having no clue how to make that work with starting a new job, he simply nodded. With his cock at her entrance, he took in the determined expression on her face, pushing in as she lifted her hips.

Again, thoughts of taking it slow fled as she continued to meet him thrust for thrust. Her sex was tight, her inner muscles clenching around him. Their gazes remained locked on each other, and a desperate need to taste her had him angle his head as he sealed his mouth over hers. His tongue moved inside her velvet warmth in movements that matched his hips.

He might not have had a word to describe what they were, but this was no casual fuck. He'd had those before, and there was no comparison. He wanted to kiss her, taste her, feel her, become part of her. He wanted to give her everything and take everything she was offering. He couldn't promise forever, but he knew he wanted more than just now.

Her legs wrapped around his waist, giving him easier access as he glided in and out until she finally began to shudder, her fingernails now digging into his back. Lifting her chin, she pressed her head deep into the mattress, groaning out her release.

As though a switch had been flipped, he tumbled headlong into the abyss with her, continuing to thrust as his cock emptied. His posture mirrored hers with his chin lifted, neck muscles red and taut, and he gritted his teeth through the most powerful orgasm he'd ever experienced.

When his body finally gave out, he dropped forward, barely able to shift slightly so that his full weight was not on her. The only sounds heard were their gasping breaths mixed with the wheezing of the ancient air conditioner in the hotel room. He wasn't sure which would give out first, the AC or him. But if it was his time to expire, he couldn't think of a better way to go.

13

Stella felt boneless. Weightless. Orgasmed relaxed. And fuckin' fantastic. Sex had never felt the way Chris made her feel. He worshiped her body with his. The sex was so far from rote and perfunctory, it made her previous lovers pale in comparison. Now, their sweat-slicked bodies entwined, and with him still partially weighing her down, she wasn't sure she could move.

"You okay, Stella?"

"Yuh…"

He chuckled, and she felt his mirth rumble from deep in his chest against hers.

"I'm not sure that lets me know anything, babe. I'm gonna need a little more to know if I need to call the rescue squad."

She managed to turn her head, her gaze now pinned on his smile. The thought crossed her mind that she could spend the rest of her life staring at that smile, especially after they'd just had sex. Tamping down that notion since she'd just told him that they didn't need to label what they were doing, she reached up and smoothed the laugh lines extending from his eyes. "No ambulance. But I think I'm going to need mouth-to-mouth resuscitation from you, just to be sure."

His smile widened, and her heart clenched at the sight. His arms around her back tightened, and he rolled a little more so that they were face to face, keeping his weight off her chest.

"That, I can do with pleasure." His nose nuzzled along hers as his lips danced over her mouth, his tongue darting out and teasing as he kept the kiss light.

He leaned back, and now the smile was on her face as she continued to trace her fingertips over his jaw. Biting her bottom lip, she whispered, "That was amazing. Not just the kiss but everything. Thank you."

His eyes widened slightly as he shook his head. "You don't need to thank me. I should get down on my knees and thank my lucky stars that for once, I wavered off my plan and decided to take this trip with you. Of course, if I was down on my knees, I can probably think of something else to do with my mouth. Which will be next on my list as soon as I can move."

She snorted as she barked out laughter. "Oh, God, if you went down on me right now, I'm not sure I'd live to see the morning." She rolled her eyes upward, pretending to ponder. "But... it would be worth it to find out. And give me a chance to do the same to you."

She watched, fascinated as his eyes darkened, the blue now resembling the sky after the sun had set. She lifted her hand to stifle a yawn that slipped out.

"As much as I'd love another round, we ought to get

a little sleep first," he said, then groaned. "Plus, I only have one condom."

She sucked in her lips. "I'm on birth control and clean, but I don't know if guys trust a woman saying she's on birth control."

"I trust you, Stella," he admitted. "And I'm clean, too. I've got my latest results on my phone."

She grinned. "Then there's nothing stopping us from a second round after we rest?"

His eyes darkened, and he grinned. "Absolutely nothing. But I need a shower first."

"Want some company?"

"Oh, hell yeah, Stella girl."

No longer as tired as she thought she was, she rolled over, straddling his thick thighs, bending to place a soft kiss on him. Lifting slightly, she said, "Let's go get wet and see what happens." She hopped up from the bed but didn't move quick enough. His hand gently slapped her ass, and she squealed as they darted for the bathroom. The shower seemed to revive them both, and once out, he placed his hands on her hips and turned her so that she was facing the counter with her ass tilted up.

With their gazes locked on their reflection in the mirror, he slid in from behind. She'd never watched herself have sex before, but with her breasts bouncing, his hands roaming all over her, and his cock sliding deep inside, they smiled in unison as they came together again.

And she silently wished the trip didn't have to end the next day.

Stella woke suddenly, rolling toward Chris and stretching out her hand which only met empty but still-warm sheets. Sitting up, she spied his silhouette to the side of the window, seeming to peek out from the corner.

"What is it?" she whispered.

He didn't reply but lifted his hand in a wait-a-minute gesture. She realized he'd slipped on his jeans, and feeling exposed, she slithered from the bed and quietly felt around for her T-shirt that had been abandoned on the floor. She had just pulled it over her head when he walked toward her.

"It's okay, Stella. You don't need that."

With her shirt around her neck leaving the rest of her body naked, she scrunched her nose. "I thought if there was something out there, maybe I should put my clothes on." Her gaze darted to the window, but with the curtains closed, she couldn't see anything. Shifting her gaze back to him, she tilted her head to the side. "Did you see something?"

"I thought I heard something."

Her hands shot to the arms of her T-shirt, and she jerked it down to her hips, his words still making her feel exposed as though something was going to come bolting into the room. "What was it?"

"I thought I heard scraping, and then there were some whispered voices. When I got to the window, I couldn't see anything. The bar next door closed at one a.m., so it may have just been employees or stragglers."

She chewed on her bottom lip and nodded. Noises in and around hotels were common, but she could only imagine that as a former SEAL, he would always be cautious. "Do you want to go out and check? I can get dressed and go with you."

He smiled, lifting his hand and grazing her cheek with his knuckles. "No, it's okay. I parked right outside the door and never saw anyone around our vehicle."

"But it gave you a weird feeling, right?"

"I'm always security conscious, babe. Occupational hazard." He rolled his shoulders back and sighed. "I wish I'd been a little more aware of who was in the bar last night, but I didn't get a bad vibe from anyone there."

She lifted on her toes and placed her palm on the smooth, warm skin of his chest. Holding his gaze, she said, "Well, you were rather distracted during dinner. If I'm not mistaken, there was a woman who garnered all your attention."

He wrapped his hand around hers, keeping it pressed to his chest while his other arm wrapped around her back. Bending, he nuzzled her nose before sliding his lips over hers. "She still does garner all my attention."

"Maybe you need a distraction from what's going on outside."

His hand slid from her back down to her bare ass, gripping her flesh. "Oh, hell yeah, babe. I'll take a distraction from you anytime."

He made quick work of discarding her shirt and shucking his jeans. She backed up to the bed, pulling him along by his hand. Grinning, they fell onto the mattress at the same time, quickly wrapping their bodies together once again.

Chris held Stella for a long time after they made love again. *Made love? Is that what we did?* It seemed more than just sex. Certainly more than just a one-and-done. More than two people who jumped each other out of opportunity. But made love?

Remembering it was Stella who'd said they didn't have to define what they were doing or them, he sighed. The problem was that he didn't want the trip to be over and them not see each other again. *We're both in California, not too far from each other. But fuck, I'm starting a new job. One where I'll travel at a moment's notice and can't always tell her what I'm doing or where I'm going.*

But the idea of not seeing her again was untenable. He hated the thought of another man sitting across the table from her, watching her enjoyment as she ate or listening to her talk about snacks on a road trip. His arms tightened as he thought about another man on the receiving end of her beaming smile or watching her walk toward him while wearing the most outlandish colors.

She shifted her body, and he looked down to see that she was still asleep. Her head rested on his shoulder, and their legs were tangled together.

Initially, it was the sounds he thought he'd heard outside that kept him awake. But now, it was the beautiful woman in his arms and the knowledge that their trip would soon be over that had him on edge. *But maybe this doesn't have to be the end. Maybe we can keep seeing each other. Occasionally. Like friends. Or maybe more than friends. Or maybe...*

Heaving another sigh, he knew the night would not yield any answers. At least, not until they could talk and he could find out if she was even willing to see him beyond this journey.

He finally fell asleep with the sound of her gentle breathing puffing warmly across his chest.

14

Chris rested his hands on the steering wheel as they pulled away from the hotel parking lot after lingering over breakfast in the nearby diner, which had been after Stella had woken him up with her mouth around his dick. He'd returned the favor before they'd rolled in the sheets again. And then they'd showered. Just as he'd started the SUV, Stella had run back into the hotel's reception area to purchase some snacks for the road to add to her stash. And then ran back to pee again before they hit the road.

Glancing to the side, he couldn't keep the grin from his face. What had driven him crazy three days ago was now, well... just Stella. Funny, unique, smart, sexy, and completely endearing.

"So..." she began, dragging out the word as she glanced toward him.

"Yeah?"

"I know you said we'd get to San Jose today. I just wondered if you'd decided what route we'd travel."

Her normal confident exuberance appeared subdued, and he wondered if she was hating the end of their journey as much as he was. "Well, um... I looked yesterday and didn't know if you'd like to take any side trips or preferred to go straight to your home."

"Side trips?" she asked, sitting up straighter, her voice perkier.

"Yeah, like maybe get off the highway and see something different."

"Is that what you'd like to do?"

He glanced to the side again, seeing what he hoped was true interest. "It's just that we've gone straight through and haven't really seen a lot other than the stops for you to take pictures. I know that's what we planned on when we left Kansas City. The goal was to just get to California, but I'm in no hurry. So..."

"Yes, I'd love to!" she laughed. Placing her hand on his arm, she squeezed. "Honestly, Chris... I'd love to do anything to prolong our time together!"

"Me, too," he confessed, his heart lighter at the idea of spending more time with her. "I was going to have us get to Reno this morning, but we could head south off the highway to Silver Springs and Stagecoach, Nevada, first. Then take a road to Carson City before we continue on."

"Sounds good to me."

He was no longer surprised when two hours later Stella began the tell-tale signs of needing to stop when she started shifting in her seat. Grinning, he cocked his brow. "You should have quit after one coffee this morning."

"Oh, shut up," she laughed.

Pulling off at the next exit, he looked at the sign to see they were in Lovelock, Nevada. Parking outside the market, he decided a quick trip in would be advantageous for him, as well. When he left the men's room, he easily found her buying fresh pastries along with another bottle of water.

She looked up at him as he approached and smiled widely. "They have a baker who brings these in daily. Don't they look amazing?"

The only thing he thought looked amazing was her, but he simply smiled in return, nodding.

They'd just gotten back onto the road leading to the highway when the brakes felt loose. He tapped them several times. "I wonder when this rental last had maintenance." He grumbled under his breath, glad that the road was not crowded, but his concern increased as they continued. "We're going to have to stop, Stella—shit!" He pressed down, but the SUV didn't slow. Looking ahead, he observed a smaller road that gave him an opportunity. Thankfully, it was on a slight incline, and the vehicle naturally decreased its speed while churning up the rocks and dirt behind them.

They came to a rumbling stop, and his fist hit the steering wheel. "Goddamnit!" Jerking his head to the side, he could see Stella's wide eyes and her pale face, but other than shock, they were fine.

"What do we do now?"

"Call the number for the national rental facility and see if they can send someone out. Of course, here in the middle of nowhere, I don't know when that will happen."

They climbed out, and he looked underneath the vehicle but was unable to see how the brake line was damaged. Considering they'd been on highways and not rough terrain, he couldn't imagine how it had happened naturally and yet had no suspicion that it had not. Hearing a vehicle rumbling nearby, he stepped in front of Stella, looking to see who had approached.

An old, rusty farm truck growled to a halt, and he spied an older couple inside. The man had his window down and called out, "You folks got some trouble?"

"Yes, sir. The brakes went out, and we had to make an emergency stop. Do you happen to know if there's an auto shop or rental facility nearby?"

He turned to the woman sitting next to him, and they exchanged comments before he looked back out his window. "We're hauling some crops to Fallon, just down the way. It's a decent-sized town because of the base there. If you don't mind a ride in the back, we can take it that far."

"We'd appreciate it, sir. Give us just a minute to get our things and we'll hop into the back." He turned to Stella, realizing he'd just volunteered her to ride in the back of a truck carrying vegetables without asking if that was all right even though they didn't have a lot of choices. She was already smiling and waving toward the couple, rushing to grab all of their belongings. Shaking his head, he couldn't help breathing a sigh of relief, even as pissed as he was about the SUV.

Within a few minutes, they packed everything into their bags, and he hefted them into the back of the truck. Turning, he placed his hands on Stella's waist and lifted her easily into the air, giving her a chance to scramble amongst the vegetables, finding a place to sit. Climbing aboard, he settled in next to her. With a nod toward the older man, they drove away, leaving the brakeless SUV still sitting on the dirt road.

Their bodies swayed and bumped together, and he looked down as a giggle erupted from Stella. She beamed up at him as the truck continued to bounce along the road.

"Gotta say, Chris, you sure know how to show a girl a good time."

"Hell, girl, this trip was your idea. I'd say you're the one who knows how to take a man for a ride!"

It felt good to laugh, then he leaned back and pulled out his phone. While on the road, he made a call to the rental company, finally making it through their ponderous phone tree and getting to someone who initially pissed him off when they asked if he'd run out of gas. Finally, they agreed to send notice to a local auto shop to tow the vehicle to the nearest town. They also confirmed that they had a small branch in Fallon, Nevada, if the other vehicle was not able to be repaired quickly.

By the time he finished, they were halfway to Fallon, and he glanced toward Stella again, seeing her pink cheeks when she handed him a bottle of water. "You need a hat. We'll get one when we get to town."

She nodded before she rested her head on his shoulder. The noise from the truck made it almost impossible to carry on a conversation, so he leaned his head to rest on top of hers, his mind still running through the scenarios as to why the brakes failed.

Once in Fallon, they thanked the older couple, who smiled and waved away their efforts to pay. They'd been dropped off at the rental facility where he checked to make sure that a new vehicle would be ready for them soon, glad that the young man working behind the counter was much more helpful than the person at the national phone center.

"Why don't we see if we can leave our luggage here and do a little sightseeing?" Stella asked. "I saw the sign for the Naval Air Station, and I just looked up to see that they had places visitors could go."

"Sure, you can leave your luggage here!" the young man said. "You can lock it in a closet if you want to. I'm the only one who works here. In fact, you can walk straight down this road just a quarter of a mile, and you'll come to the gate for the station. They've got great airplane exhibits. I always used to go there when I was a kid in school and loved it."

It didn't take long for them to walk to the station and have a short tour. Chris kept glancing down toward Stella until she finally huffed and asked, "What's wrong?"

"Nothing," he replied, shoving his hands into his pockets. She tossed a narrow-eyed glare toward him, and he sighed. "Okay, okay. I just realized that seeing displays of old Navy airplanes isn't exactly what you'd like to see."

She circled around until she was directly in front of him and reached out to place her hands on his waist. "Chris, first of all, you spent the last several days making countless stops just so that I could take pictures of the scenery. So, it's hardly a chore for me to let you see something that's interesting to you." Her fingers squeezed slightly, and she stepped closer, her head tilted back as she held his gaze. "Secondly, we're just making the best of a weird situation with the vehicles. Turning something crappy into something good. And third, I really like you. I know we didn't label us, but I'd at least like to think that we're friends. Therefore, anything that you're interested in interests me."

Her words had the effect of both warming and sending a chill through him. Knowing that she liked him, wanted to spend more time with him, and considered them friends, he reached out and pulled her closer, her cheek resting against his chest. But the idea that they were only friends, even if he couldn't figure out a way for them to be more, sent an ache straight to his heart. Not knowing what else to say, he held her for a moment, then, as they separated, linked fingers with her as they wandered around to the other displays, snapping both pictures of him next to the planes and a few selfies of both of them with the hills in the background leading to the snow-capped mountains of the Sierras.

Going back to the rental facility, the young man looked up and smiled. "I've got a new SUV for you. Old man Jackson who owns the auto shop called to say that he'd towed in your other vehicle. Said it was the damnedest thing, but you must have run over something that cut the brake line."

"Cut the brake line?" Chris said, his eyes narrowed. "We were on the highway, so there was nothing that should have caused a problem."

The young man blinked, then scrunched his face. "I thought that's what he said. You can talk to him if you want to, but he said it's going to take a while to get it fixed. I called my supervisor, and he said we were to give you a new vehicle."

Now, fully suspicious that the brake line might have been tampered with, Chris stood in indecision, an emotion he didn't normally have. Feeling a hand on his arm, he looked down to see Stella staring up, a crinkle between her brows.

"Is there a problem? Can't we just take the new vehicle?"

Reaching up, he squeezed the back of his neck. "Yeah, babe, sure. I just don't like having a puzzle with no answer. There's no reason the brake line should have been severed for any reason. We were on the highway, not going over any rough terrain, and yet there's no reason why someone would have done it on purpose."

"On purpose? But... but..."

"I didn't say that's what happened. I'm just wondering."

"Are you thinking about the hotel last night? When you thought you heard something?"

He knew Stella was smart, but her perception was

greater than he'd realized. Nodding slowly, he admitted, "Yeah, it's crossed my mind. But if someone was just being an asshole, then the sooner we get away, the better."

They thanked the young man, and while she filled out the new paperwork, he loaded everything into the new rental SUV. Getting back onto the road, he glanced at the time, and even though he wanted to keep going, he didn't want Stella to exist on snacks. It didn't take long to get to Stagecoach, Nevada, where they stopped at the Stagecoach Grill.

He glanced down at the salad sitting next to the fried chicken on Stella's plate. Lifting his brows, he grinned. "Needed a vegetable?"

She laughed and nodded. "I know! I know! We were just in a vegetable truck, and I could have pigged out on some of their fresh, straight-out-of-the-garden veggies!" She glanced down at her plate. "I love fried chicken, and the spicy fries are fabulous. But after three days, my body is going through vegetable withdrawal. I figure these carrots, lettuce, tomatoes, broccoli, and cucumbers can go a long way to making me feel like I'm doing something healthy."

Now that it was mid-afternoon, the crowd wasn't large, but as he glanced out the window toward the parking lot, he observed quite a few pickup trucks parked all around their small SUV. A white panel van had pulled up to the side, the driver talking out his window to someone standing nearby. He watched them for a moment, uncertain why his attention was drawn to them. His gaze swept back through the other patrons in the restaurant, searching for anyone he might have seen before but came up blank.

"What's going on?" Stella asked softly.

She had a crinkle between her brows, and he wanted to reach across the table and smooth it with his thumb but hesitated. "Probably nothing. I just keep getting the feeling that there's something I'm missing."

"Missing?"

"It's hard to explain. You develop skills when you're out on special op missions, and you learn not to ignore the little things that are going on around you. Someone's voice and mannerisms. Someone that doesn't look like they belong. Someone's clothing, vehicle. Anything that alerts you that something might not be right and you should be prepared. It's those kinds of skills that can make the difference between a successful mission or a failure."

She sucked in her lips as her eyes moved out the window and then back. "And you still think someone tampered with the brakes? Like someone from the bar who might not have liked our looks or didn't like tourists or just were drinking and did it as a dare?"

He held her gaze, amazed once more at her perception. "Yeah, maybe just like that."

She opened her mouth as though to speak again, then just nodded. "I'm finished eating, so we can leave whenever you're ready. Let me just go to the ladies' room, and then we can be on our way."

He wanted to tell her to take her time. Order dessert if she wanted. Have another soda, even if it would make her need to stop an hour down the road. But instead, he offered a chin lift in agreement. He watched as she slid out of the booth and made her way to the restroom. It didn't take long for her to reappear, and with his hand resting lightly on her lower back, he scanned the area as they left. Still seeing nothing untoward, he wanted to get back on the road and hopefully away from whatever had his senses on alert.

15

The topography changed slightly as they neared the Sierra Mountains. A few small evergreen trees were beginning to join the scrub brush that still dotted the area. The flatlands that had given way to rolling hills were now becoming craggy. Out the windshield, he observed the white-capped mountains in the distance with the forest-covered lower mountains closer to them.

"It's so beautiful here, isn't it?" Stella asked.

"Yeah, I was just thinking the same thing. Although, I'm glad to be making it across during daylight." She nodded her agreement, and he pressed on. "I know we were going to get to San Jose today, but with the car problems of earlier, it'll be really late, and I thought we might—"

"Hell yeah!"

Chuckling, he looked over to see her nodding enthusiastically. "You don't mind another night with me?"

Rolling her eyes, she tapped her chin as though

having to think. "Let's see. Another night with a hot former SEAL, big shot security whoever-you-are, who is great in bed… uh… yep, I'm all ready for that!"

Laughing, he nodded toward her phone. "Okay, Miss-good-for-my-ego. See what you can find. I'll let you choose where we stay."

"Chris, the last time I did that, you ended up in a campground cabin!"

"I've slept outdoors all over the world, so if you think that was a hardship, think again. Anyway, I had the best time, so obviously, you're good at going with your gut and finding something perfect."

She tapped away for a few minutes, then said, "I've got it! We can get to Placerville and stay in the Historic Cary House. It dates back to the eighteen-hundreds, looks elegant, and is said to be haunted!"

"Jesus, Stella, you're the only girl I know who'd get excited about a haunted hotel," he laughed.

"Doesn't that sound great?"

"If it's got you, then yes, absolutely."

"Okay, it's about fifty miles east of the center of Sacramento. We can stay there tonight and then…" her voice trailed off as she swallowed, then added with less enthusiasm, "then you can drop me off at my place."

He tried to think of something to say, but his mind was muddled. He didn't think there was time in his life right now for a relationship. He was only subletting an apartment in the same complex as a buddy but would need to find his own place soon. He needed to meet with his new boss and get started with the new job, willing to give it his all. And that didn't even include needing to spend time with his mom.

Shooting a glance to the side, her head was slightly turned away, a smile no longer playing about her lips. He wanted to bring the smile back. But she deserved a man who could focus on her. *I don't even know why I'm thinking about this! I've only been around her for a few days, how could I feel anything other than laughs and lust?*

For a moment, he considered his suggestion that maybe it was better if they just headed straight through to the coast, letting him drop her off at her place, even if it was late at night. Another glance to the side and he squelched that notion. "So, tell me about this haunted hotel," he said, hoping to restart the spark from her.

She twisted around, held his gaze, and her lips quirked upward. Feeling the tightness in his chest ease, he couldn't remember ever meeting anyone who stayed happy as much as Stella or who got over sadness as quickly.

"Well, this one site says that it has paranormal activity, but it doesn't tell me anything specific. It does say that the décor and woodwork match its original. It was a grandiose place for prosperous travelers to stay and even was host to Mark Twain and Ulysses S. Grant. Oh, even Elvis Presley stayed in the hotel! Hmm… it seems that a few murders were known to have occurred in the hotel back in its wild west days, so maybe that's who still lingers, walking the halls at night."

Chris relaxed as he listened to Stella chat about the hotel and caught her enthusiasm for staying there tonight. As they continued on their way, evergreen forests grew along the side of the road, and he turned the heat on as they drove over the highest part of their day's journey. As they continued, she called out when they crossed into California.

The two-lane road had little traffic, making it easy for Chris to keep an eye on their surroundings. After a while, he noticed the same pickup truck had stayed right behind them even though he'd slowed to give them an opportunity to go around earlier. There was nothing overly suspicious, especially considering pickups were as bountiful in the area as the scrub brush covering the craggy hills around.

Flipping on his blinker, he slowed near where a small overlook jutted out. Stella swung her head around, but before she asked, he said, "Thought you might like a picture. Plus, it will give this guy a chance to move on past us."

She twisted around to look out the back window as Chris pulled onto the wide shoulder. "They've slowed down, too."

He jerked his gaze to the rearview mirror, his keen attention now pinpointed on the truck that had now moved over and started to pass. The sound of gunfire rang out, and the SUV lurched to the side. "Fuck! Get down!" he shouted as he battled with the steering wheel. The SUV hit the guardrail, but he managed to keep it on the shoulder and not go into the ravine. Grabbing Stella's upper body, he forced her head down to the seat, ducking as well so that his body covered hers.

"What? What is it?" she cried, her words muffled with her face shoved into the seat.

"They shot at us," he growled. Having planned on plane travel only, he had no weapon with him. Gritting his teeth, he lifted his head just enough to see the truck had continued down the road. He'd only gotten a partial license plate number, but right now, he had more important things to worry about, such as what the fuck they'd hit and if they were coming back. He ordered her to stay down and moved to open his door.

Her hands clawed out, grabbing onto his arm. "No! No, don't go! What if they're still there? I don't want you to get hurt!"

His brain had immediately slid into mission mode, but her words caused him to hesitate long enough to explain, something he'd never had to do with his team members. Leaning back over her, he placed his mouth near her ear. "Stella, I need you to trust me. I know what I'm doing, but I've got to see what's happening or I can't protect you. So, stay down, let me assess what's going on and figure out our next step. But be prepared for us to make a run out into the hills if we have to." He felt her fingers squeeze his arm. "I'm going to take care of you, okay?"

She jerked her head in agreement and loosened her fingers. He checked the windows again and observed no vehicles on the road. The way the SUV listed to the side, he had a bad feeling he knew what would meet his eyes, and as he climbed out and looked down, he was right. *Goddamn fuckers shot out the left rear tire.* It only took a few seconds to see that the right rear tire had gone down considerably. Without the ability to put on more than one spare, they were fucked. *Someone wanted to ensure we were stuck out here, which means these assholes are coming back.*

He lifted the back of the SUV and opened his luggage, shifting things around so that what he needed could fit into his carry-on bag, making sure not to leave anything of value. "Stella, you need to take what you need but also what you can't afford to have taken. Take anything that might identify you," glad when she immediately followed suit and shifted her belongings around so that she had her carry-on bag and purse. Snagging her bag, he jogged to the passenger side where she stuffed water bottles and snacks into a large tote.

"Come on, babe. They've shot both tires. With no other cars in sight, they'll be back. I've got no fuckin' weapon, so we need to get out of here."

Grateful she didn't ask questions but hastily grabbed the rest of her things, slung her purse over her body and grabbed for her bag.

"I've got this," he said, holding their bags in his hands.

"But—"

"Come on. I'll explain more as we go," he ordered gently.

Giving a nod, she hurried to his side and fell in behind him. He tossed their bags down the short ravine and then turned to help her keep her feet as she skidded along the loose rocks. Once at the bottom, he grabbed the bags, and they walked quickly over the dirt toward the nearest hill, staying close to the scrub brush and trees. A scan of the area had shown an outcropping of rocks that would give them initial cover. Once there, he'd have a chance to assess and analyze the situation. Looking over his shoulder, he first checked the road and saw no activity, then dropped his gaze, glad to find Stella keeping up with him. Her sneakers wouldn't provide a lot of protection over the hard-packed dirt and rocks, but they were a lot better footwear than if she'd had on sandals or flip-flops.

She looked up and caught his eye. "I'm okay."

"Good. I was just checking." They hiked upward, keeping out of sight from the road while zigzagging between the trees. Making it to the rock cover, he checked the area then had her sit where she would be hidden. He crouched down next to her so that he'd also be hidden. Her face was turned up toward him, her lips pressed together.

"Here's what I know, Stella. I was suspicious of the truck when it didn't pass us earlier, but it must have been waiting until there was no traffic around. They got off two shots, hitting the back tires."

"That's kind of weird luck for them, isn't it?"

His jaw tightened. "My guess... they're experts with firearms. They probably hoped I'd lose control and we'd go down into the ravine. Or they knew we'd be sitting ducks and they could come back."

"So, you don't think it was random? Like just some guys out being stupid and shooting out somebody's tire?"

"No. Not at all. It was too precise. Too calculated. Combine that with a cut brake line? Someone wants us gone. But there's nothing I'm involved with, so I can't imagine it has anything to do with me—"

"Me?" she squeaked. "You think it might have something to do with me?"

"No, not you, babe. I can't imagine as an artist you'd have someone shooting at you." He scrubbed his hand over his face. "But fuck if I know what they want."

"Can I ask why we came out here? Couldn't we wait for another car to come to help us?"

He reached over and tucked a strand of hair behind her ear. "Stella, honey, you can ask anything you want. Waiting by the car for someone to come pick us up was too much of a risk. If they come back, and I feel like they will, then I wanted to be out of there."

"But won't they just start looking up here?"

"They might. That's why I wanted to get up here so that I could keep an eye on the area and no one would sneak up on us. Hopefully, they'll think that maybe we hitched a ride with someone like before, and they've lost us."

"Can we call the police? I mean, those people can't just go around shooting at people," she said, her expression tight.

"First, I'm going to call a friend who works for my new boss. I want his input on what's going on and what our best course of action is. And while that's happening, I want us to get to the next hill, which has better visibility and cover. Can you make that?"

She looked to see where he was pointing and nodded. "Yeah, that shouldn't be hard." She glanced at their bags. "But I don't want you to have to carry both bags."

"I carried a lot more than this as a SEAL. Believe me, this is nothing."

She opened her mouth as though to argue, then snapped it closed. Holding his gaze, she nodded. "Okay, fearless leader. Show me the way."

He chuckled and shook his head. She had to be scared shitless but was giving him no grief, instead making him grin. Not having or willing to take the time to figure out what that meant, he stood and reached out his hand to gently pull her to her feet.

Stella was panting, wishing she'd spent more time exercising than sitting at her pottery wheel. Of course, it was hard to deny the amount of time she spent working considering that was what paid her bills. But right now, her legs were feeling the effects of little time spent in the gym as she climbed over the hard-packed rocky ground.

And she had to admit that the vista would have been more beautiful if she was just taking a picture for inspiration. In her present circumstances, the colors were not very inspiring. A few clouds floated across the sun, but for the most part, she was grateful for the shade of the sparse trees that dotted the hills.

Looking in front of her, she couldn't believe how Chris was not showing the effects of their trek. No perspiration stains on his shirt. No heaving chest while gasping for oxygen. No slowing down. They'd only been walking for forty minutes, and she was already a sweaty, stinky mess.

Glancing behind her, she could no longer see the road and hoped that was a good thing. On one hand, if she couldn't see the return of the truck, then they wouldn't be able to see her, either. But then, Chris and she wouldn't be able to flag down any assistance, either.

Stumbling over a stone in her path, she righted herself, grateful she hadn't fallen to the ground. Chris stopped suddenly, and she bumped into the back of him. "Sorry," she mumbled, still trying to catch her breath.

"You okay?"

She looked up, wondering if his question was serious. From his non-grinning expression, she ascertained that he was completely serious. "Um... yeah?"

At that, he lifted both brows, still staring. "You shouldn't be asking me if you're okay."

"I guess I was just surprised that you had to ask. I know you can hear me sucking wind back here, tripping over rocks, and I'm fairly sure you can tell I'm sweating like I've run a marathon. So, if these were normal circumstances, I'd have to say that I wasn't okay. But since I'm alive after having been shot at, I'd say that I am okay, if *okay* is taken in the truest definition of the word."

She continued to stare upward, mesmerized as his lips quirked ever so slightly. He stepped closer, cupped the back of her head with his large hand, and leaned down to kiss her forehead. "I've only met one other person who could make me smile in the middle of a fucked-up situation. He was a teammate and a good friend. Other than him, that honor goes to you, babe."

Her heart was still pounding rapidly from the steep climb, but she couldn't help but smile. "I'll take that as a compliment and a good one, at that." She looked around, seeing scrub brush and craggy rocks in every direction, but her gaze snagged on darker clouds forming to the west beyond the Sierra Mountains. "So, what's our game plan?"

"If you think we can go a little bit further, we're going to make it to the rocky overhang up there. There's more shade now, but when the sun begins to set, it's going to get cold. I'll get hold of my contacts and see how best for us to get the hell out of here."

She looked back down in the direction they had come and wondered if they'd have to make the trip back down to the road if he had a friend who could come pick them up. She'd considered calling her parents, but the last thing she wanted to do was place them in a dangerous situation. *Nope, Chris is definitely the right person to handle this mess!*

"Yeah, I can make it," she assured and hoped she wasn't speaking with overconfidence.

He tapped the end of her nose as his gaze held hers. "I love the way you scrunch her nose when you're trying to figure something out. Gotta tell you, it's cute as hell." He hefted their bags and turned, continuing up the path.

She stood for a moment, staring at his back before she followed. *Great. Just what every woman wants to hear. My best feature is a scrunched nose, and I'm cute as hell.* She also realized that while he said she made him smile, he didn't deny that he could hear her gasping or smell her perspiration.

Shaking her head at the ridiculous thoughts moving through her mind, she hastened her steps to catch up. Knowing someone had shot at them should be first and foremost on her mind, not whether she was cute with a scrunched nose. Focusing on anything other than how tired she was, she figured it was better to let her mind roam to crazy ideas than to start screaming at the idea that someone might want them dead. A shudder ran through her whole body, and she once again pushed down that idea.

Glancing ahead, she could see the outcropping of rocks growing closer, and she hurried her steps, desperate to sit down and rest.

16

Chris made sure he checked the area for wildlife, then nodded for Stella to sit in the shade. She immediately arranged their bags so the water and food would stay out of the sun before leaning back against another rock. Letting out a groan as she stretched, he tried to ignore the sound that so resembled the little noises she'd made the previous night. *Jesus, stay focused!*

"I know you noticed the dark clouds earlier," he said, staring down at her.

She nodded, then sighed. "I thought maybe it was some weird mountain-sky thing that had to do with my ninth-grade earth science class that I didn't pay attention to because I was more interested in art class. But I have a feeling you're going to let me know exactly what those clouds mean."

He snorted, shaking his head, finding it hard to focus when Stella constantly caught him off guard with her wit. "We're on the west side of the mountains, and this area gets more rain. Looks like it's coming soon.

The good news is that it might keep whoever is after us away. And it shouldn't be too bad of a rainstorm. Bad news is that we'll get wet."

"Well, I guess that good news still falls under the aforementioned category of *okay*."

He dropped his chin and stared at his boots, losing the battle to not grin. Finally, he lifted his chin, seeing her still staring up at him. Squatting next to her, he leaned forward, placing his lips on hers lightly. "Good to hear," he mumbled as their breaths mingled. He stood and said, "I've got to make a call and need to keep an eye out. You stay here, and I'll just be right on the outside of these rocks."

Pulling out his phone, he quickly dialed, glad when it was answered almost immediately.

"Chris! How's it going?"

"Gonna need some help, Rick. Got a situation."

"What's up?" Rick asked, his voice immediately serious.

"Fuckin' crazy-ass story, but let me give the basics to you." In a hasty synopsis, he explained meeting Stella and that his decision to drive to California involved her. Then he rolled into the vandalism on the brakes of the first car and the shooting of the other. "And now, we're stuck on the west of the Sierras. We're hidden in an outcropping of rocks and have trees around although not thick."

"Coordinates?"

He had already checked using his phone and gave them to Rick. "We've got food and water, but I've got no weapon if they come looking for us. Me? Hell, I could either take them or get away, but with Stella..."

"Got it. I'm calling it in to Carson, and I'll get back to you with a plan."

"Roger that." He disconnected the call and then turned back to check the clouds, seeing them approaching along with the falling sun. His gaze scanned the area, but whoever was after them was nowhere to be seen.

"So, I take it your friend and the... uh... new employer are some kind of super-duper rescue people?"

He looked down and chuckled. "Yeah, I guess that's a good way of putting it." He sat near her, his angle giving him a view of the hillside below. "It's a private security company. They provide security and also do investigations."

"Lighthouse Security Investigations West Coast. I remember seeing that when you first showed me your identification. Interesting name."

"The company was started by a man who had served with my boss. He's based on the East Coast and partnered with my boss to open a second base located on the West Coast."

"So, I assume the security isn't exactly basic bodyguarding?"

He hesitated, looking out as the rain started. They squeezed underneath the stone overhang, providing as much protection as he could. Glad it wasn't a storm and the rain should pass quickly, he turned back to her.

Not quite sure how much to say, he knew the basic information would be acceptable. "The security isn't the type you're probably thinking. Security systems, the ones that go way beyond what most people would think. Government contracts. Investigations that go beyond your typical private eye."

She nodded slowly, drawing her knees up and wrapping her arms around her shins as the rain pelted just beyond their bodies. "It sounds like a job that would fit you very well."

While her words could seem almost trite, he knew they were true and appreciated that she recognized that in him. "It does. And thank you. I take that as a compliment."

"Good because it was meant as one." She glanced out as the sky grew darker. "What now?"

"We wait. I'll get a call back to let us know what the plan is."

She stretched her legs out in front of her, a rueful chuckle leaving her lips. "It just dawned on me that I should say, 'Welcome to California.' I guess this isn't exactly the way you thought you'd come back, is it?"

Shaking his head, he agreed. "Might not be the way I thought I'd come back, but coming home was never easy."

"Tell me about that."

His gaze jumped to hers, his chest squeezing tightly. One thing he didn't talk about with others was his family. When he'd left California, he'd left. Thankfully, no one in the military gave a shit about where he'd come from, who his parents were, or the decisions he'd made. For a moment, he considered blowing off Stella's question, but staring into her guileless eyes, he felt a pull both toward her and with her that he'd never felt with anyone before.

"I was actually in California a few months ago to interview and accept the position with LSI-WC. It was a working visit, only for the purpose of employment. Before that, I hadn't been back to California in three years, and that was to bury my father. Before that, I hadn't been back since I left home at the age of eighteen to join the Navy."

"Why do I get the feeling there's more to you staying away than just being in the military?" she prodded softly.

"You'd be right. The night before I left was the last argument my father and I had. Typical of the relationship we endured. He called me a loser for joining the military instead of following in his footsteps. Loser and a few other choice words. I walked out and never came back until I got the call from my mom that said he'd died." He winced for a number of reasons, one being that he wished he'd spent more time with his mom.

He had no idea what Stella's reaction would be. Would she look at him in disgust? Tell him how wrong he'd been? Accuse him of abandoning his mother? It was hard to hold her gaze when he feared what he'd see in her eyes.

"I can't imagine what it was like for your father to say those words to you. The horrible words that made you leave and not want to come back. I'm so sorry that he never got the chance to see what kind of man you are. How amazing his son is."

Her words soothed over him, filling cracks and

fissures he didn't realize he had. Her voice held a touch of pity but not in excess. Instead, it was her way of turning it around, making him proud. Blowing out a breath, he added, "Thank you. But I still need to face my mother. She didn't deserve me staying away."

"Home is the place where when you go there, you have to finally face the thing in the dark." She blinked, jerking slightly as though surprised the words had come. "I'm sorry. That's just a quote from Stephen King, and it popped into my head. It probably wasn't what you wanted to hear—"

"No, you're right," he acknowledged, his gaze still pinned on her. "There's a lot I have to face here. But then, I should admit that the home I grew up in is no longer where she is."

"Tell me… tell me about *you*."

He tore his gaze away from the intensity of her inquiry. He didn't know what this pull was he had for her. They'd even agreed not to try to label it. But he'd never wanted to unburden himself as much as he did right now. Shifting to a more comfortable position, he looked over at her, discovering safety.

"My father. Doctor Charles Andrews. The number one cardiac surgeon in Los Angeles and the surrounding area. He was sought after by people who had money and influence and was never without a patient list that didn't include the *who's who* of politicians, celebrities, and the wealthy. We had a huge house. Cars. Housekeeping staff. Private schools. Everything you'd expect a man of his stature to have as he planned for me to finish college, get into medical school, and follow in his footsteps."

A rueful snort slipped out as he shook his head. "The one thing I did not have was a nanny. Contrary to what many might expect, my mother was no society arm candy. When he was young and still in college, he met the beautiful Eileen McCarthy. Mom was educated in business and interior design, a career that she worked in until I was born and then gave up willingly to be a full-time mom until I started school. She was always there for me, every game, every school event. She then worked part-time but had no problem offering her many services to the charitable causes she was passionate about and my father deemed worthy. Mom was strong and independent, the perfect partner for him. She supported him, loved him, and allowed him the freedom to have the career he wanted without selling her soul in the process. The crazy thing is that you might think he was a nasty piece of work to her, too. But he wasn't. She wasn't a doormat, and he didn't treat her like one. But the one thing she wasn't able to do was to convince him that I should live my own life even though God knows she tried."

"She protected you?"

He nodded slowly. "She did. Although, my father was good about getting his digs in when she wasn't around. I honestly think she was the only person in his life that he knew wouldn't put up with his shit."

"He loved her," Stella said softly.

"Yeah. Funny, I never really thought about them as a couple."

"I don't think most children do. At least not until we're adults and have more clarity and understanding."

"You're very wise for someone so young," he laughed.

She reached out her foot and tapped his leg with her purple sneaker. "Hey, I'm almost thirty."

"Oh, then you're just a baby!"

"How old are you?" She leaned forward as though counting the lines on his face.

He barked out a laugh. "Probably not as old as I look." Seeing her lifted brow, he admitted, "I'm thirty-two. I did fourteen years in the Navy, the last ten as a SEAL." She remained quiet, not peppering him with questions, giving him a chance to think. To remember.

"When I was in high school, my father did everything he could to keep me from wanting to join the military. Looking back, I can't say that it was my life's dream, but doing anything to piss him off certainly was. When I turned eighteen, I signed with the Navy and left a month later. We had a huge argument where he essentially told me that if I joined up, I was no longer his son."

Stella leaned forward, her hand landing on his arm, her fingers wrapping around his wrist. She said nothing, but her offered support reached into the cold recesses deep inside. He turned his palm upward, and she slid her hand down, linking her fingers through his.

For a moment, he stared at their connection. The simple touch of palms together and fingers linked. It was such a common gesture, one that he'd rarely engaged in beyond high school. And yet now, the calming peace he felt with her small hand tucked tightly with his made him realize how alone he'd felt for a very long time.

"How did he die?"

"Would you believe that the premier cardiac surgeon died of a massive heart attack? No warning. No previous problems. He and my mom were at their country club, playing golf. They had just finished and were heading back to the clubhouse. As horrible as it was, I know she was glad to be with him at the end." Lifting his gaze, he yearned to tell her more. "When I came home for my father's funeral, I felt changed once I went back to my team. My mother seemed older, and I had a lot of regrets that in walking away from my father, I'd walked away from her, as well. It's not that we didn't have any contact. She and I would call or video chat often, but the realization of how much time had passed hit me. Add on top of that a fucked-up mission that went sideways, killing one of my teammates and injuring others because of poor intel, and I was ready to get out. By then, I'd already talked to my friend Rick, and when I was still stationed in Virginia Beach, his boss was in the area and we talked a lot. Next time I had a chance to take leave, I came to California to interview, and he offered me a position as a Keeper when I got out."

She cocked her head to the side, her brows lowering. "Keeper?"

"Named after the old Lighthouse Keepers, guiding others to safety."

"Wow, what an analogy." She smiled, then said, "Your

mother must be thrilled that you're moving closer to her."

"After my dad died, she sold their estate, claiming that she didn't need anything so large and ostentatious. She moved to Carmel-by-the-Sea, and from the pictures I've seen, she has a lovely condo with a beautiful view. She's made new friends, seems to have a full life, but has admitted that she can't wait to see me more often." He shrugged and held her gaze. "So, going back to California is like going home, but not the home of my past. Just to the new home where I make it."

By now, the rain had passed, and they had only gotten damp but not soaked. Nodding toward their bags, he said, "See if you can find something to wrap up in. I don't want you to get chilled."

She rummaged around, finding a sweater and sliding her arms through the sleeves while he jerked on a light jacket.

"And you have a place already?" she continued.

"Sort of. I'm going to stay with Rick for a few nights until I can get a sublease signed. The complex where he lives has a tenant leaving for a few months and needs someone to stay there. I thought I'd start with an apartment and see what's around before I decide to buy anything. Plus, I need to make some decent money with LSI-WC first. I've done a good job saving money while in the military, but I'm going to need a couple of bigger paychecks to feel like I can look for a house."

"That makes sense," she said, nodding. "Everything is so expensive. You should see my place although I guess you will when you take me there. I have a tiny apartment over my studio, which is basically in a garage."

It was on the tip of his tongue to say that he very much wanted to see her place and even hoped that he might visit her there, but his phone vibrated, immediately drawing his attention. Connecting, he said, "Talk to me."

17

As Chris took the phone call, Stella shifted on the hard rock under her ass. With the tall trees around, the sun had already passed beyond them, deep shadows surrounding the stone slab outcropping where they were hiding. While talking, Chris had maintained his vigil, and she could only imagine that it was both easy for him as a former SEAL to handle threats and yet difficult since she was with him.

The adrenaline had long since left her body, leaving her drained. She leaned her head back and closed her eyes while still listening to Chris' grunts as he mostly listened to his friend. She couldn't imagine why someone wanted them dead. *Certainly not about me! I'm a nobody potter, and he's been involved in government missions.* Not that she knew anything about what he would have done other than news, TV shows, and movies.

After Chris agreed with a few more *'roger thats'* and disconnected, she opened her eyes. He was tapping into his phone, so she remained quiet while he continued to work. Finally, he looked up, his eyes searching hers. She blinked, hoping she was showing him whatever he needed to see to feel confident that she could handle the next steps. "So, fearless leader. What's next?"

His lips quirked, and he said, "We're going to stay here for a couple of hours until they can get to us."

Her brow furrowed, and she glanced out toward the wilderness around. "If you tell me they're going to swoop down in a helicopter, lower a rope, and haul us out of here swinging over the treetops, I'll certainly go along but can't say that it would be the best part of our journey."

"Fuck, Stella," he chuckled. "I never know what's coming out of your mouth. But you're not that wrong. Rick and a couple of the Keepers will fly into Sacramento, then helicopter in. They won't have to lower a rope because they've found a meadow not too far from here. But we want to stay undercover until they're closer."

"Wow."

He lifted his brow and repeated, "Wow? I'm not quite sure how to interpret that."

"I'm not sure under the circumstances there are a whole lot of ways to interpret that. I guess *wow*, I can't believe someone was really after us. And *wow*, that you're a security hotshot with security hotshot friends who can swoop in and save us. And I suppose *wow*, this was so not the trip I envisioned when I thought about driving halfway across the country."

"That's a lot of *wows*," he said, his lips still curving

upward. He leaned forward and cupped her jaw with his hand, his thumb sweeping over her cheek. "I'm not going to let anything happen to you, Stella."

She leaned into his palm and nodded. "I know that. I might have only known you for a couple of days, but I know the kind of man you are. I trust you, Chris."

"Why don't you lay down? Close your eyes and at least rest. I'll wake you when we need to head out."

She started to deny that she was tired but knew it was ludicrous. Feeling sure she'd never be able to sleep, her body felt weighed down, exhaustion pulling at every muscle. She shifted, laid her head on her bag, and closed her eyes. She had no plans of falling asleep. *I'll just rest for a few minutes.*

Chris squatted at the edge of the mountain overlook, staring out into the dark. A dark so black it was hard to see his hand in front of his face. But when he lifted his chin, the stars above glistened with a brilliance that made him wonder if he'd ever noticed them before. *What the hell? Christ, I'm thinking about stars?* He figured if his former SEAL brothers could hear his thoughts now, they'd laugh their asses off.

He wasn't supposed to be there. *I should have been in California by now.* The road to get to this place had not been in his plans, and he always stuck to his plans. But ever since he'd left Virginia Beach several days ago, nothing had gone according to schedule. *What was it the strange lady in the Atlanta airport USO said?*

"The destination isn't as important as the road you take to get there. Learn to enjoy the journey." Blessing... that was her name.

Scrubbing his hand over his face, he squeezed his eyes shut, forcing those thoughts to the side. Taking another careful look around, he listened for any sound of danger. The night was quiet, and that should have eased the caution holding a grip on him. Instead, it just made him more aware of possible dangers. Someone was out there... someone who wanted them dead.

A movement and the sound of a soft snore drew his attention to the rock slab next to him. His gaze drifted down to the woman curled up on her side, her head resting on her hands as her palms clasped together. She was sleeping soundly on the hard rock. A small smile curved his lips at the sight of her yellow-blonde curls escaping from her lopsided braid, her wildly printed shirt, and purple sneakers. And if her eyes were open, he knew he'd be staring at a blue so pure it was like looking at the ocean off the coast of Greece on a sunlit day. *Christ, I'm losing it.*

If he believed in voodoo shit, he'd wonder if Blessing had cast an incantation over him. Sighing, he shifted his ass to the ground next to her. He hoped the only danger that might get to them tonight was his own imagination.

Stella woke to a gentle hand nudging her. She blinked several times, then jerked awake, her body protesting its stiffness while her mind remembered where she was and why. Chris was next to her, his face close, his gaze intense, and his expression full of concern.

"What's happening?" she whispered, fear lancing through her.

"I want you to stay here—"

Her hand snapped out, her fingers gripping his arm.

"Someone's out there, and I'm going to see if our way is clear. But I need you to stay here, Stella. Promise me. "

She wanted to argue and beg him to stay as her heart beat faster. Instead, her eyes widened in silent pleading.

"Promise me," he repeated. "I'll come back for you, but I want to get to them before they try to get to us here."

"Your friends…"

"They're coming, but I don't want to wait. Stay here and stay safe. Promise."

Her head jerked up and down. "I promise." Gripping him tighter, she demanded, "And you promise me that you'll come back safe, too."

He dipped his chin. "I'll come back. I promise." He leaned closer, his lips sealing over hers for just a few seconds before he moved back and slipped over the edge of the rock into the darkness.

She lifted her hand, which had been holding onto his arm, and touched her fingers to her still-tingling lips. She leaned forward, peering out, but could see nothing. Without any light, she wasn't sure what she could do but knew she couldn't sit still. With determination, she shifted to her knees and felt around for the few items she'd taken out of their bags and shoved them back in. The evening chill made her fingers ache, but she pushed through the pain. When he came back, she wanted to be ready.

Once that task was complete, she sat back on the hard rock, now wondering how she ever slept on that surface. Not willing to risk the light from her cell phone giving away her position, she had no idea what time it was or how much time had passed since Chris left.

Suddenly, she heard a noise, but before she had time to squeak, Chris jumped from the overhang above, landing deftly next to her.

"Sorry, babe, I didn't want to startle you," he whispered, his voice full of urgency. "We've got to go."

He reached for the bags, and she grabbed the smaller ones, looping them over her shoulder. She followed him out, nerves zinging through her body, making her hyper-aware of the sound of her sneakers on the rocks and each breath seeming to ricochet down the mountain. They didn't go far when he halted and she tripped slightly, trying not to run into the back of him.

"We wait here."

She glanced around in the dark, not seeing that *here* was anywhere special. Leaning closer, she whispered, "Why?"

"The helicopter has landed—"

"I thought we'd have to walk to get to the meadow."

"We were, but plans have changed. Two of the Keepers are coming in to get us."

She swiped her hair from her face, the darkness keeping her from reading his expression now that he wasn't as close. She glanced around again, then shifted her gaze back to him. She had so many questions but pressed her lips together tightly to keep from blurting them out. She needed to trust him. She *did* trust him.

"The Keepers have the equipment to see in the dark. There was a pickup truck parked close to our SUV. Only one person was observed inside, but others might be around. So, to make sure we don't stumble into an ambush, the Keepers will come to us."

She leaned forward and placed her hand on his jaw, feeling the tension underneath her fingertips. "You hate this, don't you?"

A huff of air blew heavily from his lips. "Let's just say that I'm not a fan of waiting for someone else to take care of what I know I can handle."

"But you came back for me."

"Absolutely," he said without hesitation.

He jolted, his head jerking to one side. She mimicked his behavior although she heard nothing and, staring into the dark, saw nothing. He reached out and grabbed her hand just in time to keep her from yelping when two creatures suddenly appeared. Her fingers clenched tightly as her other hand slapped across her mouth to hold in the gasp threatening to erupt. Seeing the smile on Chris' face helped her to breathe easier although her heart was still pounding erratically.

He clasped hands with one of the huge men whose faces were hidden behind large goggles and whose body was covered in dark camo. He offered a chin lift to the other man, and as both goggled faces turned toward her, she remained quiet, having no idea what the proper protocol would be for a middle-of-the-night, middle-of-the-wilderness rescue. The two nodded toward her, then turned their attention back to Chris, handing him a pair of goggles, as well. One of the men leaned toward her and she instinctively stepped back, but he merely took her bag and hefted it onto his shoulder.

After a few seconds, Chris inclined his head toward them, and assuming that meant they were going to follow, she nodded. They fell into line behind one of the men, the second man moving behind her. Chris stayed close with his arm around her as she stumbled along. She wished she had a pair of night-vision goggles also but wasn't about to stop and ask.

The terrain leveled, and the men's pace increased. Not stumbling as much, she began to think she'd gotten used to the idea of trotting along in the dark when she stumbled to a halt at the sight of a huge dark object in front of them. With the moonlight shining over the meadow, she could now see they were heading toward a helicopter. Without having a chance to become frightened at the idea of flying over the terrain in the dark, Chris led her to the side where the door slid open. Tossing his bag onto the floorboard, he turned and grabbed her by the waist, lifting her easily into the air.

Another pair of hands reached down and took her from him, settling her feet onto the floor of the aircraft. Turning around to offer thanks, she looked up at another tall man whose face was also hidden behind the same goggles, except this time, the man had a wide grin, eliciting smile from her.

Chris deftly climbed into the helicopter, followed by

the other two men who'd met them, and then the door slid shut.

"Let's get you buckled in and get airborne, and then I'll introduce you."

Dim lights exposed a pilot and copilot seat in the front and four seats in the back. Moving to the one Chris indicated, she pulled her crossbody bags over her head and set them on the floor. Sitting down, she watched as he buckled the strap across her waist and then the ones that crossed from her shoulders. Next, he handed her headphones with a small microphone attached.

"You good, Stella?" Chris asked. "You'll be able to hear us and speak even with the noise of the bird."

Nodding, she said, "Remember, this is my first uh... *bird* ride. It had better be a good one."

Laughter came from the first man Chris had greeted as he smiled at her and then looked toward Chris, who was now settled into the seat next to her. "I like her, man."

"Thank you," she interjected. "For liking me and for coming to get us."

"Sounds like you've had quite the trip," one of the other men said as the pilot began flipping switches and the sound of the blades began to roar.

Chris chuckled. "I'd like to introduce Stella Parker. Stella, this is my new boss, the man who runs everything, Carson Dyer. And the man with a wide grin is my good friend, Rick. The man at the controls, also with a grin on his face, is our pilot, Hop."

She greeted the three, then gripped the arms of her

seat tightly as the helicopter lifted into the air, soon banking to the left as it turned and swooped over the treetops. Considering it was dark outside, she hoped they were going over the treetops.

"You good?" Chris asked again.

She nodded as she twisted her head to look at him in the faint lights of the helicopter's interior. "Yeah. Although, I think my stomach just took a flip-flop." She leaned closer and whispered, "I assume he can see where to fly in the dark?" As soon as the words left her mouth, she rolled her eyes. "That was really dumb, wasn't it? Airplane pilots fly in the dark all the time."

"Nothing's dumb, babe," he said. "This is all new for you, so ask whatever questions you want to." He reached over and took her hand, linking fingers and holding tightly.

She looked down at their connection, loving the feel, as always. She'd wanted to hold his hand when they lifted off but was afraid PDA might not be appropriate or even wanted. Glad that he was holding on, she smiled. The Keepers began talking amongst themselves, and she remained quiet but was glad she could hear what they were saying. Considering everything that had been happening to them, the last thing she wanted was to be left in the dark. Especially since she had no idea if she'd see Chris again once they landed. Or where they were even heading to.

She had so many questions to ask, but now, uncertainty kept her silent. In truth, maybe it was more fear than uncertainty. When they'd just been traveling together, she discovered early on that Chris was somebody she'd like to know better. After a couple of days, it was evident he was somebody she'd like to have in her life. And while sex didn't have to mean everything, with him it had meant something. But before they'd had a chance to explore more, their lives as well as the trip had been upended. Not having a clue as to his thoughts, she didn't want to ask them now with an audience. So, instead, she held his gaze and offered a small smile, gaining a finger squeeze from him in return.

18

"What have you found out?" Chris asked.

Carson twisted around in his seat and faced Chris. "I've got Jeb and Leo on highway cameras, seeing if they can find the black truck that shot out your tires. There's a white pickup that's been driving slowly near where your SUV was left. Nevada plates. One driver, male. He was either very curious about your SUV and why it was left there, or he was waiting to pick up someone nearby. Jeb's working on that, as well. We weren't willing to risk Ms. Parker's safety by staying in the area to keep an eye on him. I made the call that it was better to get you two out of there."

Chris nodded, disappointed that they didn't have any more to go on at the moment but glad that Carson took Stella's safety at as high a priority as he did. He glanced to the side, knowing that Stella could hear what they were talking about, but she remained quiet, her gaze cast downward. Ever since he'd met her, she was always so open, and it felt strange not to know what she was thinking.

Continuing, Carson said, "We've called in the authorities for your rental. My contact at the FBI will be there at first light, and they'll take possession of the vehicle and secure the rest of your luggage if it's still there. What I'd like to do is get a jump on the investigation, and to do so, we'll head to LSI unless you have an objection."

Chris caught Carson's meaning, especially since his new boss' eyes cut over to Stella. He wasn't sure how to answer. He and Stella hadn't talked about what would happen after they got picked up. *Is she expecting to go back to San Jose now? Will she be upset if we go to LSI first?* Uncertain what to say, he wasn't surprised when Carson didn't beat around the bush.

"Ms. Parker?"

Her gaze jumped up to Carson sitting in front of them. "Yes, sir?"

Carson grinned and shook his head. "You can call me Carson."

She smiled and nodded. "And please call me Stella."

"All right, Stella. Our plans right now are to head straight back to our headquarters. We're located on the coast, about eighty miles south of where you live. If you insist, we can take you to your home. We still need to interview you and Chris, and it would be easier on our home turf. But I realize you've had a trying time—"

"It's fine, Carson. We can certainly go wherever you'd prefer to interview me. I want to help all I can. All I ask is that at some point, I need to call my parents and let them know when I'll be home. I haven't called them since all this happened, but don't want them to worry since we usually talk often."

"Absolutely," Carson agreed.

"I'll take you home, Stella," Chris said quickly, hoping she wouldn't disagree. "I'll have to borrow a vehicle because buying one was one of the first things I was going to do when I arrived in California, but I'll drive you up to your place in San Jose as soon as we get finished with our interviews."

She turned her face toward him and beamed, the now-familiar smile that had started out several days ago as enduring and was now an expression he couldn't imagine not having in his life. She nodded and said, "That'd be great. Thank you!"

He looked down at their still-linked fingers, feeling her squeeze him lightly. He didn't care that Rick and Carson could see that this woman meant something to him. He had no idea what would happen when this was over but hoped she was going to remain in his life. Remain as a *big* part of his life.

"So, did you ever figure out why on earth these guys were after you?" Rick asked, interrupting Chris' thoughts of Stella.

Forcing his attention back to the others, he shook his head. "No fuckin' clue. We had almost no conversations with anyone. No altercations with anyone. We were on the road, stopping for gas and snacks and food, and stayed at a couple of hotels and in a campground another night. There no reason for someone to come after us."

"Did anyone take an interest in Stella?" Rick continued as he turned toward her. "I guess I should be asking you that, Stella. Anyone flirt with you that you had to shut down? Anyone try to get close that made you uncomfortable?"

She shook her head. "No, no one. Not since the airplane, and Chris dealt with him when we drove off together. Everyone I met on the road was friendly. I'm easy going and don't have a problem talking to people. We weren't around anyone that made me feel weird."

"Okay," Carson looked toward Chris. "This man from the airplane… he a possibility?"

Chris shook his head. "Guy was a letch but no threat. I can't see him following and doing anything. He was more the kind who'd take advantage of a young woman traveling alone, not go after the two of us with a weapon."

Carson nodded. "Okay. I trust your judgment. You guys get some rest, and as soon as we get back, we'll have the others with us. My fiancée is waiting on us, Stella. You'll be able to take a shower, have some food, and even take a nap. I know you're exhausted, and we're going to make sure that you're taken care of."

She thanked him before turning her attention back to Chris. He leaned closer and said, "It's going to take a couple of hours, so you should try to rest." There was so much more he wanted to say but didn't want an audience for a meaningful conversation. She held his gaze, then nodded, settling deeper into her seat before she closed her eyes. He breathed a sigh of relief but knew that not only did he face his first investigation with LSI as the victim, which was not the way he wanted to start off his employment, but he also had to face his relationship with her, which was undefinable, and he had no idea when it might become more definable.

Two hours later, they landed. The sky was still dark although to the east was the faintest hint of approaching dawn. Chris grinned as Stella stretched and yawned. She looked adorably confused for a few seconds before realizing they were on the ground.

"Oh, my goodness! I can't believe I went to sleep!"

He'd let go of her hand sometime while she slept but reached back over to squeeze her fingers. "I'm glad you did. You were exhausted."

Her brow furrowed as she looked at him. "What about you? You have to be just as tired."

"I'm used to going longer with less sleep."

Now it was her time to grin, and she rolled her eyes. "Macho super-op, right?"

"Something like that," he laughed. The door slid open and, already unbuckled, he assisted Stella with her straps. He moved in front of her and hopped to the ground, turning to lift her easily. Rick followed with their bags, shaking his head as Chris attempted to reach for them.

"I got 'em, man," Rick said.

They fell in line toward a large, black SUV and climbed in. Carson was behind the wheel with Hop in the front, Rick and Leo took the second row of seats, and Chris and Stella were in the back. Chris was curious, assuming Carson would not take them to the LSI headquarters. Not that it was an off-the-grid, completely secret location, but he figured Carson didn't entertain non-LSI persons there.

As the sun rose just enough to cast a pale blue hue to the sky, they drove to a small building. Carson parked outside, and with the bags left in the SUV, the others alighted from the vehicle. With his hand on Stella's lower back, Chris guided her inside, following Rick.

Immediately hit with the scent of coffee and cinnamon, his mouth watered, and he felt Stella perk up, as well. "That's gotta be for us, babe."

They moved into a room that had several tables with chairs, all filled with men that he recognized as other Keepers. Along the wall was a counter with an industrial coffee pot and several large platters filled with cinnamon buns and other pastries. A woman in nursing scrubs with her hair in a neat braid turned and smiled.

"Hey!" She smiled widely and walked directly to Stella. "I'm Jeannie, Carson's fiancée. He told me a little about what was happening to you all, and I wanted to make sure I had a chance to greet you before I headed to work. I'm a nurse in a family medical practice nearby. Please, have some coffee and pastries that Rachel brought over. She works for Carson also and will stop by in a little bit to make sure you have everything you need."

"Wow, thank you. This looks amazing." Stella smiled toward Jeannie, then cast her pleading gaze up toward Chris. Interpreting her expression, he offered a slight chin lift before turning to Jeannie.

"This is great. I think first, perhaps, we could both use a trip to the restroom."

"Of course, I should have thought about that," Jeannie agreed. "Follow me."

With a nod to the others in the room, he guided Stella out of the room and down the hall. She mouthed, 'Thank you,' and he grinned. A few minutes later, they were back in the conference room where they filled mugs full of coffee, and each grabbed a pastry before sitting down, turning their attention to Carson.

He began by addressing Chris. "I know this isn't the way you expected to start work here with us."

Chris nodded, his face heating, but he was relieved by the friendly chuckles from the others in the room. "You're right, and I should apologize for that—" Immediately, the chuckles turned into heads shaking and denials which was a relief.

"No apology needed," Carson said, then turned his attention to Stella. "For a more formal introduction, I'm the head of the Lighthouse Security Investigations West Coast. We are a private security firm that is also licensed to investigate, taking private and government contracts. I'm aware that you know that Chris was on his way here to begin working for us. So, while your trip was not what you expected, I can assure you that I only employ the best. Therefore, Chris was able to see to your safety, and now you have us in your corner, as well."

She nodded, pressing her lips together, her gaze darting from Carson to Chris. He wanted to reassure her, but considering this was his first true meeting with LSI, he was uncertain of the protocol.

Chris had no doubt Carson could read the emotions

on Stella's face as he continued, "This building is a place where we can meet with others who are not one of our employees. It's not a hideout, and you're certainly not being kept here against your will. We wanted you to have a chance to eat and rest as you talked to us before Chris takes you back to your apartment in San Jose."

She nodded and smiled. "Thank you, both for your hospitality and for making me feel safe after what happened."

A man sitting nearby with an open laptop looked over at them. "I'm Jeb, and I've been running through highway camera feeds to see who may have taken a shot at you. With the partial license plate that you were able to give, Chris, it looks like I might have a hit. There's a truck that includes that license and fits the description that belongs to Jonathan Markham. He's an electrician who lives in Winnemucca, Nevada."

"Winnemucca?" Stella repeated, turning to look at Chris. "That doesn't mean anything to me. We passed so many road signs that I couldn't tell you where that was."

"Me either," Chris admitted. "Do you have a photograph of him?"

Jeb turned his laptop screen around, showing Jonathan's driver's license. He stared at the photograph, shaking his head slowly from side to side. Glancing toward Stella, he observed her doing the same.

"I don't recognize that man or that name at all," Chris said. "But we stopped at numerous gas stations, diners and fast food, a hotel—"

"And the campground," Stella interjected.

"Yeah, and a night in a campground. Lots of people

around, lots of pickup trucks, but I can't come up with one reason why that man or anyone would want to try to take us out."

His glance moved around the room, seeing Carson rub his chin and a few other Keepers in what appeared to be deep thought. He knew there had to be a connection. One attempt on them with cutting the brake line could be chalked up to vandals, random criminal activity, or just dumb luck. But that combined with having their tires shot out meant someone was after them.

After several more minutes of ideas being bounced around with no resolution, Carson placed his hands on the table and then pushed himself to stand. "Chris, Stella, we're going to keep looking at this. But I know you have a life to get back to. Chris, I know you were going to stay at Rick's apartment until you could move into your own place, and I'm offering you the use of one of our SUVs to take Stella home."

"Thank you, Carson, that's more than generous."

Carson waved away his thanks. "You're a Keeper now." His gaze moved between Chris and Stella. "Stella, it's been a pleasure, and we'll keep you informed on what else we can tell you."

She stood and graciously thanked the Keepers, and it didn't pass Chris' notice that when she beamed her smile toward them, they all had a huge smile in return. She headed back to the ladies' room, and he turned to the others.

"I know you said it didn't matter, but I hate like hell that this was my introduction to you. I'll take Stella back to her home in San Jose and come straight back.

I'll get my stuff stowed away at Rick's later, and then I plan on coming back and being ready to start."

"Hell, Chris," Leo said, his gaze penetrating. "You don't have to rush on our account. Take time to make sure Stella is settled and do whatever you need to do for her."

Disconcerted, he shook his head. "We're not... we haven't... it's not like that."

"Could have fooled me," Rick said, his grin wide.

Leo lifted his brow as he added, "Looks like you're going to be in for my Relationship 101 class."

Carson barked out a laugh. "Coming from someone who's just been in Leo's *class*, I can at least vouch that I walked away *with* the girl after trying to walk away *from* the girl."

"Thanks, but I'm coming into this job wanting to give one hundred percent. Like I said, it's embarrassing that I have to bring a case to your doorstep on the heels of my arriving... or rather, that my arriving had to involve a middle-of-the-night rescue by you all. But once I get Stella to her home, I'll head back here and be ready to start."

With that said, he walked out into the hall, realizing that he should have been more careful to make sure Stella didn't overhear what he'd said. Considering his feelings about her were all over the place, it didn't feel right to acknowledge something was between them to his new coworkers when, in fact, she might not feel the same. It was true that he wanted to give his new job his entire focus but wasn't ready to discuss his conflicting emotions with her. Glad to find the hall empty, he leaned against the wall until Stella walked around the corner. Her eyes landed on him, then behind him, where the other men were leaving the room. Her smile seemed guarded, but he knew she was running on exhaustion and fumes.

Stepping over, he placed his hand on her shoulder, giving what he hoped was a reassuring squeeze. "You ready to leave?"

She nodded, her eyes glancing up to his but not holding his gaze. "Yeah, I feel like I could sleep for years."

"All right, babe. Let's hit the road."

She snorted and shook her head. "God, who could ever imagine that *hit the road* could bring such drama?"

He laughed and swung his arm around her shoulder as they walked outside. Clicking the locks on the SUV Carson provided, he checked to make sure her bags were in the back and climbed in behind the wheel.

The last leg of their journey was about to happen when he'd drop her off at her home. Several days ago, that was all he'd planned on doing. Even now, he knew that's what had to happen. He just wished he could tell the ache in his heart to get on board with the plan.

19

Stella sat in the passenger side of the huge SUV, trying to think of something to talk about. She'd spent the last several days talking almost nonstop, but now the only words in her head were the ones she'd heard Chris speak.

"We're not... we haven't... it's not like that." "I'm coming into this job wanting to give one hundred percent." "But once I get Stella to her home, I'll head back here and be ready to start."

She wasn't sure he could have made it any plainer that his interest in her was now over. She pressed her lips together and stared out the side window, blinking back the tears that threatened to spill. It wasn't that she thought he was ready to declare undying love and ask her to spend forever with him, but she thought they'd forged a friendship with the hope of something more. The ache in her chest bloomed, and she wondered if she looked down if she would see blood oozing from what felt like a stab wound. Giving her head a little shake, she grimaced. *Jesus, Stella, stop it! You thought it was something, he didn't. You had good sex... okay, great sex, but that's all it was.*

After several minutes, her frustration ebbed slightly. They'd never made any promises, so he'd broken no vow. They'd only known each other a few days, so he'd broken no trust of friendship. And while their chemistry was phenomenal, he'd broken no unspoken rule that said great sex had to equal forever. She realized if all she had of him was this trip's memories, she'd cherish them.

"Hey, are you okay?"

Chris' words startled her out of the mental maze she'd been running around in. Jerking her head around, she plastered a smile on her face. "Yeah, sure. Just ready to get home, that's all."

"Yeah, I guess you're looking forward to putting this trip behind you, aren't you?"

His voice held a strange timbre, one she couldn't define. It almost sounded like regret, but that emotion wouldn't fit with the words he'd said to his new coworkers.

"So, you must be excited to have your own place soon."

"I'll stay for a few days with Rick just to make sure it's what I want, but the sublease apartment is in his complex. I looked at them online, and they look fine for now. Nothing I'd want long-term, but for a few months' lease, I can handle it."

"He's a good friend."

"The best," he nodded. "I sent him the details I

wanted for a vehicle, and he's already scoped one out for me. All I have to do is go in, sign on the dotted line, write a check, and I'll get the keys from the dealer. It's usually hard when you move into a new place, but having him here has made it a lot easier."

"Carson seems like a nice man, and his fiancée, Jeannie, was very sweet." It felt strange to make conversation when what she wanted to do was fling herself into his arms. But if this was all she could have of Chris, she wanted it.

"I was impressed with him when I first met him. Everything I've heard about LSI lets me know that they are a premier company to get with. I'm really lucky."

Unsure how to respond, she was glad that they'd driven into an area that had more traffic, and she guided him to where she lived.

She finally felt as though she could breathe easier when they turned onto her street. She knew the area wasn't the best, but it was what she could afford. She pointed to a building that looked like an old, two-story garage. "You can park there. That's my car."

He parked, then leaned forward as he looked at the building through the windshield, his brow lowered. "You live in the garage?"

Her back stiffened. "Rent in this area is killer, and I'm just an artist. I can hardly afford to live in anything fancy."

His head swung around quickly, his gaze pinned on her. "I'm sorry, Stella. I wasn't being condescending."

Her shoulders slumped as her anger fled. "I'm sorry, too. I'm just tired. The garage is my studio where I work, and it holds my kilns. I also work at one of the art schools as a teacher and am able to use their facilities, as well. Sometimes I prefer to create alone, so this works best. My apartment is up there, over the garage." Clicking the buckle, she once again plastered another smile on her face. "Well, thanks for bringing me home. I realize this trip was... well, sort of not at all what you expected when you volunteered to accompany me. But I certainly appreciate everything."

"I want to come up."

"You don't have to—"

"I want to. I'll bring your things in. I want to check and make sure everything is okay. Please, Stella."

She pressed her lips together again, forcing her head to bob up and down in a nod. "Sure!" she agreed with what she hoped sounded like enthusiasm. "I'll give you the grand tour." She threw open the door and hopped down, waiting as Chris grabbed her bag from the back. Leading him up the side stairs, she observed him looking around.

"I know it's not much, but, well, it's home."

"I just noticed there wasn't any security."

At the top of the landing, she had her key in the doorknob but cocked her head to the side as she held his gaze. "This area isn't too bad. Plus, I know it looks crappy on the outside, but that helps with security, I suppose. Downstairs, the kilns are too heavy for someone to cart off, and up here doesn't look any better off from the outside."

Throwing open the door, she stepped into her haven, grinning as she heard his exclamation when he crossed the threshold. The wooden floor was old but clean and polished, with colorful rugs covering some of the surfaces. In one corner was her kitchen, complete with counters and cabinets, a sink, a small oven and stove top with microwave overhead, and a refrigerator. In the other corner was a double bed, a brightly colored spread covering the sheets with pillows piled against the headboard. A door was next to it, standing open, exposing a small bathroom. Near the front was a table with four chairs, and on the other side was a flatscreen TV facing a small sofa, coffee table, and comfy chair with a floor lamp next to it. And above, skylights gave the small space an open feel.

"Holy shit, Stella! This is beautiful!"

It felt good to be home, and she inhaled deeply the scent of the potpourri in one of her pottery bowls filling the air. Smiling what felt like a genuine smile for the first time in hours, she turned toward him. "Thanks. It's small, but it fits my needs." Laughing, she added, "And my budget!"

He set her bag down and walked around the room. She observed him as he seemed to take in everything.

Bending, his fingers ran over one of the pottery bowls on the kitchen counter. Looking over his shoulder, he asked, "Is this one of yours?"

Suddenly uncertain what he thought of her art, she hesitated. She'd never felt awkward with anyone looking at her work before but realized how much she wanted him to like it. Nodding, she sucked in a deep breath. "Yeah. That's one of my creations."

His lips curved in a smile that made her heart stutter.

"I think it's fuckin' beautiful." He glanced back down at it before lifting his gaze again. "I feel really stupid asking this, but do you sell pieces like this?"

Laughing, she nodded. "Absolutely. A few of my pieces go in a gallery, but mostly I sell online and at a number of stores in California. I don't make a ton of money with it, but I'm not exactly a starving artist." Tilting her head to the side, she asked, "Why do you ask?"

"I think my mom would love something like this." His smile drooped. "Although, I haven't been around her much in years, so maybe I don't know what she'd like, after all."

"Tell you what, Chris. Once you connect with her again and find out what tastes she has, you can let me know. I can easily ship something to her."

"I can always come and get it."

The air halted in her lungs, and they stood staring at each other, neither speaking. Swallowing deeply, she finally said, "If you want, that'd be fine. But I know you're going to be busy. I know you've got your life with LSI now."

He jammed his hands into his front pockets, opening and closing his mouth a couple of times. For a moment, the strong man seemed so uncertain that she found herself moving forward, placing her palm over his heart.

"You could stay for a little while... if you wanted," she began.

He winced as he lifted his hand and curled his fingers around hers. "I'm so sorry, but I can't."

She held his gaze, her heart aching, but forced her mouth to ask the question even though she was terrified of the answer. "So, that's it? The trip was it for us?"

He winced again, and she wanted to ease his pain even though hers was roaring through her body.

"It has to be for now," he said. "I care about you, Stella, I really do. But I'm not in a place to make a commitment right now. My whole life is unsettled, and it's gonna take a little bit before it gets settled."

"I understand," she sighed, blinking against the gathering moisture again. She stepped back, immediately missing the feel of his heartbeat from underneath her fingertips as well as the warmth from his hand. Trying to find an upbeat tone she didn't feel, she added, "Give me a call if you ever want a traveling partner again."

Chris moved faster than she could imagine, and his arms banded around her, pulling her tight. She leaned her head back, and he bent, claiming her mouth. The kiss was everything she remembered and more. Heat raced through her veins. Electricity sent tingles through her nerves. Her breasts felt heavy, and her core ached. She wanted to rub herself against him to alleviate the desperate need for friction. Instead, she simply closed her eyes and gave over to the sensations rocketing through her body. If this was the last kiss they'd ever share, she wanted to commit every nuance to memory.

Just when she thought he might carry her over to the bed, he lifted his head and stepped back. She rocked back slightly, unsteady on her feet, and immediately felt bereft of the warmth of his body. Raising her fingers to her mouth, her lips still tingled.

"Goodbye, Stella," he said with regret etched onto his expression.

"Goodbye, C... Chris." His name hiccuped from her lips as she steeled her spine against the quivers that threatened.

He walked to the door, and with his hand on the knob, he turned, his gaze pinning her in place. He opened his mouth several times, but the words she yearned to hear never came. He finally dipped his chin and walked out, closing it behind him.

She moved on wooden legs to the window and looked down. He stood at the bottom of her stairs, the expression on his face hard to read, but she thought it was still the same regret he'd shown. His face contorted as he growled, and his fist shot out, hitting the side of the wooden garage. She jumped at the noise, staring at the now-bloody knuckles of his hand. His chest heaved, and then he turned and climbed into the SUV, driving out of sight. Three days. Three nights. With this man. And her heart was already involved. And now hurting, ripped in shreds.

20

Chris' knuckles hurt, but he welcomed the pain as a way to take his mind off Stella. Driving away, heading back to start his job with LSI-WC should have made him thrilled, but all he could think of was the look on her face. Grimacing as he merged onto the highway, he inwardly cursed meeting her at a time when he couldn't offer her anything. He had no place to live that was his own and certainly no vacation days saved up to visit when he hadn't officially had his first day on the job.

As he came to the exit for Carmel-by-the-Sea, he flipped on his turn signal. It didn't take long to pull up to his mom's condo. He looked out the windshield, appreciating the simplicity of the new building so much more than the formidable estate they'd lived in when his father was alive. Instead of a brick mansion with lawns and gardens and a fuckin' fountain in the front, the pale-yellow stucco home was modestly landscaped with flowers and a few trees.

Climbing from his vehicle, he walked to her door.

Hesitating before he knocked, he wondered if he should have called first. But before his bruised knuckles could meet the door, it was flung open and his mother's wide eyes and bright smile greeted him.

"Chris?" Clapping her hands as she exclaimed, she threw her arms open and enveloped him in her embrace. He towered over her, Eileen Andrews barely coming to his shoulder. And yet, the feel of her strong hug eased the tightness in his chest. She leaned back and looked up, her gaze roaming over his face. "I'm so glad you're here."

"I'm sorry I didn't call first—"

She narrowed her eyes as she shook her head. "And when does my son need to call before he comes to visit his mother? Come in, come in!"

He stepped inside and could not help but smile, as well. The condo was furnished elegantly but in a style that was so contrasting to what he'd remembered growing up. The space instantly felt more like home than where she'd spent all those years with his dad.

A cream-colored sofa was adorned with several colorful pillows, and a bright blue blanket draped over the back. Two blue chairs sat opposite, flanking the coffee table. Through an arched doorway, he could see her small dining room table with four chairs, no longer the previous one that could hold twenty guests for dinner. The furniture was mostly cream, but she'd given it her special touch with lots of colors. Looking around, it struck him how similar his mother's true tastes were to Stella's.

"Let's go into the kitchen. Are you hungry?" Without

waiting for him to reply, she turned and led the way past the dining room and around the counter to her bright and airy kitchen. Looking over her shoulder, she smiled. "I think I'm in the mood for comfort food. Does that sound good?"

Growing up, they'd always had a cook, and it was on the tip of his tongue to tell her that she didn't need to fix any food for him. But looking at her hopeful expression, it hit him how much she seemed to want to perform the simple task. Nodding, he smiled in return. "That'd be great."

Even though it wasn't breakfast time, she was soon scrambling eggs, cooking French toast with thick slices of battered brioche, and crisping bacon. He poured both of them a cup of coffee, then hesitated, having no idea how she drank it.

She must have caught his hesitation because she inclined her head toward the counter next to the coffee pot and said, "I'll take one sweetener packet and hazelnut creamer that's in the refrigerator."

It didn't take long for them to settle at her table, the scents of delicious food surrounding them. For a few minutes, they ate in comfortable silence before she held his gaze as she sipped her coffee. "Talk to me, Chris."

Her simple request caught him by surprise. Wiping his mouth with a napkin, he tilted his head to the side. "Talk to you about what, Mom?"

"Anything and everything." She laughed, setting her cup down on the table. "I'm so excited to have you close by again. I hope we can spend more time together."

"I'd like that, too."

"When you called to tell me that you were taking a job in California, I wondered if this was going to be your new home port. I was surprised when you told me you were leaving the Navy."

"In many ways, Mom, California will always seem like my home even though I'm not in the Navy anymore. Don't get me wrong. I loved Virginia Beach, but there's something about California that feels right. I was ready to leave the SEALs, ready for a new challenge. My job with a security and investigation company lets me use my skills, pays very well, and gives me the freedom to pick and choose missions I'd like to be on."

"Then I'm very happy for you, son. And, as I said, happy for me to have you close by again." She took another sip of coffee. "And I'm hoping you'll find someone to settle down with. I know that sounds old-fashioned, but I'd love to see you get married and have children."

"I'm not sure that my new job will be very conducive to settling down." As soon as the words left his mouth, his brow furrowed as he thought of meeting Jeannie the day before.

"Not be conducive to settling down? I don't understand."

"I'm not sure I understand myself, either." They were silent for a minute as he gathered his thoughts, then lifted his gaze to see her peering intensely toward him and realized she was waiting. "I want to get used to my new duties. My new coworkers. My new boss. Be able to take assignments as they come in. I don't want to ask for days off to try to go see... uh, someone."

Her brow lifted. "Someone? The way you say that sounds rather specific."

Silence descended between them for a moment as he pondered how much to say.

"Chris, honey," his mom interjected. "I want you to be able to tell me anything."

He held her gaze and a weight eased from his chest. Unlike the relationship he had with his father, he'd always been able to talk to his mother and she'd listen without judgement. Nodding slowly, he began.

"Actually, Mom, I met someone. But nothing about it should be right. We're total opposites. At first, everything about her drove me crazy. Then we ended up taking a cross-country journey together. We met on the plane coming over here, and we had to make an emergency landing in Kansas City. It seemed like one thing after another was going wrong, and she decided that she was going to drive the rest of the way to California. Me, who always likes things planned, made a spur-of-the-moment change of arrangements and decided to accompany her."

"That does sound rather unlike you," she smiled. "I assume, though, it gave you the opportunity to get to know her better."

"She's quirky and funny. Beautiful. Smart. Overly friendly to the point that I'm not sure she's ever met a stranger. She's an artist and so are her parents. There's an ease and freedom about her that, while very different from me, was really nice to be with." As he spoke, memories began to filter through his mind, and he smiled. The way she considered travel snacks to be of ultimate importance. How many stops they'd made so she could replenish her drinks and run to the restroom. Her sitting around the campfire, engaging everyone as she made s'mores. All the stops so that she could hop out and take pictures of the scenery. The night they'd made love, and he'd worshipped her beautiful body. But mostly, it was the way her smile beamed at him that caused an ache deep in his chest.

"That smile on your face as you think about her tells me that this woman means something to you. Something more than a traveling companion."

He dropped his chin and chuckled. "Yeah, she became more." His chuckle ended, and he shook his head. "But I walked away, Mom. I told her I just didn't have time in my life right now. I know I hurt her. I could see it on her face." He swiped his hand through his hair, then squeezed the back of his neck.

"I'm curious, son. Why do you think you can't have a relationship and your new career at the same time?"

"There's so much I need to get done now, Mom. I'm staying with a friend and need to sign a sublease on an apartment. It's partially furnished but I need to get some things for myself. I'm ready to buy a vehicle. I need to start with my job and show them that I'm willing to take on any assignment and work as many hours as needed to handle everything. I mean, maybe, down the road... of course, she probably wouldn't still be single by then."

She leaned back in her chair and pressed her lips

together, slowly shaking her head. "It's amazing how much you're like your father!"

His chin jerked back as his brow lowered. He couldn't imagine anything his mom could have said to him that would have shocked or insulted him more. "You've got to be kidding me?"

"Why do you think you two butted heads so much?"

"Because we were about as different as two people could possibly be," he bit out.

She threw her head back and laughed. "Oh, Chris, that's not true. You may have wanted different careers. You may have wanted different paths in life, but you are very much alike." As her mirth slowed, she continued to hold his gaze. "Your father was single-minded of purpose. He wanted to be a cardiac surgeon, and he gave it his all. He wanted to have an impressive career and gave it his all. He wanted to have a lifestyle that fit his idea of success and gave it his all. During all of that, I supported him because I loved him and knew he loved me. And when he died, my heart broke."

His breath had halted in his lungs as he listened to the words his mom was saying and, more importantly, watched the pain of grief etch lines across her face.

Maintaining her composure, she continued. "I sold the mansion not because I was trying to erase your father from my mind but because it was no longer needed. Whether I was ready or not, I was entering into a new phase of my life and decided to move to a place that felt more like me. Older. Widowed. But still with years to live and living it my way."

He glanced around at her more whimsical decorating style and nodded. "You've done a beautiful job of that, Mom."

She lifted her delicate shoulders. "It fits me. This new me." After another moment of silence, she said, "Your father, with his infinite planning, always assumed he knew the career path you'd take. When you chose something different, he couldn't figure out how to accommodate that in his plans. I talked until I was blue in the face to try to get him to see that plans can be altered. Changed. Plans can evolve. Sometimes plans can be completely dismissed. After all, we don't all take the same journey to our destination."

He sighed again, his heart heavy. "I'm sorry, Mom. I'm sorry that you got caught between Dad and me."

"Your father was proud of you. I don't know why it was not within his personality to tell you so, but I know that he was. And I can't begin to pretend to know what words of wisdom he might impart at this particular point in your life. So, all I can do is tell you what I think. If you wait, trying to get all the pieces of your life's puzzle to fit together before allowing yourself to have a relationship, you'll end up lonely. Your father and I got together when he was in medical school, and I never once regretted being married to him, and thank God that he didn't try to get all of his life pursuits accomplished before we became a couple. If he had, we might not ever have gotten together, and then I wouldn't have the wonderful son that I do."

He pondered her words for a moment, turning them over carefully in his mind. He wanted to become an asset as a Keeper. He wanted to impress his coworkers and boss. He wanted to start the next phase of his life. But there was no denying that he also wanted Stella. "I think I screwed up, Mom. I tried to compartmentalize and think of her as just a fellow traveler heading in the same direction. She became more, and I pushed her away."

"I think it was William Shakespeare who said, 'Journeys end in lovers meeting.' Rather apropos, don't you think?"

Chris blinked, the words of Blessing coming back to him. "You know, it's weird, but I met a lady in the USO in Atlanta who said the very same thing to me. There's no way she could have known anything was going to happen to me. No way at all."

"Stranger things have happened, son. But I think the most important thing you need to focus on now is figuring out your new life and if this woman can share in it. As your mother, I certainly hope you decide that she can and will bring her to meet me soon. But as I used to tell your father, only you can choose your path and your destination."

They both stood, taking the dishes to the sink before rinsing them and putting them in the dishwasher. When they finished cleaning the kitchen, she walked him to the front door, where he once again felt the loving embrace of his mother's arms around him. "Thanks for the meal, Mom."

She stepped away but squeezed his hands and looked up into his eyes. "Now that you found your home port, come again soon to visit me. I want to spend more time with my son."

The drive back to Rick's apartment was filled with thoughts moving through Chris' mind. There was no doubt he'd decided he wanted Stella in his life, but how to make all the parts fit together, he had no idea. But as with most of his plans, he knew he needed to start with first things first: a place to stay and a vehicle.

Entering Rick's apartment with the key he'd been given, he was glad to see his friend already at home. Rick grinned, cracked open a beer, handed it to him, and said, "So, you took your girl home. Want to tell me why you look like a dog that's been kicked?"

Taking a long swig, he shook his head. "First off, she's not *my* girl. At least not right now. Hell, maybe never. But I stopped on the way down here and had a chance to see my mom."

Rick's brows raised. "How's she doing after your dad's death?"

"Actually, not too bad. She moved into a small condo, decorated it to her style, and while growing old without Dad isn't the life she envisioned, she seemed pretty good."

"I know she's gotta be fuckin' glad you're home and close by."

He nodded, taking another swig. "Yeah, me too. We had a good visit. Had a chance to catch up, and let's just say she gave me some things to think about."

"I know you said you found a sublease for an apartment in this complex, but don't rush on my account," Rick said. "I've got two bedrooms, mainly so I'd have a place when the family came to visit. Although, since my brother and his wife just had a baby, I'm not sure I could stand a screaming kid all night long."

Chris laughed. "You're so full of shit. I've seen the pictures of your niece, and she's already got you wrapped around her finger! Next thing you know, you'll be the one who wants to settle down and have babies." Rick laughed, but Chris noted that his friend didn't deny the suggestion. Not wanting to pry, he continued on. "I like this complex well enough and sent a note to the office manager. The sublease is a one-bedroom and partially furnished. Since my mom is close by and I don't have any other relatives, a one-bedroom will be fine. I'll go and sign a short-term lease. That'll give me a chance to see if I want to keep renting or look to buy. I'm also going to have you drop me off at the auto dealer after we leave our meeting in the morning. All I have to do is sign and put in the down payment. I'll have one of the discount furniture stores deliver the furniture not already in the apartment, and that'll get the biggest things off my back."

"Sounds like you've got it all planned out. By the way, Carson called. Jeb is still working on digging into the owner of the truck. He said we'll meet first thing in the morning."

Finishing his beer, he rinsed then tossed the bottle into the recycle bin. "Good by me. I'm off to the manager and then the furniture store. Hopefully, in another day, I'll be out of your hair, but I really appreciate you letting me stay."

Rick waved him off, shaking his head. "Don't worry about it. The Keepers have the same kind of brotherhood we used to have in the military. We take care of each other."

With that, Rick headed into the living room to watch a game, and Chris realized how tired he was. Glad it only took half an hour to see the apartment and sign the sublease, he headed to the furniture store and made arrangements for the delivery of the items he needed, including a bed and TV. Back at Rick's place, he took a shower, then fell into bed in Rick's guestroom, crashing early.

He slept, but his dreams were filled with images of Stella's bright smile morphing into the image of hurt he'd remembered from that morning. And when he woke, he still didn't have a clue how he could fit all the puzzle pieces of his life together.

21

Walking into LSI-WC the next morning, Chris already felt like the new job was home. He grabbed his coffee early, then started filling out some of the online information that Rachel, the office manager, would need. Almost finished by the time everyone arrived, he gave his attention to Jeb.

"I dug deeper into Johnny Markham. It seems he was at one time in the Nevada Army National Guard."

Sitting up straighter, Chris said, "We passed by there. I can't remember right now exactly where that was on our trip, but Stella and I had a short conversation about the National Guard."

Jeb nodded. "It's in Elko County, Nevada. You would have passed it before you got to Battle Mountain."

Carson looked over. "You didn't stop nearby? For gas or food?"

Shaking his head, Chris replied, "No. I remember that specifically because Stella mentioned she didn't know anything about the National Guard, and we had a short conversation about what they did compared to the military. We didn't stop again until Battle Mountain."

"What's interesting," Jeb continued, "is that Johnny was OTH discharged out of the Guard."

Everyone's gaze snapped over to Jeb, and Chris let out a long breath. "Other than honorable discharge. What the hell did he do?"

"Took me a little bit to get into his records, but he'd had some problems with showing up under the influence. Several incidents of mouthing off to superiors. Not coming in and reporting when it was his time. But the last problem was being in the munitions area when he wasn't authorized to be there."

"So, a man who likes to push the boundaries, or rather, doesn't want any boundaries," Leo said.

Carson nodded. "Jeb, keep digging on him. Where he lives. Who he works with. Friends, family. Especially, I want to know if he's continued any friendships with some of the current National Guard."

"For him to try to take me out twice, there's got to be a reason, but fuck if I know what it is," Chris said, anger rising. "There is absolutely nothing we did on this trip that would have brought us into anyone's sights. At the bar, the campground, the stops we made... nothing. But I know there's got to be some connection."

"I know you're frustrated," Carson said. "Jeb is going to keep working on it, and I'll have you monitor things along with him once you're ready." Chris opened his mouth, but Carson lifted his hand and continued. "You need to finish the paperwork for Rachel and get with

Teddy who's in charge of our grounds and munitions and equipment. I know you're purchasing a vehicle today, and Rick's told me that you signed a lease. You need a couple of days to take care of getting settled, but I know you'll be in here because you want this resolved. We're all working on this together, so remember that. It doesn't all fall on your shoulders."

He nodded, and as the meeting finished after other missions were discussed, his day was filled very much as Carson had indicated: working with Rachel and Teddy at LSI-WC, checking in with Jeb to see what else he was finding out about the man who shot at him and Stella, having Rick take him over so that he could sign the paperwork and drive off the car lot with the new SUV, and getting the keys to his apartment from the complex manager. The delivery of furniture was set for the next day, so he headed back over to LSI.

Everyone had gone except for Carson, who offered him a beer. Chris hesitated, then nodded and accepted it. "Thanks, I appreciate it." Looking around, he asked, "Am I cutting into your time with Jeannie?"

"No, not at all. She works at a clinic but occasionally does relief work for one of the nursing homes, so she'll be a little late today. Plus, even if she was here, it would be fine. She understands the unique life of a Keeper. She knows she's the most important person in my life but also knows that she doesn't need to feel competitive with the business or my friends."

"Sounds like a special woman."

Carson grinned. "Absolutely, she's a special woman. I met her on a mission."

"No kidding!"

"One of the things I learned from my partner with the original LSI in Maine is that it takes a special woman to be involved with a Keeper. And most of us have fallen for someone we met on a mission."

They were quiet for several minutes, the sun setting over the ocean, and Chris drank in the calm.

"Were you able to take care of everything today?" Carson asked.

Nodding slowly, Chris replied, "Hell of a day, but yes. Thanks for letting me have the time to get to my place and my vehicle."

"It's not easy going from active duty to retirement to a new job. I have to admit I was surprised to hear that you didn't fly all the way in and that you changed your plans to drive. But then, after meeting Stella, I can understand why."

He winced but felt that Carson needed honesty. "Honest to God, it didn't start out the way you're thinking. Sure, she's beautiful, but she just struck me as..." He hesitated, rubbing his chin. "I don't want to say that she needed looking after because that would make her sound weak. It's just that she didn't strike me as very security conscious. And heading out halfway across the country in a car... well, I just found myself drawn to her. I had the time, and I didn't mind getting to know her better. I showed her my ID so she wouldn't feel like it was such a risk although either one of us probably could have been a serial killer." A rueful snort escaped. "I tend to stick to plans, so changing them for her was something new for me." They were quiet for several more minutes, and then Chris looked to the side "Can I ask how you do it, Carson? How do you run a business, go on missions, and have a relationship?"

Carson laughed. "Hell, before I met Jeannie, I figured I'd stay single the rest of my life. I couldn't figure out how on earth to make it all work. But then I met her and realized that I wanted her in my life. There are lots of people with busy jobs, kids, and commitments, and somehow, they make relationships work. And then I thought of the alternative."

He speared Chris with an intense gaze and Chris fought the urge to squirm. "The alternative?"

"What would my life be like if I didn't do everything I could to have her be part of me? I realized I didn't like the answer. So, that just meant that I had a new mission. The first mission was to make sure she was in my life, and the second was to work with her to make all the pieces of our lives fit together."

Chris nodded, his mind whirling with all that Carson had said. He couldn't imagine never seeing Stella smile at him again. But then, he also couldn't imagine how they'd combine their divergent lives. Hearing a noise behind them, he watched as Jeannie walked around the side of the building, smiling as she saw them. She greeted him but bent to kiss Carson lightly. Not wanting to intrude, Chris stood.

"Thank you, Carson. You gave me a lot to think about."

Carson wrapped his arm around Jeannie as he stood, as well. "Just remember that I expect my Keepers to give me their best. But I do not expect them to forgo their lives and their happiness for this job. With the right woman, it's possible to have it all."

With a handshake and chin lift, he said goodbye and jogged around the building to where he'd parked his new SUV. Swinging by to grab pizza for him and Rick, he headed back to the apartment. They sat on the sofa, feet on the coffee table, pizza box sitting between them, and beers in their hands. They watched a game on TV although Chris' mind was firmly planted on what possible reason a discharged Nevada National Guardsman would have for wanting him dead. The idea that Stella could have been injured or killed made his blood run cold. Still unable to come up with a reason, he shoved down the last of his pizza, drained his beer, and decided to turn in.

It had been a long-ass day, but he'd managed to accomplish a lot. He was grateful to Rick but was looking forward to being in his own place tomorrow once the furniture was delivered. Now, in bed, his fingers hovered over his phone, wanting to send Stella a text. He missed her. Wanted to hear how her day was. He typed out several messages, deleting each of them. Finally tossing his phone to the nightstand, he scrubbed his hand over his face. *Not yet. Let me make sure there's no threat against me that could put her more at risk.*

Several days later, Stella tried to steady her mind as her hands moved mechanically over the clay. While she could easily form a pot or a vase worthy of going into the kiln to sell with her mind on anything but what she was doing, her true pieces of art needed to come from within. Granted, art could be created from anger or frustration as easily as happiness and pleasure, but staring at the circling clay underneath her fingertips, she knew it was no piece of art.

Digging her fingers in, the clay crumpled inward. With her hands still messy, she used her shoulder to swipe a piece of hair off her cheek. Dropping her chin to her chest, she sighed heavily before talking to herself. "Jesus, girl, get over it. You had fun sex with a seriously hot Chris one time. It's not like any vows were spoken, no promises made. Hell, he's not the only one-night stand you've ever had!" Jerking her head upward, she stared at the ceiling for a moment, continuing her lonely diatribe. "Yeah, but then you went and fell for him. What an idiotic thing to do!"

She had no problem admitting to herself that she'd fallen for Chris. It had been two days since she'd seen him and missing him had not slowed at all. Self-reflection and self-honesty had never been a problem for her. *But damn, if I could lie to myself, maybe it wouldn't hurt so bad.*

Staring back at the lump of clay, trying not to focus on how much it resembled what she felt like at the moment, she started the wheel again and dipped her hands back into the water. If there was one thing she was good at, it was taking care of her business.

Several hours later, she'd finished more pots and vases and placed them in her automatic kiln, which was set to ramp up the heat and then cool at the appropriate times. She stood and arched her back, feeling the vertebrae popping as she stretched. Rolling her shoulders and neck, she eased the kinks that came with the territory of being a potter. At her studio's sink, she washed off, scrubbing the clay from her fingers and hands and forearms. After a quick cleanup of the area, she pulled off the large shirt she always wore and hung it on a peg near the door.

Stepping outside, she locked the door and jogged up the side stairs to her apartment. She spent some time on her computer, looking over orders, emailing her teaching assistant, and answering a few of her students' questions. Finally, after a quick phone call with one of the gallery owners that showcased her work, she wandered to her kitchen and opened the refrigerator, finding it woefully neglected. Her stomach rumbled, and she glanced at the clock on the stove, determined that a quick trip to the grocery store would not only take care of her empty refrigerator but her empty stomach, as well.

Grateful that there was a small but well-stocked, independently owned market nearby, she quickly drove there and greeted the cashiers as she walked in. Where possible, she tried to support indie businesses, and by the time she'd made it to the bakery section of the store, she spied the owner and waved.

She chatted with several people as she wandered up and down the aisles, finding that her quick trip to the grocery store had turned into more of an enjoyable outing. After she finished shopping, checking out, and paying, she loaded her bags into her vehicle and headed home. The food and wine she planned on having that evening would not chase away her still-morose thoughts of Chris, but she hoped they would at least partially salve the heartache.

Before she took the groceries upstairs, she hurried into the studio, double-checking the kilns, pleased with how everything was working. *At least something is going right!*

As ridiculous as it was to load her arms up with groceries, she'd always considered it a silly badge of honor to make it into her apartment in one trip. When she got to the top of the stairs, the bags were so heavy, she couldn't get to her keys and stumbled against the door, which flung open. Nearly tumbling to the floor, several of the bags dropped as she righted herself. Her entrance would have been comical if it wasn't for the sight that greeted her.

Gasping as her gaze darted about the room, it was evident someone had been in her apartment. It wasn't trashed, but someone had been looking for something. The bag she'd had with her on the trip that was still sitting next to the sofa had been dumped out, the contents scattered. Items that had been left sitting on her kitchen counter were also scattered, some dropped to the floor. The items on her coffee table had been shoved to the side. She had several purses and bags that hung from hangers next to the door within easy reach for when she wanted to change bags, each having been tossed down, as well.

Becoming untangled from the handles of her grocery bags, her chest heaved. "What the hell?" She shoved her hand into the purse that hung crossways over her body, and her fingers searched for her phone to call 9-1-1. Stepping over one of the grocery bags on the floor, her fingers still fumbled inside her purse when she heard a noise and looked up.

"Wh—" she gasped again as a man stepped out of her bedroom. Black hair and dark eyes were all she could see with the bottom half of his face covered with a camouflage mask.

"Is it in there?" he barked.

She stepped back, tripping over the grocery bag, her hand flying out to grab the door frame to keep from falling.

"Is it in there?" he asked again, stepping closer. His gaze darted from her face down to her purse, then back up again.

"What? What do you want?" Frozen in place, she wanted to flee out the door but was afraid to move.

"Give it to me!" He closed the distance between them as he pointed to her purse.

Her billfold was in her bag, but she had very little cash on her. Not wanting him closer, she jerked the purse strap over her head and held it out to him. He stepped back, turning the bag upside down, dumping the contents on top of her small table, his gaze bouncing between her and the contents that had spilled out.

Turning, he leaned closer. "Where the fuck is your phone?"

It took a second for her brain to catch up with his demand, and she looked at the table, not understanding why her phone wasn't among the contents. She couldn't remember where she'd used it last. Mind racing, she kept her expression blank, afraid to admit she had no idea. She couldn't imagine why he wanted her phone but hoped ignorance would satisfy him. Slowly, she shook her head as she lifted her gaze up to him. "I don't know. It should be there. I don't know why it's not."

He growled again, making a noise but not speaking. He looked down at the bags on the floor and then mumbled almost to himself, "Probably dropped the fuckin' thing at the grocery store."

Self-preservation had reared its head, and while he seemed to be distracted, she turned and bolted toward the door, hoping that he would be slowed by the number of grocery bags littering the way out. She had just made it to the landing when her head snapped back as he grabbed her long braid. Crying out, she was jerked backward.

He twirled her body around, and while she brought her hands up to fend off an attack, she wasn't quick enough. His fist came toward her, connecting with her cheekbone. Pain exploded throughout her face just before she dropped, and the world went black.

22

Rachel walked into the workroom, making a beeline toward Carson while her gaze landed on Chris, as well. "I just received a phone call from the San Jose police department. They received a 9-1-1 call to Stella's apartment. She had a break-in and assault. She had the detective not only call her parents but wanted to call Lighthouse Security."

The air rushed from Chris' lungs as he jumped to his feet. His heart threatened to pound out of his chest as he pulled his keys from his pocket.

Carson stood and called out, "Rick, go with him. Stay in contact. Full report as soon as you get it."

As Chris darted through the door, he heard Rachel add, "The detective said the man was looking for her phone."

"Keys, bro," Rick said as they hustled to where the vehicles were parked.

"Rick—"

"No, man. You need to focus on her, what you're

going to help her deal with, and not driving. We need to get there in one piece."

Knowing Rick was right, he ground his teeth together and tossed his keys to his friend. While Rick drove, he stayed in contact with Jeb, listening as the other Keepers gathered intel from the initial report. Carson had a relationship with the governor, politicians, and state police as well as local police. He'd gotten hold of the SJPD, making it easier to siphon through the early information.

"Tell me what I'm facing," Chris ordered, his chest tight as the words left his mouth.

"Assault wasn't sexual," Carson said.

Chris elicited a heaving sigh, his heart leaping at that bit of news.

"Male, black hair, dark eyes, had a camo mask, so she can't ID him. She tried to escape her apartment, and he hit her. Knocked her out. By the time she came to, the neighbor who lives behind her had noticed her lying in her doorway and called the police. She was treated by EMTs there and refused transportation to the hospital. She asked them to call her parents and LSI."

"Why the fuck didn't she have them call me directly?" he groused aloud.

"Probably didn't have your number memorized," Carson replied. "She did the right thing. They let us know what's happening while notifying you."

He kept quiet at that. If he'd felt more rational, he would have had to admit Carson was right, but rational thinking was not close to the surface at the moment.

Dragging in a breath, he said, "We're making good time. Her parents with her?"

"The detective said that when he left, her parents had arrived."

"Thanks, Carson. Keep me up on everything."

"Keep your head, but just know I understand. Whatever happens, she shouldn't stay in her apartment—"

"It'll be taken care of," Chris assured.

Disconnecting, he glanced to see Rick was speeding along the highway but not so fast that they'd waste time getting pulled over. Glad the traffic was light, he hated that Stella was as far away as she was.

"Maybe she'll go stay with her parents," Rick said.

"Fuck that. I want her to come back with me."

"You think she'll agree?"

Scrubbing his hand over his face, he shook his head. "I don't know. I fucked things up a couple of days ago and was going to start figuring out how to unfuck them. My timelines have been moved up, but that's fine by me."

"Now, you'll just have to get her on board with that."

"Doesn't matter. She can't stay there." His words sounded final, but he knew he might have a fight on his hands. Turning to look out his window, he willed the minutes to go by faster.

After what seemed an interminable length of time, they arrived in San Jose, and he gave Rick the directions to Stella's apartment. Having lost all semblance of military precision and cool-headed ability to work a problem, he barely waited for the SUV to come to a stop before he leaped out the door. Racing around the side of her garage studio to the stairs, he took them two at a time. Not hesitating, he knocked rapidly on the door, calling out, "Stella! Stella! It's me!" As Rick came up behind him, the door opened, and Chris found himself staring at a tall, wiry man.

His dark hair was shot with silver, and his blue eyes were etched with deep worry lines around them. He placed his body in the doorway. "Who are you?"

"I'm Chris. Chris Andrews. A friend of Stella's. She had the detective call my boss." He spoke rapidly, certain that he was talking to Stella's father, and while he didn't want to push past the older man, he was willing to do whatever he could to get to her.

"It's okay, Dad. You can let him in."

Chris heard the words and recognized Stella's voice, but the tone was all wrong. It was small, not at all like Stella's bright, energetic voice. Barely giving her father a chance to step back, he rushed forward, his feet halting when he spied her sitting on her small sofa, staring at him with one eye and the rest of her face hidden behind an ice pack. Someone else stepped into the room, but he only had eyes for Stella. Gaining control over his legs, he stalked to her and then dropped to a knee in front of her.

He held her one-eyed gaze, then slowly lifted his hand to the one that was holding the ice pack and gently pulled it from her face. It was only his medic training that kept him from gasping. But even though he'd seen and treated knife wounds, gunshot wounds, broken bones, burns, and all manner of combat injuries, he'd never wanted to wail as loudly as he did right then at the sight of her swollen, bruised cheek. Her hand was shaking, and he held it tightly. Keeping his voice steady, he asked, "Did they check you for a concussion, babe?"

His calm voice seemed to settle her, and her hand stopped shaking. "Yeah, they did. It doesn't appear I have a concussion even though I was knocked out. But they gave me the information on what to look for."

"And you don't want to go to the hospital? Maybe for x-rays?"

Her brow scrunched, then she winced. Just the sight of her in pain had him grind his back teeth in an effort to keep his countenance steady.

"No, I really don't. My cheek hurts, but nothing's broken. I know you probably think that's dumb of me not to go—"

"Not true, Stella. I want you to do whatever makes you comfortable. I just know that sometimes decisions can be made hastily, and then later, you might feel differently. The offer stands to go to the hospital at any time you feel that you need to."

"That's what the paramedic said. They gave me a list of things to look for and told me that if I didn't feel well or had any symptoms, then I should go." Her gaze moved over his face, but he had no idea what was going on in her mind.

"You must be Stella's parents. I'm Rick, a friend of Chris'. We both work for Lighthouse Security Investigations."

Realizing he'd focused entirely on Stella, he stayed on his knees in front of her but twisted around to see that an older version of Stella had walked into the room and was standing next to her dad.

"Mom. Dad. This is Chris Andrews, the man I told you about. He's the… friend who traveled with me. He and Rick work for a private investigation company. These are my parents, Harvey and Beatrice."

"Keep the ice on," he said softly before standing. He held out his hand toward her parents. "Mr. Parker. Mrs. Parker. It's nice to meet you, but I'm sorry for the circumstances." Beatrice tried to smile, but it didn't reach her eyes as worry appeared to be the only emotion she could muster. And with what had happened, he completely understood.

"Please, call us Beatrice and Harvey. Stella told us how good you were to accompany her on her drive. We were hoping for a chance to be able to meet you and thank you personally."

"There's no need for thanks. I had a wonderful time getting to know Stella." His gaze swung back to the sofa, seeing her with the ice pack on her lower cheek, both eyes on him. "We developed a close friendship. One that I have no intention of turning my back on." He didn't miss the way her eyes widened, but that was all he was willing to say at the moment. Anything else needed to be said between them when they were alone.

"We got here as soon as we could," Harvey said. "We simply can't imagine why anyone would want to hurt Stella. Or why on earth they thought there was anything here to steal."

"I'm just sorry it took me so long to get here. I left as soon as I got the call." He stepped back to the sofa, this time sitting carefully next to her, not wanting to jostle her body. "I'm glad you got the message to us."

"I had the detective call you and my parents since I didn't have my phone with me."

Remembering what was said as he raced out of headquarters, he looked back over at her. "The person who was in here waiting on you was looking for your phone. Is that right?"

She nodded, chewing on her bottom lip. "He dumped my purse out, but it wasn't in there. I was scared and couldn't think where I'd had it last, but then he hit me, and I haven't had time to try to figure it out. The police asked me, but I don't know." She twisted her fingers together as her hands lay in her lap. "I can't imagine why he wants my phone. There's nothing on it. I have texts and calls between my friends, business acquaintances, and a few gallery owners. And pictures." A rueful snort slipped out. "My pictures. Chris, you know what that's like. Sunsets. Mountains. Colors. Vistas. Panoramic views. Even different colors of wood. Hardly worth anyone wanting to see."

He wanted to ask more but knew he needed to move slowly and take care of getting her out of her apartment first. Rick sat on one of the kitchen stools nearby as Beatrice and Harvey sat down, as well.

Harvey's gaze darted between Stella and Chris. "Sweetheart, I know you want to visit with your friends, but your mom and I feel like we need to get you out of here and back to our place."

Realizing he couldn't wait, Chris jumped in. "Stella, I want you to come back with me." She startled, her eyes jumping over to him, wincing again. Continuing, he said, "Whoever did this might come back here looking for your phone. We don't know why he wants it, and you don't want to bring any trouble to your parents' door. Plus, you know we can protect you."

"Protect? Protect her in what way?" Harvey asked, leaning forward, his gaze intense.

Rick started to speak, but Chris gave a quick shake of his head. If he was going to have a permanent place in Stella's life, he needed to build trust with her and with her parents. "I'm a former SEAL, recently employed with an exclusive private security and investigation firm. We have the means to provide security as well as assist in the investigation of the crime against her."

Harvey and Beatrice shared a look, slightly relaxing their stiff bodies, and with the sighs that slipped out, he could tell they were glad that someone would look out for her.

Pressing his luck, he reached for Stella's free hand, drawing her gaze back to him. "Stella, I want you to come back with me. If nothing else, we're friends. I want to be the one to make sure that you're safe, and I sure as hell want to work to find out who did this." Rubbing her fingers gently, he lowered his voice. "I owe you a huge apology for leaving the other day. But we can talk about that later if you'll give me a chance."

Her fingers squeezed lightly, and he held on. She sighed heavily and nodded. "I'll go with you. Honestly, I don't want to stay here now, but when can I come back? I don't feel safe here, and I hate that, but my studio is downstairs. I've got a class to teach. On top of that, I've got a showing in a couple of weeks. Granted, it's not a huge showing in a major gallery, but it's still a big deal to me."

"I know you have a life that can't just stop. But think about this: if something happens to you, all those things aren't going to mean anything. For the wonderful things going on in your life, you need to stay safe, and for now, that means not here."

"I'll need my car, and the paramedic said I can't drive for a couple of days."

"I'll drive you in your car, and Rick will drive my vehicle."

He watched her good eye as emotions fluttered through, her teeth still worrying her bottom lip.

"My parents are closer..."

Emboldened that her voice was less sure, he pressed his suit. "Yes, but until we know what that person was looking for and why, you don't want them to be in danger."

She shook her head slowly. "You're right. I don't." Sighing heavily again, she squeezed his fingers and leaned closer, keeping her voice low. "Chris, me staying with you probably isn't the right thing to do. I mean, I know you said that we're still friends, but that isn't how it felt when you left a couple of days ago."

Shifting toward her even more, he pulled both of her hands into his. "I had a couple of days without you in my life to realize I messed up. I was going to call you to talk because I couldn't stand the way things were left. I know you might not believe me, but I'm not lying. I promise if you come with me, I can keep you safe, and it'll give us a chance to figure out what we are to each other. Please, Stella, come stay with me."

He didn't realize he was holding his breath until she nodded and agreed.

"Thank God, babe." Almost having forgotten that they had an audience, he turned to look at Rick's grin and the relieved expressions on Harvey's and Beatrice's faces.

"I'll gather some things for you," Beatrice said.

"I'll help, too, Mom. I know what I need for a couple of days. And you might as well take the perishables I just bought. I don't want them to go to waste."

Chris stood and assisted Stella to her feet, glad to see that she was as steady as she was. The two women walked to the bedroom corner of the apartment, and after they filled a suitcase, they reloaded some of the grocery bags with the food that might spoil before she got back. Rick said his goodbyes to her parents, and he took the suitcase and headed downstairs.

Watching the warm hugs and kisses between Stella, Harvey, and Beatrice, Chris waited to say goodbye to them, as well. He gave them his cell phone number as well as a contact number for LSI-WC. "We'll get Stella a new cell phone as soon as we can and should give you a call. Until then, call me anytime."

Beatrice threw her arms around him, hugging him tightly, then leaned back and said, "Thank you so much for taking care of my baby. Stella means everything to us."

Harvey shook his hand and echoed his wife's sentiments. "I know how much you came to mean to Stella during your trip. I'm glad she has a friend like you."

Stella blinked back tears as her parents walked out the door, her overwhelming emotions written clearly on her face. He wrapped his arms around her, tucking the uninjured side of her face close to his heartbeat. "There's a lot I want to say, Stella. But right now, the most important thing is for us to get you to my place."

Her arms tightened around his waist, and he felt her nod against his chest. Double checking that she had everything, they walked down the stairs toward the vehicles.

She jerked and exclaimed, "My kilns! I need to make sure they've turned off."

He held up a finger toward Rick to indicate that they'd be right back, and he followed Stella through the front door of her studio. He stood to the side as she moved to the large kilns, checking dials and knobs, seeming satisfied.

"All good?" he asked.

"Yeah. Normally, I'd let them stay on longer and let them turn off automatically, but I don't want to take a chance. The pots will be okay to stay in there as the temperature lowers."

He swept his gaze around the room, a smile curving his lips at the array of supplies and finished vases, dishes, and pots she had around.

She walked toward the sink, still looking around, then grabbed a bag that was lying on the table. "Oh, I keep some sketches in here. It'll be good to have my pad with me." Her shoulders sagged. "I hate having to leave my studio and not having a phone."

His heart ached for her. Stepping over, he placed his hands on either side of her face, careful of her bruises. "Once we get to my place, I can keep you safe while we keep investigating. We've made some progress, and if we can get street security videos near here, we might pinpoint who was here."

"We'll provide an untraceable phone for her," Rick said from the doorway, drawing Chris' gaze.

"Good. Thanks, man. Okay, we're ready. I'll drive her car, and you can drive mine." He made sure she was buckled safely and shook Rick's hand. "See you there."

With that, he settled behind the wheel of her car and let out a sigh of relief for the first time in a couple of hours. They had a lot to talk about, but as her eyes closed with her head leaning back against the headrest, he knew it could all wait.

Grinning, he pulled onto the road behind Rick. *At least she's with me now. One way or the other, I'll make this right.*

23

Stella followed Chris into his apartment. When they had arrived in the parking lot, Rick had handed Chris the keys to his SUV and waved goodbye as he was picked up by another Keeper.

Now, at first glance around the room, she was startled at how stark it was. Few pieces of furniture and no personality. Remembering he had just moved, she hoped he would have a chance to decorate it so that it would feel more like home.

"Stella?"

Jumping, she hadn't noticed that he'd turned to her. "Oh, sorry. I was just looking at your place."

He chuckled. "Kind of empty, isn't it? It's just a sublease, so there's not much I can do with it. I only had to buy a bed and the TV." He hesitated and lifted his hand to squeeze the back of his neck. "Um, I need to tell you that there's only one bedroom and that's where you'll stay. I'll sleep out here."

"No way! You were kind enough to come when I

called. Kind enough to offer a safe haven. There's no way I'm going to take your bed. Anyway, I'm much smaller than you and can easily fit on the sofa."

He moved toward her, and as he stepped closer, her heart beat faster. There was no denying that their days apart hadn't decreased her body's response to him. He lifted a hand and cupped her good cheek, and she closed her eyes and leaned into his palm, grateful for the comfort he offered.

"Stella, I won't take no for an answer. Not about this. Now, let's get you settled, and you can rest while I check on what groceries I might need."

"Don't forget I've brought some things that were non-perishable."

"I'll run back down and get those in a couple of minutes."

His apartment was not large but had a wide living room window that offered a view of a nearby park. Stepping into his bedroom, which was on the same side as the living room, the window there offered the same expansive view. But it was the king-size bed that drew and kept her attention.

"Chris, your bed is huge! There's no reason we both can't sleep here." He swung his gaze quickly to her, but she continued, "You can sleep on one side, and I can sleep on the other. We'll both be comfortable and have a better chance of resting without you trying to scrunch on your sofa and me lying in here worried about you not sleeping."

"Stella, I don't think that such a good idea—"

"Are you afraid I can't keep my hands to myself? For

your information, while it will be a Herculean task, I'm sure that I can manage to stay on my side of the bed and not jump you in the middle of the night." She tried not to grin but then winced as her smile pulled the bruised and swollen side of her face.

His face hardened, and his eyes glittered. "When I get my hands on the fucker that did that..."

Before she had a chance to respond, there was a knock on the front door and a female voice calling out, "Yoo-hoo! Are you home?"

Chris rolled his eyes at the interruption. "That's Jeannie."

They walked back into the living room, and he opened the door, welcoming Jeannie inside. She carried a covered dish, and the scent drifting from it made Stella's mouth water. She couldn't remember when she ate last.

"Oh, Stella," Jeannie exclaimed, immediately setting the food on the counter and rushing over. Still wearing her nursing scrubs from her job, she immediately went into professional mode as she gently moved Stella's head so that she could get a better look at the damage. Her eyes glittered the same way Chris' had earlier. "I couldn't believe it when I heard it, and it pissed me off!"

Stella couldn't help but smile in spite of the discomfort.

"I assume the paramedics went over care and concussion protocol with you?"

"Yes, they were very thorough. I didn't go to the hospital because there didn't appear to be anything broken, just hurt. And because I know you'll ask, I held ice on my face for a long time."

"Then I'm sure I'm being repetitive, but get plenty of rest, take over-the-counter pain relief and don't be afraid to do so, and have Chris monitor you during the night just to make sure everything's fine. If you start having headaches, pain beyond what you're having now, dizziness, and anything else on the list they gave you, go straight to the ER."

"Don't worry, Jeannie. I'll take care of her," Chris promised.

"Oh, that's right. I forgot that Carson said you were a medic."

As Jeannie turned to explain the reheating of her casserole to Chris, Stella closed her eyes and dropped her chin. Hearing his soft voice and firm vow, Stella's heart flip-flopped in her chest. Her heart had broken when Chris walked out several days ago. And now, he was back in her life, saying it was for more than just her protection, but she had no idea what he wanted from her. And just being around him, in his space, *sharing a bed*, her heart was once again in danger.

Soon after, she offered a heartfelt hug to Jeannie, smiling as the other woman whispered, "These guys really are the best. They work hard in a job that sometimes makes them afraid of being in a relationship. But give him a chance, and I don't think you'll ever be sorry."

Jeannie stepped back, then waved goodbye to Chris and headed back out the door. Stella made her way to the microwave, pulling out the casserole. Sniffing in appreciation, she looked over her shoulder and said, "I hope you don't mind if I dive in. I'm really hungry. I haven't eaten since breakfast!" She opened the cabinet only to find it bare. "Oh!"

"Shit! This place had most of the furniture, but the owner took all their kitchen things, and I haven't gotten everything I need yet. I grabbed some plastic utensils at the grocery store but forgot paper plates."

"Well, if you're not afraid of my cooties, we can dig in straight from the casserole pan."

He stepped closer and grinned as he brushed her hair back from her face. "I think considering all we've *shared* before, I'm definitely not afraid of your cooties."

She threw her head back and laughed, then immediately winced again. "Damn! This shit hurts. I hope the swelling goes down soon."

His eyes narrowed and a muscle ticked in his jaw. Now it was her turn to reach up and offer him comfort. "Chris, honey, don't worry. I'm fine. Nothing that a little rest, pain reliever, and makeup can't take care of."

"I promise you, babe, we're working to find out who did this. But if I can get my hands on him first, he's going to get a taste of what he did to you."

She started to argue that if he ended up in jail, that wouldn't help their relationship but decided at this moment that silence was best. Instead, she grabbed plastic forks and held them in the air. "Who gets the first bite?"

"I do."

She handed the fork to him although she was a little surprised that he'd called dibs. She watched as he scooped up a bite of the lasagna, but instead of putting it into his own mouth, he turned it to her. She smiled just before she opened her lips and accepted the delicious bite. Moaning, she looked up to see his eyes staring intently at her. Trying to ignore the way his gaze made her feel, she focused on the meal as they continued to eat from the pan.

After they ate and cleared away the dish, he took her by the hand and led her into the living room, where they both settled next to each other on the sofa. He turned, shifting his body so that he could face her and their legs were still touching.

"Stella, I know the timing sucks. I know that I should be insisting that you take a hot bath, take your pain medicine, and climb into bed. And I want you to do all of those things, but first, I need to let you know that I'm so sorry for the way I left things the other day. And I need to beg for your forgiveness and hope that you'll give me another chance."

There was no denying that she was exhausted, the adrenaline long gone, and the delicious warm food filling her belly made her desire the bath, pain meds, and bed that he'd mentioned. But with his words, her chest tightened, and she wanted to hear everything he needed to say. "Please, go on."

His face seemed to flood with relief, and she knew she'd made the right decision.

"Thank you," he said, taking her hands in his. "I told you that as a SEAL, we planned our missions meticulously. But that didn't mean that things always went according to what we hoped. Sometimes intel wasn't good. Sometimes shit went sideways. A lot of times, we had to make split-second decisions and come up with new plans. Most of the time, that worked well. Occasionally, not so well. The last major mission that I went on was one where the intel was bad. Therefore, our backup plan was flawed, and I had some team members and friends who paid the price."

She held on to his hands, gaining as much strength as she hoped she offered.

"I found myself reevaluating my years in the Navy, my years as a SEAL, and while I wouldn't want to have done anything else, I felt ready for a change. I spent time after I met Carson figuring out what I wanted—making major decisions about getting out of the Navy, leaving my team, and starting fresh. I decided to come to California, knowing it would give my mom and me a chance to reconnect on a level that we hadn't had before, especially now that my dad had passed away. When I left Virginia Beach, I spent so much time thinking, planning, evaluating, and was so sure of what I was doing that it was very out of character for me to decide to accompany you. But in doing so, I may have diverted temporarily from my plan, but I got to know the real Stella. And even though we may be complete opposites, you got under my skin in a way that I don't want you to get out."

Stella was both thrilled but cautious. "I understand what you're saying, Chris, but what changed?"

"When we were in danger, all I could think about was keeping you safe. But by the time we got to California, it was as though everything was crashing in.

Because of the situation, I showed up at my new job not as a person ready to jump in and learn everything but as a person who was in need. That felt strange to me. Stupid, I know, but—"

"No, not stupid. You're allowed to have whatever emotions you want to have."

"Well, that wasn't how I was feeling at the time, but you're right. I was suddenly very aware of everything I needed to do."

He sighed as though the weight of the world was on his shoulders, and she longed to reach out and make it better but remained quiet to give him a chance to get all his thoughts out.

"With you, Stella, I reacted. Instead of thinking through how we could make everything work between us, I focused on what my original plan had been when it was just me. And I stupidly thought it would be best if I went back to that plan. Honest to God, I regretted that decision almost immediately. I hurt myself, but I also know I hurt you, and I hated that most of all. I talked to Carson to find out how he did it… how he managed to pull it all together, and he gave me good advice. He said he simply thought about what it would be like not to have Jeannie in his life. And he couldn't imagine that, so he decided to do whatever he could to make it work. I did the same thing."

"And what did you decide?" By what he'd already told her, she thought she knew the answer but desperately needed to hear him say it.

He let go of her hands and reached up to cup her face, so gentle with the bruises. "I want you in my life,

Stella. I want us to figure out how to make it all work. I don't want to be afraid of the long distance. I don't want to deny what I feel for you. I want us to be a couple. And I'm praying that you feel the same way, too."

She had no idea if the heart could actually sing but at that moment decided that was the best way to describe the feeling in her chest. Smiling so big it hurt, she nodded. "I feel the same way, and I want you, too."

"I know you have a life in San Jose, and I don't want to pull you away from your life. But I think if we're willing to work together, we'll be able to figure out a way forward."

He leaned closer, and she waited, anticipation cutting off all other thoughts. When his lips met hers, she melted into him. His arms circled and pulled her closer, but he didn't take the kiss deeper. Instead, keeping it light, his lips danced over hers. She groaned slightly, her fingers digging into his shoulders, but he pulled back.

"Not tonight, Stella. You need to rest and recuperate, but I'll take you up on your offer for us to share the bed. Not for sex... just for togetherness."

She nodded slowly, knowing that as much as her body wanted his, right now, she wanted his comforting presence more than anything.

"You get whatever you need, and I'll start your bath-water." He stood and gently pulled her to her feet, guiding her into the bedroom, where she soon heard the water running in the bathroom.

When he came out, he kissed her lightly again, then gave her privacy while she stripped. She stared into the mirror over the sink for a long moment, shocked at the reflection looking back. Her upper cheek was still swollen, but she was glad she'd used the ice to keep it from getting worse. She stared at the colors that now mottled her skin... red, purple, a touch of green. That ridiculous thought caused her to snort. The damage could've been so much more. Broken nose or jaw or cheekbone—or worse. She closed her eyes as her body shuddered. When she had regained consciousness, things were very fuzzy, both her vision and her memory. Now, everything was clearer, and she wished it wasn't. She hated to see that man in her mind and the fear that had choked her breath.

A knock on the door brought her back to the present. "Are you okay in there?"

"Yes, just getting in. Thanks." She stepped over into the tub and sank into the hot water, a groan leaving her lips as she was enveloped by warmth. Leaning back, she kept her eyes open so the thoughts of the attack wouldn't come to the forefront of her mind, and she finally relaxed. She was tempted to stay until the water completely cooled, but the idea that she'd be sharing a bed with Chris again, even for sleep, had her soon drying off and slipping into the purple tank top and green sleep shorts she'd brought with her. Gently applying moisturizer to her face, she brushed her teeth and walked into the bedroom, seeing the comforter and sheets already pulled back.

Glancing to the side, she saw Chris leaning against his chest of drawers, his boots now off and one bare foot crossed over the other. She walked straight to him, lifted her hands, and placed her palms on his chest, tilting her head back so that she could keep her gaze on his face. "I'm glad I'm here. I'm sorry for the reason, but I'm glad I'm here." She winced but continued to hold his gaze. "You make me feel... safe. And I hate feeling unsafe."

His hands cupped her face, and he bent low. "Babe, you will always be safe with me."

She nodded but remained quiet as his face filled her vision.

"I'm sorry for the reason that jumped ahead of my being able to apologize first. But I was going to do everything in my power to beg for your forgiveness and make sure you were here."

Her heart melted a little bit more. Leaning even closer, she welcomed his arms as they wrapped around her. "Honey, there's nothing to forgive. You weren't expecting a relationship. You weren't expecting anything to happen other than us to be travel partners. And you have a right to take the time you need to get settled in your new life. Yes, I grew to care for you quickly, but you don't have to apologize for needing space to figure things out from your perspective. I'm just lucky that you want me and it didn't take long for you to decide that."

"Babe, I knew that before I drove away from you."

She smiled, loving the feel of his heartbeat under her palm. "Let's go to bed."

He lifted a brow, adopting a stern expression. "Just to sleep. You need your rest."

"Fine, fine." She offered an exaggerated huff, then

turned and walked over to the bed. Climbing in, she immediately let out a sigh at the feel of his new mattress.

"I'll be right there," he said.

True to his word, it didn't take long for him to finish in the bathroom and flip off the lights. She watched as he stalked toward the other side of the bed, his chest bare and clad in only boxers. A few minutes later, they were each lying on their backs, staring at the ceiling with at least three feet of space between them.

As glad as she was to be there with him, a snake of unease curled in her belly. Swallowing down the fear, she whispered, "Can you hold me?"

24

When Chris heard Stella's small voice whisper her need for him to hold her, his heart clenched with anger at the reason behind her need. With frustration for the way he'd wasted days wondering how to approach her. With relief that she'd had the detective call him even when he hadn't made the first move yet. With humility that she'd offered forgiveness so readily. With gratitude that she wanted him.

He quickly erased the space between them and gently wrapped her in his embrace, tucking her face against his chest, and burying his nose in her hair. He gently rubbed his hands up and down her back, remembering the soft feel of her skin and hoping to infuse warmth to chase away the bad memories. She immediately relaxed, her body easing against his.

His cock twitched, and he inwardly cursed, willing the feel of her soft curves to not affect him. With his training, he was able to control his body while recognizing that with her in his arms, that was more difficult than it had ever been before.

Her breathing slowed, her muscles relaxed, and a sigh of relief escaped his lips that she was able to find sleep in his arms. Uncertain if he would be able to do the same, he knew it didn't matter. As long as she was safe and with him, he didn't care if he stayed awake and in the same position all night. But feeling her soft breath puffed against his chest, he soon followed her in slumber.

The early morning light was barely peeking through the blinds of his bedroom window when his eyes jerked open. After having slept deeper than he could ever remember sleeping, it took a few seconds to realize what woke him... the feel of soft kisses trailing over his chest.

His cock reacted instantly, and he looked down to see Stella lift her head and stare at him. Her thick blonde hair was messy, her face still bruised and slightly swollen, and her expression held uncertainty. And he'd never seen anything more beautiful in his life. Unable to keep the grin from spreading across his face, it must have been the reaction she needed because her body relaxed, and her smile beamed at him. She lowered her head and resumed her feather-light kisses over his chest and continued lower.

"Babe, we don't have to— oh, God," he groaned as her hand slid into his boxers. There was no hiding his erection now, and he was fairly sure there was no trick in the book to keep his cock from reacting.

"Please," she whispered as she pushed his boxers down and encircled him with her mouth.

He couldn't refuse her soft plea and allowed himself to be carried away by the lust firing throughout his body. His hands reached down, his fingers tangling in her thick hair. She hesitated, her breath hitching. "Babe? Are you hurting?" He started to lift her head off him, not wanting anything they did to cause her pain.

She lifted her gaze to him, then slowly shook her head. Sliding her mouth from him, she said, "Please, I need this. I need you. I just need to go a little slow." Before he had a chance to object, she lowered her mouth back around him.

"Fuuuuuck," he moaned. She sucked and licked slowly, taking him further and further into her mouth. He tried to hold off but knew if he didn't stop her soon, he'd blow. Another time, absolutely. But not this time. This time when he came, he wanted to come with her sweet sex clenching around him.

Losing his grip on her hair, he ab-curled, grabbed her waist, and gently hauled her up against his body until they were face to face. "I want to be inside, but don't want to hurt you, so you've got top, babe. But I need to get you ready."

She shifted up on her knees, reaching down to place the tip of his cock at her entrance. "I'm more than ready, Chris. I'm still on the pill, still clean. Is this okay?"

"This is more than fuckin' okay."

She grinned, her smile still a little wonky, but she no longer winced, which he took as a good sign. She lowered herself slowly until fully seated, and all rational thoughts fled from his mind at the feel of her tight, warm sex surrounding him.

With her hands resting on his shoulders and his hands spanning her waist, his fingertips digging into her hips, they worked together as she rose and sank over his cock. When he could tell she was tired, he lifted her slightly and took over, shifting his hips upward, creating the friction they both needed and sought.

She leaned forward so that her nipples brushed against his chest, and she gasped against his lips as the new angle intensified the sensations. He kept his eyes open, not wanting to miss a moment of their being together, a new experience for him. But then, everything with Stella was a new experience. Sex had always been just sex. But with her, his heart seemed to beat in a rhythm all its own, and he could swear it was synchronized with her heartbeat.

He forced himself to focus on her shining eyes as she peered down at him and not the bruising. This needed to be about her. This needed to be about the two of them. The idea of what he'd do if he got his hands on the man who'd hurt her flew through his mind. But just as quickly, everything fled his mind as her fingers dug into his shoulders, and her breathing became heavier. *Christ, I'm an idiot... I should have taken care of her first.*

As though she read his mind, she shook her head and mumbled against his lips. "Coming... I'm coming."

He slid one hand forward, and as his cock continued to drive into her warmth, his thumb found her sensitive nub, pressing and rolling. His tongue thrust into her mouth, sweeping over her sweet taste. She shuddered and cried out her release, and he swallowed the sound. Her arms gave out completely, and she lay on his chest, panting.

He rolled her over and kept his weight off her chest with his forearms planted in the mattress next to her, his heart threatening to explode as he thrust into her slick channel. A blinding light hit behind his eyes as he squeezed them shut, his body tense and his release overtaking all other thoughts. Dropping his head, he nuzzled her neck, still making sure not to crush her under his weight.

When he could finally catch his breath, he rolled to the side, his cock sliding out from her sex and their sweat-slick bodies crushed together. Time ceased to matter, and he had no idea how long they lay without speaking. Not that he had the energy to speak anyway.

A little giggle sounded as she leaned her head back and held his gaze. "Wow."

Grinning, he agreed. "Yeah, wow."

"I thought our first time at the hotel was amazing but sort of wondered if it was a fluke."

Lowering his brow, he glared. "A fluke? Are you calling my sexual prowess a fluke?"

She crinkled her nose. "Let's just say that it was light years better than any other experience I've ever had. Not that I've had all that much experience, but you know what I mean. So, while it was—"

"Earth-shattering?"

Laughing, she said, "Yeah, sex god. It was earth-shattering."

"Sex god. I like that. Now, about it being a fluke?"

"Okay, okay! After this morning, I can definitely say it was not a fluke!"

He leaned in and kissed her, loving her taste, loving her laughter, loving the ease felt around her. *Loving...*

There was no way he could be in love with her after only knowing her for a short while. *Or can I?* What he did know was he couldn't imagine her not being in his life.

"Honey, I'm leaking."

"Sorry, babe," he mumbled as he rolled away. She climbed from the bed, and he watched her ass as she disappeared into the bathroom. Coming out a few minutes later, still naked, he watched her gorgeous body as she bent over and snagged her panties from the floor.

"Grab one of my T-shirts. I'm ordering breakfast delivery from a diner down the road."

Her eyes lit, and her response was to saunter over to his chest of drawers and pull out a clean T-shirt. It settled over her hips, and he couldn't imagine a more beautiful sight. He headed to the bathroom, quickly taking care of his business. Walking into his living room, he pulled up the food delivery app and was just about to ask her what she wanted to eat when his phone rang. Seeing it was from LSI, he answered. "Yeah?"

"It's Jeb. Is Stella with you?"

Immediately alert, he replied, "Yeah, she is. What's going on?"

"I'm sorry as fuck that I didn't realize she didn't have it with her in her apartment, so I didn't think to search for it until Rick said something. I've got a ping on her phone. Man, you're not gonna believe this, but it's in your apartment."

His chin jerked back. "My apartment? Stella's phone is in my apartment?" He looked over as she walked into the room, the expression on her face mirroring the same surprise as his.

Her brow furrowed as her head jerked around, almost as though she were expecting her phone to suddenly appear in front of her. Looking back at him, she tossed her hand to the sides. "Where? Ask him where it is!"

"Babe, it doesn't work that way. He can't tell me where *in* the apartment it is, just that it's here." He heard laughter in the background and wondered who else was in on the call besides Jeb. Still talking to Stella, he added, "Look in your bags. It's got to be in something that we brought with us."

She ran into the bedroom, and while she began tossing things out of her suitcase, he dug through her purse, finding nothing. She ran back in, her hands once again flying out to the side. "I don't know. What else did I bring?"

He looked down and saw the bag from her studio still lying next to the front door and pointed. "Check there."

She dumped the contents into the floor, and her phone fell out amongst the art pad and pencils. "Oh, my God. I had it in the studio when I was working before I went to the store." She looked up. "I'm so glad I didn't lose it and that the bastard didn't take it!"

"Jeb, we've got it. We'll bring it in now."

"Sounds good. Carson will call in the others."

Disconnecting, he looked over as Stella was still kneeling on the floor. "We're gonna take your phone into LSI-WC. They'll go through it to see if they can figure out why someone wanted it. I hope that's okay because that may be the key to us—"

"Sure, sure. There are no secrets on it. Use whatever you can to get this person away from us."

He walked over and offered his hand, gently pulling her to her feet. Wrapping his arms around her, he stared at her injured face before holding her gaze. "Stella, babe, because of my former and current jobs, I thought this person might have been after me. But after what happened to you and him wanting your phone, it looks like you're the one they're after."

He felt her body stiffen in shock a second before her eyes widened.

"Me?" she squeaked.

He tightened his arms around her and held her close. Finally kissing the top of her head, he said, "Don't worry. You're safe now, and I want to keep you that way. Let's go ahead and get dressed, and we'll grab breakfast at a drive-through on the way."

She nodded and pulled out of his arms, stripping his T-shirt off as she hurried into the bedroom. Watching her panty-clad ass as she moved away, he sighed, adjusting his cock. *I know, I know. Not the way I wanted to spend my morning, either.*

25

"As you can see, I'm pretty boring," Stella said, her gaze darting around to the other Keepers in the room.

Chris was proud of how she handled herself, immediately handing her phone to Jeb and giving them permission to look at everything stored there. He wrapped his arm around her, tucking her into his side, making it clear that they were together.

The meeting took place in the room where she'd met them previously, and even though he'd grabbed a fast-food breakfast that they'd shoved down in the car, he was overjoyed that Rachel had provided an array of breakfast items.

It hadn't escaped his notice that as each Keeper greeted her warmly, their gazes landed on her bruised face and their jaws hardened. While they'd managed to smile, making her feel at ease, he knew they were seriously pissed.

She had related the entire incident to them in great detail, her voice only shaking slightly. "It was weird because when I should have been terrified, all I could think of was, *'Where is my phone?'* My brain was behind because I never had a chance to duck when he swung at me."

"That's probably a good thing, Stella," Carson said, his expression full of concern. "As angry as we are that he hit you, when you were unconscious, he probably felt safer to keep looking and then get out of your place. Otherwise, he may have done something more permanent to shut you up."

She sighed and Chris tightened his grip. While she munched on a muffin, Jeb connected her phone to his computer, his gaze skimming through the contents. With Leo and Rick on either side of him, they each took different information so they could work faster.

After several minutes, Leo shook his head. "The texts are all to family, friends, or coworkers, just as she said. I don't see anything out of the ordinary here."

Nodding, Rick agreed. "I'm scanning through emails and don't see anything suspicious."

"I can't see going back any further," Carson said. "Whatever happened had to have happened on their trip. And we know there's a good possibility that it happened in Nevada."

At that, Stella swung her gaze to Chris, unspoken questions in her eyes. He shook his head and mumbled, "I know you're part of this, but the investigation is still active. We've given the information to the feds, so I need you to trust us."

Her gaze remained steadfast on his for a few seconds, then she nodded, shrugging. "That's good. I'm pissed as hell at whoever is doing this, but since there's little I can do, I'm just glad that you guys have it."

He couldn't help but grin, once again impressed by her.

"You've got a lot of pictures," Jeb stated, drawing their attention back to him.

"I know," she sighed. "Poor Chris had to stop on the side of the road so many times so that I could take pictures. Most of them are for inspiration."

Chris watched as the other Keepers' eyes moved to her, and he tensed. It might not make sense, but while he may have questioned Stella's activities when they were traveling, he sure as fuck didn't want anyone questioning her methods now. But, in true Stella fashion, she continued her straightforward explanation.

"As an artist, I'm fascinated by the colors, lines, and shapes that are all around us. That's why you see so many skies, sunset, and scenic pictures. Where most of you might look up and be amazed at the beautiful sunset, I see the cloud formations, the streaks of various light, the ever-changing patterns, and the colors as they morph into each other. So, I take a lot of pictures so that I can fall back on those when I'm working those colors into my pottery."

The Keepers nodded, no one seeming surprised by her response. Jeb continued to click through and said, "I'm going to focus on the ones after that first night."

"What are you looking for?" she asked.

"To be honest, I don't have a fuckin' clue."

At Jeb's answer, she made big eyes toward Chris, and he fought a grin. *I'm with my coworkers and new boss, and*

I'm smiling. But instead of being embarrassed, he loved who she was and didn't mind the others knowing.

As the pictures were shared onto a screen on the wall, he focused his attention on them, remembering the various stops they made. After dozens of scenic shots, there were some with people around a campfire.

"Oh, that's at the campground!" Stella exclaimed.

The Keepers' attention honed in on the faces, and Chris stared, casting his mind back to that night. The night he fell for her. *But was that the night someone didn't want their picture taken?* Next to him, Stella leaned forward, her gaze pinned on the screen. She slowly shook her head before turning to him.

"I don't see anything suspicious, do you?"

He shook his head, as well. "No, I don't."

"Let's keep looking," Carson said. "We'll tag some of these and enhance them digitally."

After looking at more pictures of the bonfire, they came to the sunset pictures she took at the overlook near Battle Mountain. "The hotel manager told us of this place to view the sunset," Chris said.

After several scenic pictures, they came to the one of a beaming Stella standing next to Chris. He glanced over at her, seeing her smile.

"I forgot about that selfie I took of us," she said.

Jeb clicked through the others, then stopped. "Who's that in the background?"

Chris leaned forward as Jeb enhanced the photograph, zooming in on the truck and van down in the ravine behind them. "The day before, we'd seen some Boy Scouts out on a camping trip. When I saw these guys down there, I assumed they were campers or hikers."

"One of them waved at us, remember?" Stella said.

"Yeah, I remember," he nodded, but now a snake of suspicion moved through him. "From where we were, we couldn't see them clearly. There was nothing suspicious about them but fuck if I know what they were really doing."

Everyone in the room leaned forward, and Carson ordered, "Enhance."

Jed began typing quickly, and Chris watched as the photograph zoomed in on the vehicles and men, bringing them more clearly into view. The white panel van had no writing on the outside, and even though they could see the back doors open, they couldn't observe the license plate. But the white truck's license plate was clear.

Rick's fingers flew over his keyboard, and it wasn't long before he said, "Fuckin' bingo." Chris swung his gaze around, and Rick said, "Samuel Watson. Also an electrician, just like Johnny Markham. And guess what? Sam is still in the Army National Guard for Nevada."

"Rick…" Chris called out, his voice low, holding a warning.

Rick looked up, then his gaze shot over to Stella before back to Chris. "Shit… sorry."

Stella sighed. "I guess this is where I need to leave the room, right?"

He opened his mouth to respond, but Carson spoke first. "Stella, please understand that we're not dismissing the fact that you're in the middle of this. But we want to keep you as safe as possible, and to do that, we need to investigate freely. Whatever Chris can share with you, he will. But right now, I think it's best if you let us continue."

"That's fine. Really, I understand." She glanced up at Chris, then offered a little smile that hit him straight in the heart. "I'll just wait outside?"

"I'll walk you out and make sure you're okay." He stood and wrapped his arm around her, offering a chin lift to the others. He had no idea when Carson had signaled Rachel, but she was outside the room, ready to take Stella in hand. Bending, he kissed Stella lightly. "As soon as I can, I'll come back and take you home."

"Go, do whatever you gotta do. I'll be fine," Stella said, waving her hands in a shooing motion.

With another kiss, he said goodbye to the two women and moved back into the room. As soon as he sat down, Carson said, "Rachel will take care of her."

It was hard to suppress his grin. "Believe me, Stella has never met a stranger. Before long, she and Rachel will be fast friends."

The others grinned, and then they turned back to the screen. By now, Jeb had enhanced the picture more, and he focused on the back of the van. "Is that... coffins? Why the hell does a National Guardsman have a couple of coffins in a van? What the fuck was he transporting?"

"I was just getting to that," Jeb said. With the tap of a few more keys on his computer, he enlarged and enhanced the picture even more. The lid to one of the coffins was open, and they could clearly see it was filled with guns.

"Oh, shit," Chris cursed, the reality of the situation hitting him. "Those guys are fuckin' smuggling weapons, probably stolen from their Guard unit." Scrubbing his hand over his face, he shook his head. "We stumbled in there, and Stella took a picture. Christ, no wonder they're after us."

For the next several hours, Chris assisted as Carson and the others worked the case. They contacted an FBI agent who had a close working relationship with LSI-WC. The agent was interested and had no problem running with whatever information he was given.

The photographs were sent, Chris and Stella's information was given, and Chris had identified the exact area. Within a couple of hours, the FBI agent reported he'd been in contact with the commanding officer of the Army National Guard of Nevada. The FBI had picked up Jonathan Markham and Samuel Watson. Stunned at how fast the events were unfolding, Chris could not help but be impressed with not only the work LSI-WC had accomplished but also the obvious integrity and respect the FBI had for their work.

"How are you doing?" Rick asked, settling into the seat next to him.

"Honestly? Impressed as fuck." Squeezing the back of his neck, he shook his head. "And my career change? Jesus, if I ever had any doubt, this has put that to rest!"

Rick laughed and nodded. "I thought the same thing the first time I was with my brother at the LSI in Maine. I wondered if leaving the Navy had been the right thing until I saw how they operated. Then I knew that's exactly what I wanted."

"So, with what we provided and the fact that the Feds have already picked up Markham and Watson, what does that mean for us?"

"It means we can put this case to bed," Rick said.

Nodding, he gave voice to the inkling of disappointment that niggled inside. "Does it make me an ass to admit that as impressed as I am, there's also a letdown? Like, I thought we'd have a chance to take them down."

Rick belted out a laugh. "Nah, man. Sometimes we do get to, like the good old days. But sometimes a case is just handed over and we're done. Don't worry, though. There are plenty of others out there. We have more work than we can take, and Carson has to turn down a lot. And you already know that this was an easy one. Our work runs from security installs that can be interesting or boring as fuck. Investigations that can last weeks, end up in the field all over the world, and can bring down some serious assholes that finally get what's coming to them. And then sometimes, we land a job that doesn't take long to solve."

"And turn it over to the Feds," he added.

"Yeah, but as Carson reminds us, most of the time we do the work and someone else gets the glory. But we're in the wrong business if it's the glory we're after."

"I hear you, man, and that's fine by me," Chris said. With the Keepers all being from special ops, they all knew about staying in the shadows when the accolades were heaped on the higher-ups or politicians.

Rick stood and clapped him on the back. "At least you and that pretty lady out there can get back to whatever it is that you two started."

Chris leaned back in his chair, his gaze on the other Keepers as most of them headed out of the building and back to headquarters, but his mind was on Stella. He wanted to do exactly what Rick suggested, but a strange niggling of doubt moved through him. Unable to decipher where it came from, he figured it must be because the threat ended so quickly and he hadn't had a chance to wrap his mind around what was next. When he'd brought her to his place yesterday, he'd thought they'd have more time together to figure out what they wanted and how to make their relationship work. *That must be why I feel like things didn't get settled completely. It's not the mission... it's Stella and me.*

Standing, he headed outside, smiling as he spied her with Rachel sitting in chairs overlooking where the ocean crashed against the cliffs below. Stella was smiling and chatting, waving her hands around with animation. And a plate of snacks was on the small table between the two women. Grinning, he headed toward them, pushing aside the strange feeling in his gut.

26

"So, that's it?" Stella asked, standing in Chris' apartment the next morning.

After leaving the meeting at LSI-WC, they'd stopped at a SuperMart where she'd picked out some basic household items, grabbing some groceries, as well. Then they'd driven back to his apartment, and she'd followed him in, eager to find out what the Keepers learned. Her eyes had widened, and she was sure her mouth had hung open when Chris told her that two men had been identified from the picture Stella inadvertently snapped and it appeared to be a military munitions theft ring.

The rest of the day had been perfect as they lounged, rested, talked, and ate takeout. The night had been spent with long, slow explorations of their bodies after discovering the fun of taking a bath together. After sleeping late, she'd risen to scramble eggs and fry bacon. He'd managed the toast and coffee, and over breakfast, he'd filled her in on the latest after taking a phone call from Carson.

"Essentially, yes. Now, the FBI will still coordinate with Carson as well as work with the National Guard in Nevada."

"Oh. Um... well, good." Her words sounded ridiculous to her own ears, and she could only imagine what they sounded like to Chris. After all, she should be thrilled. While they'd had a harrowing experience trying to get away from the one who'd shot at them and she'd been traumatized by the man who'd broken into her apartment, she had thought that it would take much longer to identify the criminals. *That's good. Of course, that's good.*

And yet, there was an unsettled feeling in her stomach. Looking up at Chris, the reason was staring her in the face. She'd honestly thought they'd have more time to figure out who they were as a couple and how they were going to make it all work. Now, with the danger passed, she had no reason to stay with him, and even though he'd said he wanted them to be together, she wondered how to make a long-distance relationship work.

"So... uh... I guess I can get back to my studio?" Uncertainty laced her words.

He hesitated, then nodded. "Yeah, I guess you can."

She looked down at her empty plate and fiddled with her fork, strangely pleased to have known she was with him when he'd bought such a basic item. She liked the idea of doing everyday things with Chris. It wasn't just about taking a trip together or escaping someone while racing through the woods. It was long kisses and even longer sex. It was standing in a SuperMart debating the best snacks to buy. It was eating breakfast on the dishes they'd picked out together even if they were boring white. And now her breakfast sat like a rock in her stomach at the idea of going back to her studio by herself after saying goodbye to Chris and looking at their calendars to see when they might be able to see each other again.

"Stella?"

She lifted her head to see him staring at her, and she waited.

"I meant everything that I said to you. I have to confess I thought you'd be able to stay here longer, but that sounds selfish, doesn't it? That sounds like I'm saying I wanted you to still be in danger so that you need to be here."

She reached over and placed her hand on his, a rueful smile playing about her lips. "No, that's not self-ish. To be honest, I've been thinking the same thing."

He hesitated, then a slight grimace crossed his face. "Things are going to be kind of rough for a little bit. I have no idea what kind of training Carson is going to put me through or what kind of missions he's going to assign to me. I know there will be some travel. I know I often won't get a lot of heads up before I get an assign-ment. And I realize that for a starting relationship, that sucks."

She nodded slowly. "I've got a gallery showing in two weeks, so I'm going to be busy as well. I thought I was going to have to do long-distance final organizing with the gallery owner, but it will be a lot easier if I can be there in person." She shrugged, adding, "It's a small gallery and a small showing, but it's all just my work, so that's kind of cool."

"Babe, I think it's very cool," he enthused.

Her hands fiddled in her lap before she lifted her gaze back to him. His blue eyes were mesmerizing, and she felt pulled into their depths, wanting more of him. "I know with everything you've got going on here, you might not make it, but if you wanted—"

"Tell me when and where, and I'll be there. I'm pretty sure I'll still be in training for a couple of weeks, so I shouldn't have any problem making it."

Relief filled her chest, and the nerves in her stomach settled just a bit. "Good, I'm glad. It's not fancy or anything. You don't have to dress up. She's just having some hors d'oeuvres and wine and beer."

He stepped closer, and her breath halted in her throat as she felt the warmth coming from his body. "And I promise we won't have to wait two weeks before we see each other again." Lifting a hand, he cupped her cheek, his gaze roving over her face. "I could kill the fucker for doing this to you."

"I guess it's better that you didn't. I'd hate to see what you look like in prison orange even if it is one of the colors in a beautiful sunset."

He laughed and lowered his head. "Yeah, you're probably right. But I confess I thought there might be a chance that I could go after this guy and was looking forward to teaching him a lesson to stay away from my girl."

Her hands reached out to his waist, her fingers clutching the soft material of his shirt. "Is that what I am?"

"God, I hope so, Stella."

She smiled, the tightness in her chest easing. "Then I am. And while it will take both of us working together, a lot of patience, and a lot of coordination of schedules, we can make this relationship happen."

His head had now lowered until his lips were a whisper away from hers. "Hope like hell you think it's worth it, babe."

He hesitated, and she lifted on her toes to close the gap. Sealing her mouth over his, she melted into him as his arms snaked around her, pulling her tightly to his chest. Like all their kisses that stole her breath, she gave in to the multitude of sensations that swept over her. Tingling nerves moved through her body, centering on her breasts and core. Shaky legs she wasn't sure would keep holding her upright. The velvet feel of his tongue gliding through her mouth, tangling with her tongue. The hard body underneath her fingertips as they traveled up and down his back.

Lust and love warred deep inside. The lust she understood, even welcomed. *But love? So soon?* As their bodies pressed together and the kiss flamed higher, the two emotions swirled together then clearly separated in her mind. *Lust? Absolutely. Love? Oh yeah.*

Smiling in the middle of their kiss, she stopped thinking and gave herself completely over to her heart.

Driving back to her house, she thought about everything that had happened and everything that had been said. With the radio turned down low, she talked aloud, finding it worthwhile when trying to work through a problem.

"He wants us together. Does that mean long-distance? He can't move to where my studio is because he needs to be close to his work. Is it fair for me to move? But then, I'm independent. I can create anywhere. God, I'd have to move everything from my studio though, including my heavy kilns. But that's what moving companies are for. Yeah, but they're expensive. Maybe a few of the Keepers with trucks could help? Shirtless... yeah, that'd be worth photographing for *inspiration*." She snorted at the thought. "Lighthouse Movers."

She reached over and stuck her hand into the bag of snacks Chris had offered before she left. Crunching on the cheese crackers, she grinned at the memory of how incredulous he was at the beginning of their journey when she'd explained the importance of travel snacks. *Now, he gives them to me.*

"What about the classes I teach? But then, they're only one night a week. And San Jose isn't the only place with art schools."

She changed the station on the radio, settling for a station dedicated to indie musicians as she continued to munch on crackers. Her fingers were getting slightly orange from the snack, and she dug into her purse for a tissue while driving with her left hand. "I need to teach him about driving snacks versus passenger snacks."

Wiping her fingers, she decided that all the pondering she was doing required eating regardless of orange fingers, so she grabbed another few crackers and munched some more.

"Do I really want to stay in my tiny apartment with my studio crammed inside a garage?" Her gaze shot out over the beautiful vista all around. Glimpses of the ocean to the west. Lush green grass and distant mountains to the east. The idea of having a new studio with more light and the chance to travel this area in search of inspiration filled her. Sucking in a quick breath, her lips curved widely at the thought of being with Chris for more than just the times they could squeeze in together.

"I'm falling for him… oh, hell, who am I kidding? I've fallen. But is it smart to think of moving in together so soon? Well, no one said it had to be *now*. Date first. Get used to each other. Let him become acclimated to his new job. See how it goes."

Taking a huge gulp of the diet drink he gave her before she left, she rolled her eyes. "Yeah, right… like I really want to wait!"

Her phone rang, and she glanced to see his name on the ID. Snatching it from the cup holder, she hit the speaker button, then placed it on the seat next to the snack bag. "Hey, sweetie, you'll have to talk loudly because my phone is in the seat on speaker. I don't have a fancy-ass vehicle with Bluetooth like some people I know."

The sound of his deep laughter came through and filled her small car. "I don't want to distract you, babe. Just wanted to say that I already miss you."

Her heart squeezed, and her smile widened. "I've been talking to myself for the past hour," she blurted.

There were a few seconds of silence before he said, "Um... okay."

"That's what I do when I travel by myself. I talk. Just like when you were with me, only you aren't with me, so I talk."

Laughter met her ears again. "Okaaaay," he drew out. "You want to share what you were talking about so I can pretend I'm there with you?"

"I was trying to decide what we should do. You know, about being together. It's two hours between where you are and where I live. But that's okay. I don't want you to think that I won't make the trip. It's just that I was trying to think how long that would work before it might get old." Silence met her again, and worry snaked through her. "I'm not saying this right, Chris. I'm so afraid of saying the wrong thing that I'm just blabbing instead."

"Stella, babe, you're scaring me here. We were together an hour ago, and I thought we were on the same page. Please, just say what's on your mind."

Wincing, she hated that she'd given him cause to worry. "Chris, honey, I'm sorry. I'm messing this up." Pulling her thoughts together, she settled her mind. "I suppose, as I was driving, I was thinking about how much I want to spend time with you. And then I thought about the trip, and while it's not the worst thing to have two hours between us, I was thinking of how to make it shorter. You can't move from down there, and my studio is up here—"

"Stella, we'll make it work—"

"I know."

"You know?"

Laughter bubbled forth. "Yeah, I know. We've been apart for an hour, and I miss you so much already. So, while I'm not proposing we make any major life plans right now because Lord knows you have enough going on, and I've got commitments, all of which we need to—"

"Stella!" he interrupted. "What are you saying?"

"Oh… well, I can create my art anywhere, honey. To be honest, I had already been thinking of finding a new place for a studio anyway."

"Are you saying what I think you're saying?"

She could hear the hope in his voice, and her heart leaped. "Well, not right now. But if things keep going for us like I think they are, then I don't want us to keep heading up and down this road, stealing just a few nights here and there. And of the two of us, I am more mobile in where I reside. So, as long as I can find a place for my studio… I'll move."

"Thank God! Damn, babe, I thought you were breaking up with me."

"We were just together an hour ago, so why on earth would I break up with you?"

"Yeah, well, I was afraid that you'd convinced yourself in that hour that I wasn't worth the trouble."

"You? Chris, you're the best man I've ever met."

There was a heartbeat of silence before his low voice growled, "I wish you were here so I could let you know how much those words mean to me."

A giggle slipped out. "Then you can show me the next time we're together."

"That's a promise."

"Oh, I've got to go. I see the sign for my exit, and I need to change lanes. Love you!" Her finger tapped 'Disconnect' as she signaled and changed lanes quickly, having to take the exit ramp faster than she'd intended. Her purse tipped over, and several things fell onto the floorboard. Glancing down, she grinned, seeing her cheese crackers remaining steadfast on the seat.

Continuing toward her home, the last words she'd said replayed in her mind. *Love you? Love you? Oh, shit! I let the words slip out right before I hung up!* The desire to bang her head on the steering wheel was strong, but now, heading into traffic, she could only shake her head and hope he hadn't heard the words. Not that she didn't think she meant them, but that was not the way she wanted to say them.

Reaching her hand over into the bag of crackers again, she pulled them out and shoved some into her mouth, unheeding the orange residue coloring her fingers.

27

"Love you."

Chris stared at his phone for a few seconds, questioning whether or not he heard her correctly. *Was that a declaration of feelings for him? Or just a hasty talk-to-you-soon-goodbye-end-of-conversation comment?*

"Hey, you okay?" Leo asked, walking past him.

"Yeah. Uh… sure, yeah." He shoved his phone back into his pocket and focused on the screen in front of him. Leo had been working with him on the security installation part of their business.

"We just analyze the clients' needs and match that to the best contractor that installs the actual system. We don't do the installations ourselves. We also only take certain clients with certain needs. Just 'cause someone's got more money than God and thinks the world is after them, they don't necessarily get our attention. LSI-WC sometimes takes on clients with serious security needs who can't afford the best."

"And who monitors when there's a live security feed?" Chris asked.

"It depends. We contract with some of your security companies that provide twenty-four-seven camera monitoring. We also monitor if it's an active case that we are investigating."

Chris quickly absorbed everything that he was being taught, satisfaction morphing into excitement at the idea of what he would be doing with the team that Carson had created. While Leo answered a question from Jeb, Chris leaned back in his chair, looking around. Years ago, he couldn't wait to leave home and had been glad to have his base on the eastern coast. Now, he felt like this was home once again.

Rachel hurried in, her gaze going immediately to Carson. Everyone's attention was pinned on her, and Chris felt the hairs on the back of his neck stand on end, reminded of the last time she'd entered that way to tell them that Stella had been attacked. Then Rachel's eyes cut toward him before she zeroed in on Carson again, and Chris felt the punch straight to his gut.

"The FBI liaison is on the phone for you, Carson."

Chris watched as Carson immediately picked up his phone, turned his back to the others, and said, "Talk to me."

Other than the sound of his heartbeat, which he felt sure everyone could hear, the room was silent. Chris listened as Carson kept his side of the conversation low. Finally, saying, "We're on it," he hung up and turned around.

Pinning Chris with a hard stare, Carson said, "While

under questioning, Sam Watson pointed toward the contact who would receive the guns. He claims he doesn't know the person's name, just met him for the first time at the hand-off location Stella managed to photograph. Says the man has a Slavic accent, maybe Russian."

Years of SEAL training allowed Chris' chest to barely move even as the air fell from his lungs. His face was impassive, but his heart beat wildly as he waited for more.

"Digging, they've connected Sam and Johnny's small-time munitions thefts to a larger case the Bureau has been working on—Russian cartel moving stolen guns out of the country and getting them into the hands of whatever faction will pay the most."

"Stella..." he choked out. "Surely the cartel realizes that she knows nothing about any of this."

"With the FBI working on identifying the contact and the cartel's munitions theft ring now halted, the Russians may go for payback. You've mentioned that she used her credit card several times on the trip, and—"

"Fuck, they could have ID'd her from that." His stomach dropped at the idea.

"They might go for her just to make a fuckin' state-ment," Rick said, already taking to his feet while clapping Chris on the shoulder. "I'll get the bird ready."

Chris jumped up and pulled out his phone, calling out, "I'll get hold of Stella." With the phone to his ear, he grimaced. "Dammit! Why doesn't she answer?"

"Leo, you're with Rick and Chris again," Carson

ordered, and with a nod, Leo steered Chris out of the room and down the hall to the equipment room.

"Grab what you need," Leo said, already pulling his weapons and body armor off the shelves.

Falling into mission mode with the attempt to push all thoughts of Stella from his mind, Chris grabbed what he thought he'd need. Then, looking at the equipment and weapons he'd taken, the idea of needing to use those to keep the woman he loved safe hit him. White-hot anger flowed through his veins, fueling his determination. Looking up as Carson walked in, he speared his fellow Keepers with a hard stare and nodded. "Ready."

Carson walked out with them but kept his instructions to a minimum. Chris was grateful for the show of confidence as well as the acknowledgement of professionalism. He wasn't about to fuck things up for LSI-WC, but nothing was going to keep him from making sure Stella was protected, as well.

Within thirty minutes, they were airborne. They would land at a private airstrip, and Carson had an SUV waiting for them courtesy of an old Army buddy of his.

He knew enough about the Russians to know that they would want someone to pay for the interruption of their munitions pipeline. It wouldn't matter who, but vengeance would be sought and meted out. Chris kept trying to call Stella, but her voicemail was all he could reach. Finally, closing his eyes, he prayed they got to her in time.

Stella parked next to her garage studio and cut the engine but didn't alight from her car. Instead, she sat and stared out the windshield at the familiar view, looking at it with a new perspective. The building she lived and worked in was old, with not enough windows to allow natural light. With her workspace, materials, equipment, and kilns, there was little room for storage of her finished work. Lifting her gaze to where her apartment sat above the garage, it no longer held quite the same appeal that it had when she'd first moved in and was thrilled with her independence. While she'd personalized the studio apartment, making it homey and a reflection of her, it was still a tiny space.

Looking out the side window, it was easy to see why her rent was cheap. Rundown buildings and a neighborhood that had seen better times, and considering her landlord didn't spend any money on upkeep, he could afford to rent the place at the price that was right several years ago. But now, her business was flourishing and growing with each showing. It would only be a matter of time before her landlord would start raising her rent, and she had no doubt he still wouldn't make any improvements.

The idea of starting a new relationship didn't frighten her. The idea of change, leaving the familiar, and embarking on a new journey filled her with excitement. Climbing from her car, she sucked in a deep breath and let it out. *Get my next orders filled. Have my gallery showing in a couple of weeks. Visit Chris and find a place that would work for my studio. Then turn in my notice to my landlord and get ready to move.* She happy-danced her way around the front of her car, threw open the door, and grabbed her purse and snack bag. Opening the back, she pulled out her other bags and slammed the trunk.

With her arms loaded, she halted at the bottom of the steps, remembering the last time she was unprepared. Setting everything down except her purse, she had her pepper spray in her hand as she went up to the top of the stairs. Breathing a sigh of relief at her still-locked door, she entered cautiously, looked around to see that it was empty, then dumped her purse on the floor. Running back down the stairs, she grabbed her other bags and jogged back up to her apartment.

She walked to the refrigerator and stared, wishing that something amazing would appear. When that magic didn't happen, she grabbed the milk. Standing at her small counter, she poured cereal into a bowl, doused it in milk, and had the breakfast of champions for lunch.

Fatigue pulled at her muscles, but the desire to pack up some of the orders that had come in kept her from face-planting on the bed. She quickly printed off the order list, then locked her apartment as she left. Jogging down the stairs once again, she entered her studio. Just like she'd looked around the outside when she first parked, she now stood with her hands on her hips and carefully moved her gaze around the space. The garage had seemed so large when she'd first rented it, excited to call it her studio. But with the addition of two larger kilns, another table for work-space, more shelving for supplies, and a separate area for packing the pieces to take to the post office, it was cramped.

With a sigh, she moved to the packing table and began sorting. She took great pride in packing her pottery to ensure that it would arrive at its destination in one piece. Flipping on the old radio that had been left in the garage when she took it over, she sang along as she made sure to wrap each piece carefully.

A tickling on the back of her neck caused her to look over her shoulder, but there was nothing behind her. Rolling her eyes at her overactive imagination, she turned back to her work. After taping the next box, she felt the same tickling sensation. This time, a man's face was visible through the window in the door of the garage. A little scream emitted, but he simply waved.

Walking closer, she pressed her lips together as he waved from the other side of the glass. He appeared middle-aged with dark hair, silver just at the temples, and a square jaw. She could only see the top half of him but spied he was wearing a white buttoned shirt, dark suit coat, and dark tie. He wasn't smiling but didn't seem like he was pissed about anything. *My bills are paid, so he can't be from a collection agency.* "Can I help you?" she called out.

"Miss Parker?"

"Uh... yes?"

"I saw your name on some work from the Shannon Gallery in town. I wanted to requisition a piece, and they gave me your studio address."

He spoke with a heavy Slavic accent, and she had to lean closer to understand. She had several smaller pieces at the gallery in town but was surprised they gave out her address. She felt sure that the owner was aware her apartment was over her studio, but perhaps one of the employees wasn't. She hesitated, then sighed. If someone wanted to pay to requisition a piece of work from her, she hated to turn them down. She was no longer a starving artist, but the word of mouth about her work from a satisfied customer who had the money to pay for a private piece was valuable in and of itself. Sucking in a deep breath, she smiled. "Um, sure."

She flipped the lock on the door and pushed it open. She stepped back to the table, reaching for one of her heavy vases, ready to wrap it before it would go into the box. "I was just packing up some of my orders. I have a showing in two weeks at another gallery that I'm still working on, but depending on what your request is, I might be able to fit it in before that showing. If not, then I would work on it soon after—" Her words halted as she glanced back at him and now spied the gun in his hand pointing toward her. "What? I have nothing to steal! I don't keep any money here!"

"I'm not interested in money Miss Parker."

She stared at his face, the icy blue of his eyes holding her attention. For an instant, she thought of Chris' blue eyes, but this man's could not be more different. As this man stared, she was filled with a sense that he would kill at will and barely blink. Her mouth was suddenly as dry as cotton as her gaze dragged from his face and dropped to the weapon. "What do you want with me?" Her words were shaky, mirroring her knees locked so she wouldn't drop.

"Because of you, I lost something that my employer is not happy about."

"I... I don't know what you mean. Was it a piece of pottery? If something got lost, I can replace it with another piece." The temperature seemed to drop in the room even though a bead of sweat rolled down her back.

"Do not play games with me, Miss Parker. I don't like games."

Shaking her head from side to side, she struggled to catch her breath. "I'm not playing a game. I don't know what you lost."

"I don't know if you are that stupid or if you think I am," he said.

At that, she remained silent, realizing nothing she could say to that comment would make him happy.

"My employer lost a great deal of money when the shipment was taken by the authorities. And all because of a simple photograph you took at a very inopportune time."

Understanding slammed into her, and she gasped. "Oh, God. I... I don't have anything."

"I have decided that you are stupid," he said, shaking his head slowly. "Of course, you don't have the weapons here. But I didn't come for the weapons. Federal agents have those, and I can't get my hands on them. But you will be my recompense."

"Me?"

"Guns are not the only thing my employer cares about. He has... varied interests. While you won't be of equal value to what he lost, I'm certain he'll find a way to put you to use. And it may take some of the pressure off me if I can bring him a worthy prize."

Fear poured through Stella's gut. She didn't know exactly what he was implying, but she'd read enough about criminal organizations in the news to know that if he took her away from her studio, she would never be seen again. And she'd never felt so alone.

Icy cold moved through her, and she dropped her gaze back to the gun in his hand. *He'll never let me go. Whatever he has planned for me or whoever he's taking me to, they'll never let me go.* She shivered at the thought of her parents having to go through life wondering what had happened to her and her heart pounded. Then the image of Chris moved through her mind, and her chest seized at the idea that he'd try to search for her, never knowing where she went.

The ice water in her veins froze, and she faced him, rage making her shake as much as fear. "No."

28

Having landed at the private airport, Chris leaped from the bird, the others right behind. The SUV was waiting, the keys inside. Leo climbed behind the wheel and Chris punched Stella's address into the GPS. Looking at the monitor, he let out a breath. ETA eight minutes. No matter how short, he knew his heart would threaten to beat out of his chest for the entire trip.

"If she's there and no threat is evident, we'll get her out," Rick said from the back seat. "Do you think that'll be a problem?"

"We'd already talked about her moving," Chris admitted. "Not so soon, but she'll do what she needs to do for protection."

Rick grabbed his phone. "Carson's calling."

"FBI has identified Stan Lovochek. Jeb is sending his photograph now. His uncle is part of the Alekhin Bratva. Based in California but have fingers everywhere as evidenced by the military munition thefts."

"Got it, boss. We're close to her place. We'll have you on our radios."

As Rick disconnected, Chris pointed for Leo to drive down a street. "This will take us to the opposite side. We can get in without being in view of her apartment or studio." He knew none of them had any idea what they'd be facing. It could be a perfectly fine Stella who'd misplaced her phone and wondered why they were showing up with firepower. Or it could be her in trouble again.

He just prayed the Russian didn't know who had unknowingly brought the thefts to an end and if he did hadn't found her yet. "Here," he said, and climbed out as soon as Leo had stopped the SUV.

Slipping to the back alley soundlessly, he raced to the stairs leading to her apartment. Glancing to the side, he spied the door to her studio barely open. Stepping closer, his heart dropped as Stella's voice, harder and colder than he'd ever heard, said one word.

"No."

Taking a step back, he flattened against the building, then signaled as Leo came from behind and Rick came from the other side. Rick dropped below the view of the window and pulled out a camera snake, barely sticking the tip to the side of the windowpane. Chris slid out his phone to see the camera signal that was being sent to LSI-WC as well as the three of them in the field. Stella was standing next to a table with several boxes, pottery vases, and bowls. And just to the side was an unidentified suited man who began to speak.

"You are not making a wise decision, Miss Parker."

Based on the intel from the FBI and heavy Slavic accent of the man, Chris recognized him as the man the FBI was after, Stan Lovochek. Looking closer at a different angle Rick was providing, he could see the weapon pointed directly toward Stella. *Fuck!* They could take him out, but none of them had a good angle for ensuring Stella's safety during the takedown. Looking over at Leo, the three Keepers communicated with hand signals. He wished he could let Stella know he was outside without her giving him away. He knew with the image being sent back to LSI, Carson would notify the FBI, but he wasn't about to wait.

Stella's voice came through again. "You're wrong. You'll never let me live, or if you do, my life won't be worth anything. I'd rather you give my parents something to mourn now than to always wonder what happened to me."

Using the image Rick was sending, Chris prayed that Stella would react the way he needed her to. Without making a sound, he stepped to the door, allowing the barest hint of him to show through the sliver of the opening with his weapon raised to the back of Stan. Keeping both of them in his sights, he never saw Stella's gaze move from Stan so he wasn't sure if she was aware of anything other than what was directly in front of her. Waiting until he got the signal from Rick and Leo that they were ready, he waited with hardened nerves and steel determination. For a few seconds, it felt like so many missions he'd been on before. But seeing her standing up to this piece of shit, knowing she was scared out of her mind but not yielding, he made a vow.

No one points a weapon at Stella and gets away with it. Unable to get a clear shot, he ground his teeth and waited. *Move a step to the side, asshole.*

Stan barked out a laugh. "I think my boss will be amused with you, after all. He likes strength... at the appropriate time." He stepped closer to her, then shifted his weapon and fired into the back shelving that contained some of her work, sending shards of pottery flying out.

She jumped and stumbled backward as a scream erupted. Her hand landed on a large vase, and without hesitation, her fingers curled around the top to keep it from falling. Then, in a flash, she swung the pottery toward Stan's arm, hitting him with all the force she could muster. He staggered, giving Chris the opportunity needed to make a clean shot.

He aimed and fired, hitting Stan in the shoulder, and watched as he cried out, dropping the gun as he fell to his knees. Pushing the door open with such force it swung back and slammed against the wall, Chris rushed in as Leo and Rick followed, their weapons drawn. They rushed past him to subdue Stan, but Chris was rooted in place, his heart pounding as he stared at Stella, his gaze raking over her, making sure she wasn't bleeding.

"I'm fine. I'm fine. I'm fine," she gushed, the breathy words barely audible. Stella's eyes were wide as she stood still, her face a mask of shock. She looked down for a second at the man now on the floor with Leo's knee in his back, then turned. Closing the distance, she raced forward, and Chris swept her into his arms, pressing her tight, feeling her body shake. Hearing Rick call for an ambulance, he reluctantly set Stella's feet down to the floor. Cupping her face, his gaze continued to rove over her features to ascertain she really was whole and in his arms. "Christ almighty, babe. Fucking hell."

She pressed her lips together as her eyes never left his. She glanced down, but the last thing he wanted was for her to look at Stan and be reminded of what almost happened.

Curling his arm around her shoulders, he steered her outside. There, he held her close again. "Stella, talk to me, babe. I need to hear you."

"I didn't know what to do... I hit him... I hit him," she blurted, her wide eyes exposing her shock.

"It's okay, babe. We got him."

Her head jerked up and down as her hands gripped his arms. "He shot... he hit one of my pieces."

"Fuck, Stella, he could have shot more than just a vase."

Her head jerked up and down. "I know. I know..." Her breath was shallow and her pupils still wide.

"Get her out of here, man," Leo said softly, his gaze on her.

The medic in Chris clicked into place as he recognized Stella's shock that Leo had already ascertained. He steered her over to the stairs leading to her apartment. Assisting her up, he settled her onto her sofa and then grabbed a glass of water.

Sipping the water and keeping her hand tucked tightly into his, she appeared to calm. By the time the police and FBI arrived, she was able to give a full statement. His eyes flashed when she admitted opening the door to Stan, but she threw her hands to the sides and retorted, "What criminal comes to kidnap someone wearing a suit?"

"Damnit, Stella, not all criminals wear black clothes and black hoods!" he argued.

She rolled her eyes, and he didn't know if he wanted to kiss her or grab her up and run off with her. Probably both. Staring at her, his heartbeat hastened, and it had nothing to do with fear. Her lips curved upward, and he realized a grin crossed his face, as well. *Yeah, definitely both.*

Two weeks later

Chris stood to one side of the brightly lit gallery, a beer in his hand. If anyone had told him a month ago that he'd be at a small art gallery showcasing a local artist's pottery and actually enjoying it, he'd have called them crazy. But the jazz music in the background, the table with wine and beer along with hors d'oeuvres that looked like real food, and people meandering about wearing casual clothes set off a great vibe.

And the beautiful woman at the center of the event that had captured and held his attention from the moment he'd first seen her on the airplane in Atlanta was walking straight toward him. Her beaming smile lit up the room, scoring straight through his heart. He set his beer bottle on the table next to him so that both arms could wrap around her as she came closer. She leaned back and held his gaze, her eyes alight with excitement. "It looks like it's going well, babe. Congratulations."

"I can't believe how many people came. Thank God the news didn't pick up a story about what happened or I might be overrun with curiosity seekers and not serious buyers or art dealers."

Because of the ongoing investigation, the FBI had handled the media surrounding Stan's arrest and kept Stella's name and studio out of the press. Still worried that Stan's uncle and the Alekhin Bratva might come after her out of retaliation, Chris breathed a sigh of relief when Carson let him know that through his contacts, he'd offered a warning to the cartel: *Stella is under LSI-WC protection.* Still uncertain, Chris had been satisfied when Carson added that Stan's uncle assured him no one would go after her. He considered his nephew's actions worthless, risking the bratva when the munitions were already gone.

Lifting his gaze over her head, he took in the sight of her parents beaming with pride while talking to his mother, who'd been delighted with her invitation. So delighted that she'd wrangled more invitations for a few of her friends, knowing they loved art and had deep pockets.

He stood with Stella in his arms for another moment

until she was called away. He inclined his head and grinned. "It's your night, babe. Go have fun."

Carson and Jeannie moved through the crowd and stood next to him. Clinking his beer bottle to Carson's, he greeted, "It was really nice of you two to come."

Carson smiled, wrapping his arm around Jeannie. "We're family. At least, that's what I hope I impart to all the Keepers."

Chris nodded. "Then you're a success in more ways than one because that's exactly what it feels like."

Jeannie's smile was wide as she looked around. "I had such a good time tonight. Stella's work is beautiful, and I've already bought one piece and commissioned a special order for another." She slid her eyes toward Carson. "And when it arrives, you can't see it until I'm ready for it to be unveiled!"

Laughing, the three shook hands before Carson and Jeannie said their goodbyes. Stella moved back to him, her eyes bright. "Jeannie just commissioned a piece that would have the colors of the sunset with a lighthouse cut out on the side. Doesn't that sound amazing?"

"I wondered why she told Carson he couldn't see it until she was ready."

"I think it's going to be his Christmas present."

"You probably should make more than one because Rachel will want one as well."

She was called away again, but first, she lifted on her toes, her hands resting on his shoulders. Not one to turn down an invitation, he kissed her lightly before she darted away to greet someone else.

His phone vibrated, and he looked down to see the

USO group text. He, Scott, Dylan, Cal, and Nolan occasionally send messages, keeping up with each other's lives.

Scott: **How's the showing?**

Typing in return, he replied: **Couldn't be better. Lots of people buying her work, it's casual and serving beer. My kind of art show.**

Dylan: **Who are you kidding? You'd be there in a tux if she wanted.**

Nolan: **And drinking fuckin' champagne.**

Cal: **And eating crap on little crackers.**

Chuckling aloud, Chris shook his head. **Yep. And with a smile on my face.**

Scott: **How's she doing after everything?**

He'd filled them in on the events, accepting their concern as well as relief that everything had turned out okay. **She's great. Moved in with me, and after showing, will move her studio down as well.**

Dylan: **Holy hell, you don't waste any time.**

I finally figured out where my home port is. It's wherever she's with me.

Cal: **So the journey Blessing told you about came true.**

He thought back to the things Blessing had told him when he'd met her at the airport USO and knew that if any of his decisions that day had been different, he wouldn't be where he was standing right now. Her quote, "It is good to have an end to journey toward, but it is the journey that matters, in the end," had played over and over in his mind. His finger hovered over his phone, but he looked up to see that the showing was coming to an end and people were starting to leave. Stella had said her goodbyes and was now standing with the gallery owner, her parents, and his mom. She lifted her gaze, her brilliant smile hitting him in the heart as it always did. Glancing down, he fired off one last text.

Absolutely. And from what you all say, the same happened with your journeys home too. TTYL – time to take my girl home.

Shoving his phone into his pocket, he stalked toward her as she hurried his way. Their arms wound around each other, and he kissed her soundly.

"This is so amazing," she said, her face turned up toward his. "But I'm tired. You ready to go home?"

Lifting his head, he stared into her beautiful eyes and nodded. "I'm definitely ready to take you home." And just as he'd told his friends, his home port was wherever Stella was at the end of each journey.

Don't miss the next Long Road Home books:
Home Base (by Abbie Zanders)
Home Fires (by Cat Johnson)
Defending Home (by Caitlyn O'Leary)
Searching for Home (Kris Michaels)

Don't miss the Lighthouse Security Investigations West Coast books:
Carson
Leo
Rick

ALSO BY MARYANN JORDAN

Don't miss other Maryann Jordan books!

Baytown Boys (small town, military romantic suspense)

Coming Home

Just One More Chance

Clues of the Heart

Finding Peace

Picking Up the Pieces

Sunset Flames

Waiting for Sunrise

Hear My Heart

Guarding Your Heart

Sweet Rose

Our Time

Count On Me

Shielding You

To Love Someone

Sea Glass Hearts

Protecting Her Heart

Sunset Kiss

Baytown Heroes - A Baytown Boys subseries

A Hero's Chance

Finding a Hero

For all of Miss Ethel's boys:

Heroes at Heart (Military Romance)

Zander

Rafe

Cael

Jaxon

Jayden

Asher

Zeke

Cas

Lighthouse Security Investigations

Mace

Rank

Walker

Drew

Blake

Tate

Levi

Clay

Cobb

Bray

Josh

Knox

Lighthouse Security Investigations West Coast

Carson (LSI West Coast)

Leo (LSI West Coast)

Rick (LSI West Coast)

Hope City (romantic suspense series co-developed

with Kris Michaels

Brock book 1

Sean book 2

Carter book 3

Brody book 4

Kyle book 5

Ryker book 6

Rory book 7

Killian book 8

Torin book 9

Blayze book 10

Griffin book 11

Saints Protection & Investigations

(an elite group, assigned to the cases no one else wants...or
can solve)

Serial Love

Healing Love

Revealing Love

Seeing Love

Honor Love

Sacrifice Love

Protecting Love

Remember Love

Discover Love

Surviving Love

Celebrating Love

Searching Love

Follow the exciting spin-off series:

Alvarez Security (military romantic suspense)

Gabe

Tony

Vinny

Jobe

SEALs

Thin Ice (Sleeper SEAL)

SEAL Together (Silver SEAL)

Undercover Groom (Hot SEAL)

Also for a Hope City Crossover Novel / Hot SEAL...

A Forever Dad

Long Road Home

Military Romantic Suspense

Home to Stay (a Lighthouse Security Investigation crossover novel)

Home Port (an LSI West Coast crossover novel)

Letters From Home (military romance)

Class of Love

Freedom of Love

Bond of Love

The Love's Series (detectives)

Love's Taming

Love's Tempting

Love's Trusting

The Fairfield Series (small town detectives)

Emma's Home

Laurie's Time

Carol's Image

Fireworks Over Fairfield

Please take the time to leave a review of this book. Feel free to contact me, especially if you enjoyed my book. I love to hear from readers!

Facebook

Email

Website

ABOUT THE AUTHOR

I am an avid reader of romance novels, often joking that I cut my teeth on the historical romances. I have been reading and reviewing for years. In 2013, I finally gave into the characters in my head, screaming for their story to be told. From these musings, my first novel, Emma's Home, The Fairfield Series was born.

I was a high school counselor having worked in education for thirty years. I live in Virginia, having also lived in four states and two foreign countries. I have been married to a wonderfully patient man for forty years. When writing, my dog or one of my four cats can generally be found in the same room if not on my lap.

Please take the time to leave a review of this book. Feel free to contact me, especially if you enjoyed my book. I love to hear from readers!

Facebook

Email

Website

Made in United States
Troutdale, OR
06/02/2024

20281503R10184